6/25/07 K
$24.95
Amzrv
3w/co

warped
TL
8-18-74

The Diary
of
Mattie Spenser

Sandra Dallas

The Diary
of
Mattie Spenser

WHEELER
PUBLISHING, INC.
ROCKLAND, MA

★ AN AMERICAN COMPANY ★

Published in Large Print by arrangement with St. Martin's Press in the United States and Canada

Wheeler Large Print Book Series.

Set in 16 pt Plantin.

Library of Congress Cataloging-in-Publication Data

Dallas, Sandra
   The diary of Mattie Spenser / Sandra Dallas.
      p. (large print) cm.(Wheeler large print book series)
   ISBN 1-56895-523-5 (softcover)
   1. Large type books. 2. Frontier and pioneer life—Colorado—Fiction.
3. Women Pioneers—Colorado—Fiction. 4. Colorado—Fiction.
4. Large type books. I. Title. II. Series
[PS3554.A434.D53 1998]
813'.54—dc21   97-47196
                                                                  CIP

For my beloved Dana
Child of love, child of hope

Acknowledgements

For historical help, I am indebted to Larry Cox, Todd Ewalt, John Hutchins, Stanley Kerstein, Lee Olson, Nell Brown Propst, Roy Coy at the St. Joseph Historical Society, Rebecca Lacome at the National Park Service Homestead National Monument, Don Dilley, Augie Mastroguiseppe, and Barbara Walton at the Western History Department of the Denver Public Library, Jerry Sloat in Ft. Madison, Syrma Sotiriou at the Treasured Scarab, and Judy White at Zion Book Store. Thanks to Regan Arthur, my skillful editor at St. Martin's, to Jane Jordan Browne and Danielle Egan-Miller of Multimedia Product Development for their faith and enthusiasm, and to steadfast friends Robbie Spillman and Libbie Gottschalk.

The Diary
of
Mattie Spenser

Prologue

My next-door neighbor, Hazel Dunn, who is ninety-four, is moving into a retirement home. Ever since she signed the contract to sell her house, she's been bringing me boxes of china and old books, along with a few wonderful family heirlooms—lace-trimmed linens, a worn paisley shawl, some Indian beadwork, and a lacquered laptop desk that her grandmother brought west in a covered wagon. Hazel's only son died as a boy, and she has no other close relatives. So I'm not depriving anyone of an inheritance by accepting her family's things, she says.

Of course, she could sell the stuff to a dealer, but Hazel's a generous soul, and she knows how much I love antiques. Besides, what would she do with the money? she asks. She could live to be 150 with what she's got socked away. I think the real reason she doesn't want to sell the keepsakes, however, is that she dislikes the idea of people pawing through her bedding and schoolbooks and Victorian valentines, holding them up to curiosity.

Sorting through all the stuff has been quite a job for Hazel because she's lived in the house forever. It's huge, and every room is cluttered. Her parents designed the home for balls and big dinner parties. They were members of the Sacred Thirty-six, Denver's fashionable social set at the turn of the century.

That's the group that snubbed the Unsinkable Molly Brown, until she emerged as the heroine of the *Titanic* disaster in 1912 and they had to invite her over. Hazel remembers "the poor Unsinkable," as her mother called Molly, showing up for tea, dressed in a skunk-skin coat, poling herself down the sidewalk with a shepherd's crook. Later on, Molly and Hazel's mom got to be good friends.

When Hazel married Walter Dunn, he simply moved in with Hazel and her mother, Lorena, by then a widow, "just like Harry Truman did," Walter always joked. The two of them lived quite happily in Hazel's bedroom until Lorena died in 1959, at the age of ninety. Then they got the master suite. After Walter broke his hip, he and Hazel closed off the second floor and turned one of two parlors into their bedroom. Walter died two years ago, and realtors have been hounding Hazel to sell ever since.

Although Hazel looks and acts twenty years younger than her age, she's wise to go into a home where someone can keep an eye on her, because she refuses to slow down or take precautions. Sooner or later, she's bound to fall. All the neighbors are sorry about her decision, however, because Hazel is a hoot, more fun than anybody on the block. She's also a treasury of neighborhood history, remembering, for instance, when Dwight Eisenhower married Mamie Doud, who lived over on Lafayette Street. Mrs. Doud, Mamie's mother, was a good friend of Lorena's, too.

Our block has become part of what the

realtors say is Denver's most desirable young urban professionals' neighborhood, and those of us who moved here long before there was such a thing as a Yuppie are skeptical about the couple who've bought Hazel's house. They've announced they'll gut the place, put in a fifty-thousand-dollar kitchen, and paint the brick mauve. I'm upset about the changes, but Hazel doesn't seem to mind that the house will lose its historic character. She never was crazy about the place, but by the time her mother died, she'd lived there too long to be comfortable anywhere else. Besides, as Walter put it, "Bess Truman didn't sell her mother's house."

Of course, we're all worried that before she can move into the retirement home, Hazel will hurt herself lifting boxes and hauling junk from the attic to the alley, but she won't let anybody help her—shoos us away, in fact, when we go over on some transparent errand. Hazel's not just being stubborn. Sorting through one hundred years of family accumulations is traumatic, and she's got her pride. Hazel's never been one to show emotion, and she doesn't intend to start now. She didn't shed a tear at Walter's funeral. The only time I ever saw Hazel cry, in fact, was when I rushed over to tell her that John F. Kennedy had just been shot. She'd already heard the news on the radio, and she was sitting in the kitchen, sobbing. Sharing our grief that day became one of the many bonds between us.

Although Hazel won't let me help with the heavy lifting, I've been keeping an eye on her as she makes trips back and forth from the house to the Dumpster, or runs up and down the stairs of the carriage house—which never once housed a carriage. Hazel's conservative father owned a car when he built the place, but he wasn't convinced that automobiles were here to stay. So he erected a carriage house instead of a garage, in case horses made a comeback.

Since I try to keep track of where Hazel is, I knew that she was in the attic of the carriage house when she called out to me in an alarmed voice one afternoon. I was gardening, and I rushed through the gate that connects our yards, yelling up through the open hayloft door, "Are you all right?"

"Come up, dearie," Hazel cried in a voice that held more exasperation than panic.

Nonetheless, I took the narrow stairs two at a time, and I found Hazel bent over in the center of the room, at about the spot where the new people intend to put in a hot tub.

"I've gotten so clumsy lately. I let the trunk lid slam shut on my dress, and now I'm caught. I can't reach over there to lift the lid, and if I try to pull out my dress, I'll rip it. Can you believe it, pinned to a trunk by my skirt!"

I carefully lifted the lid, and Hazel straightened up, examining her skirt for tears. I ran my hand over the soft black leather of the old trunk. It was handmade, put together with brass nails that had turned black with tarnish. The inside was lined with mattress ticking, now soiled and torn. An oval brass plate on the front of the trunk was engraved M.F.M.S., Mingo, C.T."

"The trunk belonged to my grandmother. Those are her initials," Hazel explained when she saw me rubbing my hand over the ornate lettering. "Mingo is in the eastern part of the state. It's almost a ghost town now. The C.T. isn't Connecticut. It stands for Colorado Territory. Grandmother came out here before Colorado was a state, which means sometime prior to 1876." Hazel dropped the hem of her skirt. "No harm done, except to my pride. All that trouble for nothing, too. There wasn't a thing left in that trunk. I must have cleaned it out last week."

"Yes there is," I said, peering inside. "Over there in the corner. It's a book." I reached inside and picked up a worn leather volume that lay on the mattress ticking. "Maybe it fell out of the lid when it slammed shut. There's a sort of hidden compartment in the top. Look." I pointed at a four-inch square of cardboard, covered with a trunk manufacturer's label, which hung down from inside the bow-top lid. It had covered an opening. "That stick lying in the bottom of the trunk must have held the flap shut. See, it goes through the two brass loops on either side of the opening, to pin this piece of cardboard in place." I held the label flat against the lid and pushed the stick through the two loops. "It's pretty obvious, so it's not really much of a hiding place."

Hazel removed the stick, let the label flop down, and thumped the lid, but nothing else fell out. "Apparently not, because that's the only thing in here. No hidden treasure."

I didn't laugh; I was too busy examining the

5

little book I'd fished out of the trunk. It was well worn, but its marbleized edges were still a brilliant mix of red, blue, and black. A flap on the back cover of the book once held it shut by sliding into a leather loop on the front, but the loop was gone, replaced by a rusty safety pin. Hazel wrinkled her nose when I handed her the volume. "I'm so tired of old books. My family read them all the time and saved every one. Give me television any day." Instead of taking the book from me, she pointed to a pile on the floor. "Toss it onto the heap with the rest of the trash, unless you want it."

I started to throw it into the pile. Hazel had already given me a dozen leather-bound books, and they were in better shape than this one. If I kept on accepting things from her, I'd be in Hazel's spot one day, having to sort through it all and dispose of it. Still, I liked the little book, and cleaned up, it would look pretty propped up on my parlor table. I could always throw it out later. So I thanked Hazel, and I slid the flap out of the safety pin to open the book. I turned it to the late-afternoon light coming through the hayloft door and examined the rich paper on the inside cover. It had been creamy once but was now a warm tan, speckled with as many brown age spots as Hazel's hands.

"Mattie Fay McCauley Spenser." I read the name written in big flourishes on the paper.

"That would be my grandmother. Is it her Testament?"

"No," I said, turning the pages. "This is

handwritten. It must be a journal. You ought to keep it, Hazel. It's family history."

I handed the book to Hazel, who held it up close to her eyes. "Well, so what if it is? I'm the last of the family, and someone else will just have to throw it out when I die. Besides, I can't read a word of it. What's in pencil is smudged, and the ink entries are faded. Look how small the writing is, and it's cross-hatched, too."

When I didn't understand what she meant, Hazel held out the open diary to me. "See, she wrote on the page the usual way. Then she turned the book sideways and wrote across the original writing. People did that back then so they could double the number of words they put on a page. Imagine being that hard up for paper." Hazel closed the book and held it out. "Why don't you go through it. With your interest in history, you might find it amusing. It must be grand-mother's overland journal. She came west in a covered wagon right after she was mar-ried. If the diary turns out to be any good, you can always give it to the library."

I shrugged. "If you don't care about my snooping into your family's past, why should I?" I said, putting the diary into the pocket of my gardening smock. Then I scooped up the pile of trash and followed Hazel down the steps.

"Now, dearie, you don't have to read it if you don't want to. Give it to me and I'll just toss it into the Dumpster," Hazel teased, knowing I was hooked.

I patted my pocket and said, "You don't fool me. Damn it, Hazel, I'm going to miss you when you leave. We've been neighbors for thirty years. Why do I have to replace you with someone who likes purple brick?"

Hazel looked up, startled, and I thought I saw dampness in her eyes before she turned away. I tossed the trash into the alley, then saw Hazel safely inside her house before going back to my side of the fence. I was no longer interested in gardening. The journal had taken care of that. Not that I minded. It was nice to have a reason to sit in the shade with a glass of wine, instead of working in the hot sun. I went to the kitchen for the wine, but before I took down the glass, I opened the book and read the tiny writing on the first page, turning the journal to catch what Hazel'd called the "crosshatching." As I did so, I looked up and caught sight of Hazel through her kitchen window, which faces mine. I made a mental note to buy a curtain so I wouldn't have to stare into a fifty-thousand-dollar kitchen.

I love feminist history, have read a number of women pioneers' journals, in fact, and know that they fall into two categories. Most were for public consumption. They were lengthy letters written on the trail, then sent to the folks back home to be read aloud to friends and neighbors. Parts of them were even printed in the local newspapers. Rarer were the journals women kept for their eyes only. Having no women friends with whom they could confide during the hazardous overland trip, women used their journals as confidantes, recording private thoughts they never expected anyone else to read. Flipping through the pages of Hazel's journal, catching words such as *parturition* and *marriage bed,* I was sure her diary fit into the second category.

I turned on the light over the sink and read on, slowly deciphering the entries word by word. I poured the wine and picked up the glass, then started for the patio. Then I changed my mind and went into the guest room that serves as my office and computer room.

Reading the journal would be slow going, so I might as well transcribe it onto my computer as I went along, in case I wanted to refer back to something. In fact, I could print out a copy and tie it with a ribbon to give to Hazel as a farewell gift. I was pleased with the idea, knowing how surprised Hazel would be. Or maybe she wouldn't be. Maybe she'd known all along that's exactly what I'd do. Hazel, you are a sly old fox, I thought. I turned on the computer, and while I waited for it to warm up, I returned to the kitchen. Reading the journal would take time. So I picked up the bottle of wine, held it up to the kitchen window in a salute to Hazel, and took it into the office with me.

Chapter 1

May 9, 1865. Fort Madison, Iowa.

My name is Mattie Faye McCauley Spenser. I am twenty-two years old, and this is my book. It was given to me on Sunday last by Carrie Collier Fritch on the occasion of my marriage to Luke McCamie Spenser. Carrie says I am to use it to record my joys and sorrows, and to keep a thorough record of our wedding trip overland to Colorado Territory and the events in the life of an old married woman. Then I'm to send it back to her.

Well, maybe I will, and maybe I won't.

I was married in my navy blue China silk with the mutton-leg sleeves, a sensible dress, because I am not given to extravagances. Besides, there was not time to make a proper wedding ensemble, since Luke was anxious to be married and on our way out west. As I did not care to begin my new life with a matrimonial squall, I dutifully agreed, although meekness is not in my nature.

This marriage happened so fast that it took away my breath. I had no idea Luke thought of himself as my beau. Everyone believed I was a confirmed old maid, destined to do no more in life than spend my afternoons tutoring refractory scholars in grammar and penmanship, as I have done for two years. At

11

best, I might have wed Abner Edkins—perhaps I should say "at worst," because Abner never was my choice, and if the truth be told, I would rather be an old maid than *his* bride. Still, I have Abner to thank for my wedded bliss. Luke said Abner confided in him that he had plans to make a proposal of marriage to me before the week was out. So although Luke had supposed he would wait a while longer before declaring himself, my Darling Boy came to the farm ahead of Abner and made known his intentions. That was exactly four weeks to the day before our marriage.

I was swept off my feet, as the saying goes, for I had never expected to make such a handsome match. Luke is by far the best catch in Lee County. He spent two years away at normal school before leaving to defend the dear old Union. His is a noble character, and he was one of the first to join up from Iowa, proved his mettle at Shiloh, where he was felled by a bullet. He spent several weeks in the Valley of the Shadow of Death, then was discharged and sent home to recuperate on the family farm, where his parents hoped he would stay for good. Luke's father owns many sections of land, on which is situated a fine house. It is much larger and grander than our humble farm, although I think ours more cheerful.

But farming at Fort Madison is not for Luke. He tried it for a time, but when he was fully recovered from his wounds, he went away to claim a homestead in far-off Colorado. Then he returned to claim a wife. I've known

Luke all my life, but I never thought of him as my lover. I had believed him to be Persia Chalmers's suitor because they have been keeping company ever so long. So imagine my surprise when the wife he desired was Self!

Luke is of a good build and height, just over six feet, with hair like the stubble left in the fields after haying, and eyes as luminously blue as agates. When he smiles, the right side of his mouth curves up more than the left. He has a pleasant countenance, and his face is not so plain as mine. Unlike my life's partner, I am plain all over. My form is too thin, my face too square, and my forehead broad. Being somewhat over five feet eight inches in height, I am too tall ever to be considered a looker. Handsome is the best I might be, and then only on special occasions, and in poor light.

My plainness does not bother Luke. He says it is an asset, since we will be living in a Godless land, where men become crazed where women are concerned. I would not want to cause him vexation by attracting admiring glances, so it seems that neither one of us has to worry about me on that score. Well, it's the first time I ever was glad to be plain.

"You are a suitable cook and well made for work, and you'll have plenty of that where we're going. You are a strong-minded woman and not given to foolish ways. I'm glad you're not the kind to attract men like bees around the honey," he said when he proposed. "I'm bound for Colorado, and if you're agreeable, you may come, too. I'm clean in my ways and a Christian, and I promise to be the best husband I know how. So if you'll agree, Mattie, I'd be proud to take you as my wife. I require a yes or no right away."

It wasn't a pretty speech. Surprised and pleased though I was, I wished there had been a little less common sense, and more passion to his proposal. I suppose a prudent man (and Luke is that) should choose a wife with the same expert eye he turns on a cow. Still, I chided him a little before giving my answer. "You didn't say a word about love, Luke Spenser," said I.

He rebuked me, and rightly so. "I thought you to be a practical girl. If it's words you want, you ought to wait for Abner. He'll be along directly," replied he. Then he blushed and added, "I'm not much for that kind of talk, but do you think I would be here if I did not have feelings for you?"

Well, having studied mathematics to discipline the mind during the two years I spent at Oberlin College, I think I *am* a practical girl—practical enough to know Luke might find another if I did not reply at once. And perhaps it was best he spoke his mind in such a direct way, giving me a clear view of our future together instead of sugarcoating it with silly speeches. I believe Carrie is right in saying that strong men are not given to declarations of love, anyway.

So I meditated on it for a few moments. Marriage is life's most serious step for a woman, and the proposal, catching me unaware as it had, seemed to call for contemplation.

Still, at that instant, I knew he had won my heart and should have my hand, as well. I replied promptly, in the manner of his proposal, "You suit me, Luke, and so does your proposal."

What does not suit me so well is this business of the matrimonial bed. I've never seen a man stark before, and it was an odd thing, though not so much of a surprise. (He has six toes on each foot, which I have not mentioned to him, as Luke does not care to be teased. Nor did I laugh at his skinny legs when first I saw them sticking out from under his nightshirt.) But it was the act itself that disappointed. Carrie had told me not to expect too much, but still, I had hoped for more. There must be a reason the cows crowd the bull, and the sows the boar. I wonder what a pig knows that I don't.

The first night, Luke did not touch me at all, which I blamed on the excitement of the day and his respect for my feelings, since I was not only ignorant of what would happen in bed but also frightened.

The second night, he thrashed about, hurting me a little. Then it was over. I'd judge it took a minute, no more than two, at most. So it is not a serious loss of time. Carrie promised I'd get used to it and even grow to like it, but I doubt that. I shall be happy to dispense with it when we have as many children as we want. I thought there would be kissing and hugging, but except for a peck on the cheek at our wedding, which embarrassed me so much that I wiped it off, Luke does not seem

15

inclined to show such affection.

I precede myself. The wedding was in the dear little Methodist-Episcopal church where I grew up and until a week ago taught Sunday school. It was decorated with white lilacs and white candles. Luke gave me a ring of gold with a cluster of garnets set in it.

I asked Carrie to attend me so that there would be no cause for jealousy among my sisters from my choosing one above the others. Besides, Carrie is exactly my age and has ever been my dearest friend, and I wanted her beside me as I took the first step into my new life. Luke chose Abner to stand up with him, but Abner pouted so during the service that he almost spoiled the day. I was bound he should not do so, for it was *my* day. So I told Abner I thought Persia was sweet on him. That cheered him somewhat, although I know he would rather have me than her. Just think of it! Two men prefer me to Persia Chalmers!

Afterward, Father said, "How do, Mrs. Spenser," and I turned to Luke's mother, which made everyone laugh, except for Mama Spenser, who frowned. It is a good thing we are to leave for Colorado soon, or I would have my work cut out for me on her account.

My own dear mother outdid herself with the tasty repast following the service. And my beloved Carrie made splendid bride and groom cakes. She hugged me as soon as the deed 'twas done and said now we were both old married women. O, I am sad at the thought of leaving her, but "a woman is supposed to cleave to her husband," I told her. That was

16

when Carrie whispered not to expect too much in bed for a while.

The night prior to our wedding, Luke gave me a little trunk made of black leather, lined in blue-and-white ticking, with a cunning compartment hidden in the lid. I like it fine, and I will use it to store my favorite things, including this journal.

In turn, I presented Luke with a yellow silk vest that I had fashioned myself and embroidered all over with flowers. I had stayed awake late into the night to make it, and I was rewarded when Luke wore it at our ceremony. He seemed quite pleased when Persia admired it. I fancied she was jealous of me for snatching Luke away, because the saucy girl told me she'd never seen a bride in such an ugly dress.

"Why, Persia, what would make you say such a thing?" I asked, more from surprise than annoyance.

"Why would I say such a thing?" she repeated. "Because it is true."

So I returned the "favor," and when no one was watching, I stuck out my tongue at Persia. Cry shame! Marriage has made me bold.

⌒

May 17, 1865. Overland Trail, Missouri. Fifty-four miles west from Fort Madison.

We are off! Four days on the trail!

We had planned to leave the third day after our wedding, but dear, thoughtful Husband said he would give me more time for my good-byes, for who knows when we will ever see our loved ones again? Nonetheless, I was anxious to be away, since I did not want people looking at me in the way they do at all brides. It was bad enough staying with Mother and Father Spenser and knowing *they* were watching. And listening!

I thanked Luke for his consideration and did not let on that I knew the real reason for not leaving as scheduled was that he was not satisfied with the provisions. Then there was that business about the pigs. Luke had bought a sow from a farmer for us to take along, but she swolled up and did not look as if she could make the trip. I was just as glad to be rid of her, because I don't fancy driving a pig to Colorado. Maybe Luke changed his mind, for he asked for the return of his money instead of a second pig. I've learned this much about Luke: He demands satisfaction in all things, and that makes me wonder why he chose me for his life's companion, as I am far from perfect. I pray he does not regret our marriage, as I will not. I should be quite out of sorts if he tried to return me like the pig, so I shall be careful not to swoll up.

After we agreed to be engaged, we spent every waking moment in preparation for the trip to Colorado. I gave much time to the cooking and drying and salting of food. There were quilts to be finished—I hope Luke knows his haste is responsible for my failing to have the thirteen handmade coverlets required of brides—and, Lordy, what a lot of packing and unpacking, then packing all over again. Luke, who is the cleverest of men, told me to store my prized Delft plate and other breakables in the barrels of flour, cornmeal, and sugar.

Husband warned me I could take only the most practical items. We had many a merry discussion of what fit his term of "practical," and as he insists I am to be an obedient wife, he got his way. At least he thinks so. Oh, I am learning a great deal about men! I have taken my little japanned writing desk, which fits snugly on my lap, for I place the highest value on letters to and from home (as well as recording events in this journal). And hidden among the pots and pans are these little items I consider indispensable, though Husband may not: the pillow cover Carrie made from cigar silks, the hair wreath from Aunt Sabra, and, of course, my velvet bonnet with the cunning flowers. Bonnets are my especial weakness. I brought along a sunbonnet, too, but it is an ugly, hateful thing. I wore it all last summer in the fields, but now that I am Mrs. Luke Spenser, I've grown vain and hope that I shall never have to wear it again.

I insisted on taking my little walnut commode, which was Grandmother McCauley's and is filled with my clothing and our bedding. It is the repository, as well, for my Holy Bible and *Dr. Chase's Recipes, or Information for Everybody,* for which I gave a dollar. Sister Mary tucked in scraps of rose madder-dyed goods for a quilt and pillow slips trimmed in lace. She and the other girls at home worry that I will not have pretty things in Colorado Territory, but I say I don't need them. The way

Luke describes our new homestead, I think it will be prettier than anything I could take with me.

This little book comes, too, hidden in the secret compartment of the trunk. Luke has not seen my journal yet, and I do not propose to show it to him, since I could not confide in it if I knew Luke were to read my words—although I do not think he could do so easily, since when I finish writing across a page, I turn it so that I can write crosswise over the entry. I do not like keeping secrets from my "guardian and master," but I fancy he may have one or two from me. We have so much to learn about each other. Of course, this means I may write only during moments when Luke is not around. Just now, he is off discussing oxen with the men.

There are not so many prairie ships headed for St. Joseph as earlier in the season, since it is very late in the year for emigrants to embark. Besides, some travelers take the stage and are then outfitted on the Missouri. Luke felt we could do better with our money by buying some of our farm implements at home and avoiding as much as possible the gougers at St. Joe. It is not the most direct route, says Husband, but we can get the best provisioning there. The wagons we see are pulled by oxen, but we are transported by six grays, which Luke's father gave us as a wedding present. They are as handsome a team of horses as there ever was, but more suited to carriages than to a Conestoga. I confided such to Luke, for I know as much about a farm as any man, but he said he hadn't solicited my opinion. He has asked everybody else's opinion, however, about whether to swap the horses for mules or oxen when we get to St. Joe. I shall try to do as Carrie warned me, keeping my mouth shut and managing Luke in other ways.

We had been married nearly a week before we pulled out. Though we were early astir, Mother, Father, and my three sisters and two brothers were there to see us off. They slept only a few hours before rising for chores and hurrying to the Spensers' place, where Luke and I were nearly ready to embark on our adventure. I miss the folks dreadfully already, especially the girls, as we were always a merry group—and Carrie, too. She begged me not to forget her, and she said if we did not meet again in this life, we would surely be together in the next. Luke frowned when I pointed to the ground, meaning Hell, but Carrie and I broke into fits of the giggles.

As we started off, my youngest sister, Jemima, who is six, ran after the wagon, crying for her "sugar." Luke stopped, but I could see he was vexed at doing it. So I let her love my neck and gave her the briefest of kisses. She had to content herself with waving us out of sight and shouting, "Ho for Colorado!"

Luke did not scold her, however. I suppose it was because his mama carried on more than anyone, clutching him and begging him not to go. Mother Spenser wailed that she would never see her boy again, which suits me. He is the apple of her eye, and I know she is not pleased that Luke chose me for a wife. I know so because she told me herself, saying I was too headstrong. My husband will miss her, but not I. Luke's father is a quiet old gentleman, and the wife is the rooster in the hen roost.

I received my first word of praise from my husband at our first campfire supper, and many since. Luke pronounced me a fine camp cook, although at the end of the day, I think he is so tired and hungry, he could eat a roasted wagon wheel. He does not know that most of what we've eaten was cooked before we left and packed away. Still, if I may say so myself, my campfire biscuits are quite tasty and not a bit scorched. A lady who is camped near to us today tells me that out on the prairie, where wood is scarce, I will have to cook with "buffalo chips," which are the dung of the bison. She advises me to look for the dry ones, saying they will make a white-hot fire. Well, not I! We'll eat our biscuits raw before I stoop to that. I resolve to keep a sharp lookout for firewood along the trail.

One concession I have made to travel is to hem my skirts a good two inches above what is proper in Fort Madison, and I spent my first evening at campfire with my needle. As I generally travel by shank's mare during the day, my skirts, if left long, would quickly wear out from being dragged through the dirt. Luke taught me the army trick of coating the insides of my cotton stockings with soap to keep from getting blisters.

Now that the terrible War of the Rebellion is done (and our hero, the martyred Mr.

Lincoln, cold in his grave), many soldiers are moving west, both Unionists who are looking to improve their situations, and Rebels, who have lost all and must begin again. The Homestead Act, which allows each man 160 acres for a small fee after he lives on it for five years (Union soldiers may count their years of enlistment toward that goal), allows all a fresh start. I think we have a wise government.

Still, not everyone we meet is going to Colorado. Some are returning, telling us the territory is a fraud. We camped beside a family traveling home to Ohio. They had "Pikes Peak or Bust" on the cover of their wagon, which they had crossed out and replaced with "Busted by Golly." Luke says these "go-backs" are not so numerous as in the early days, when gold-seekers went west with wheelbarrows to pick up rich nuggets. The family seemed very poor, with only crackers soaked in water for their supper, so I shared with them a fresh peach pie, brought from home—the first they'd tasted in over a year. The man said he would starve before he ever ate another dried apple pie, and he taught us this ditty:

> I loathe, abhore, detest, and despise
> Abominate dried apple pies.
> Give me the toothache or sore eyes
> Instead of your stinking dried apple pies.

Ho for Colorado!

*May 29, 1865. Overland Trail, Missouri. Two
hundred ten miles west from Fort Madison.*

We go like the wind! Twenty-one miles
yesterday, nineteen today. Even the birds do
not fly so fast. At this rate, we shall be there
before we start. We measure the distance by
use of a clever brass instrument called an
odometer, which is attached to the wheel of
the wagon. Luke says in the early crossings,
emigrants tied a kerchief to the wheel and
counted its revolutions, then multiplied that
number by the circumference of the wheel,
thereby determining the daily distance.
Keeping track of the kerchief would make me
dizzy and cause me to fall out of the wagon,
I think.

So far, it has been good roads and good
weather, inspiring us to name last night's
stopping place "Camp Comfort." Luke says
things will not be so nice once we leave
Missouri. Enjoy the trees now, says Husband,
because they will not last. Fine, I say, for
pleasing to me are meadows and a far view.

Every meal is a picnic. We eat breakfast
around the campfire. Dinner is served in the
shade of our wagon. For the evening meal, I
spread a gutta-percha cloth on the ground and
lay it with the remaining food prepared at
home. Last night was so warm, I prepared only
a cold supper. But I unpacked two of our
good plates and served slices of Carrie's
groom's cake for dessert to celebrate our
three-week anniversary. I have become very

economical, using leftover biscuit dough from the supper to bake a pone during breakfast, which we eat at our nooning.

We pass many fine farms and kind people, who sell us fresh milk and butter. One afternoon, whilst Luke repaired a wheel, a farmer stopped plowing and offered his help. Then his wife brought a pitcher of refreshing well water. They are recently married themselves. Since she was new to the country, with few friends there, she begged us to stay to supper and to camp in their barnyard, but Luke replied we must be on our way. I asked pertly what difference did an afternoon make, but Luke looked at me sternly. Then the wife and I exchanged knowing glances. I did promise to obey him, but, O, will I ever learn to hold my tongue?

On the whole, Luke is the most indulgent of husbands. He stopped once to pick me a nosegay of wild daisies, knowing they are my favorites. When he wasn't looking, I plucked off one daisy's petals to see if he loves me, and I was rewarded for destroying the flower with the knowledge that "he loves me not!"

Luke does not raise his voice, and he finds fault but seldom. He is punctual as a clock, works harder than any man I ever knew, even Father, and keeps himself clean, for which I am thankful. I couldn't abide a smelly old bachelor of a husband. He insists that we observe the Seventh Day, though I think that is mostly so the fagged beasts can rest. I observe the sanctity of the Sabbath by scrubbing our clothes and straightening the wagon and baking as much as I can for the week ahead.

I also clean myself as well as I can, for we get very dirty. I washed my hair the day before our wedding and keep it braided tight, so there is no need to wash it again until we are settled. It is said there is no Sunday west of Missouri. I hope that is not so, for I look forward to a proper day of rest and worship each week after we reach our new home.

I realize now I knew little about this husband of mine when I accepted his proposal. Marry in haste, repent at leisure, the saying goes, although that isn't what I mean. I am not the least bit sorry I said yes to Luke, but I think I was not very well prepared. Luke smiles but does not laugh at my little jokes, and he detests being teased. When I made eyes at him once, he told me it was not becoming of a married woman to flirt, even with her own husband.

Now that Luke's "dear mama" is not in the next room listening for the rattle of corn husks in the tick, Luke takes more time with the matrimonial act. He enjoys it, but I still think it overrated. I wish Carrie were here so's I could question her. She confessed to me that sometimes she was the one to ask for "it." Well, I never will.

When I asked Luke whether I satisfied him, he didn't answer for so long, I supposed he hadn't heard. Then he replied, "You'll do."

"Do I do something wrong?" I hoped he'd ask how I felt about the matter. Then I might be brave enough to tell him I wished he'd hug me a little, instead of turning away when he finishes, but I guess I was too bold.

"It shouldn't be talked about."

So I will be satisfied with Luke in other ways. If hugs and kisses were so important to me, I could have married silly old Abner, who always wanted to spark. I blush to think of being under the covers with him!

Here is one thing we both enjoy: music. I never knew until we married that Luke cared the least about singing, but he has a beautiful, clear voice, and I can always hit the note, so we enjoy many an evening's singing by the campfire. We discovered our mutual interest one night when I hummed "The Old Rugged Cross" as I put away the supper things. Luke joined right in with the words. Then I did the harmony. "It seems I married a fine musician," he said, and started off on "Lorena," which he learned at Shiloh, and "Arkansas Traveler" and "Darling Nelly Gray," and by the time we were finished, we had sung more than a dozen old favorites.

I caught Luke watching me one day when I was gazing out across the countryside, and he said, "Colorado is different from Iowa. I wonder if you'll like it much. Perhaps it is too near sunset for you."

That description nearly took away my breath. Of course, I shall like it. I shall love it! I thank God every day for my new husband and my new life.

June 11, 1865. Camp Noah, St. Joseph, Missouri. Two hundred twenty-three miles west from Fort Madison.

Today is my birthday. I am twenty-three years old, and little did I think on this day a year ago that my next would be celebrated with a new husband on my way to a new territory. My Darling Boy awakened me this morning with a bouquet of wildflowers, still wet with rain. Then he presented me with a breast pin containing a cunning locket, the nicest I ever saw, gold with garnets. Since I had said nothing, I did not even suspect he knew it was my birthday. But I had not counted on Mother and Carrie. I should have known they would not let the day go by without notice, and they had given gifts to Luke before we left.

From Mother came *The American Frugal Housewife*, along with a note, in which she said she would not allow me go to housekeeping without it, and also wishing me many happy returns of the day. Carrie gave me a needle case, embroidered by her own hand, and filled with needles of various sizes. It will prove most useful. I discovered when I hemmed my skirts that I had brought with me ample pins and threads but just two needles. We are like two halves of an apple, Carrie and I, just alike. I hope Luke will prove to be as faithful a friend as she has always been.

Luke bought the breast pin yesterday on his visit into St. Joseph, where we are camped, for it comes in a velvet box with "Jas. Felty, Jeweler, St. J." on it. I had supposed he was only posting my letters and shopping for the remaining things we need for our new home.

I blush to think how vexed I was yesterday when he ordered me to stay with the wagon whilst he went into the center of town. I said it was necessary for me to purchase certain provisions, as only a woman knows how much should be spent on them. Why, I told him prudently, I had observed a sign advertising ham available at twelve cents the pound, and butter for two bits, and I knew I could do better. At those prices, we will have to find a gold mine to pay for our trip to Colorado.

My secret reason for wanting to go, however, was to see the delights of St. Joe., for as we passed through the town, I had glimpsed the touts in front of gambling halls, luring in the Negroes and beardless boys, and I heard the minstrel girls promenading the streets, singing, "O, California, that is the land for me." To my disappointment, Luke said it was generally known that St. Joe was a "den of abomination" and said 'twas no place for a lady, although it appears to be no more shocking than does a Mississippi River town, with which I am well acquainted. When I replied as much, Luke said, even so, someone must stand guard over our possessions, since the people hereabouts are Secesh in their sympathies and are not to be trusted. I grumbled because it seemed the greater danger was guarding my person against the "Mormon flies," as the horrid willow bugs are called. Now

I know it was not to protect me from abominations that Luke insisted I stay at camp, but to allow him leisure to select a gift for me.

There was another reason for his solitary trip, and of this one, I am not so pleased. Luke did not want my interference when he disposed of the horses, though he would have come out better had he had it. When he returned, I told him he had made a poor bargain in exchanging the team for two pairs of oxen, a buttermilk named Red, an "Alice Ann" horse, and a milk cow. The grays are worth $500, while oxen may be had for $125 the pair, and when Luke admitted he had traded straight across, I told him he had been plucked in the manner of the chicken.

I intended to say more, but I could see Luke was angry with me, so I bit my tongue. O, Lordy, I shall have a mighty sore tongue before I get used to marriage.

I tried to make up for my harsh words by putting aside the cold supper I had set out and cooking a hot meal, but there was a smart sprinkle of rain, a regular Baptist downpour, which wet the provision box clear through, even though it was wrapped in oilcloth. I had to sprinkle gunpowder on the kindling before the lucifers (which are kept in a corked bottle, or they should have been useless) would cause it to light. I stood in the rain with only an umbrella over me whilst I kept the fire going, for I could not wear my rain cloak. Before we left Fort Madison, I had waterproofed it with melted wax and spirits of turpentine, in the Chinese method, and I feared if I put it on, it would catch fire and I should be burnt to a cinder. To myself, I named this place "Camp Misery."

The sight of his wet and smoky wife, her clothes soaked and damp hair escaping from its net, softened Luke's heart, for when I set out our plates under the India rubber cloth he had attached between the wagon and two poles, he pulled me down beside him and told me I was game. He said he could not see Persia standing out there in the damp to cook his supper. I considered it odd Luke would mention Persia, because I have scarcely given her a thought since we left home, but I was glad for any compliment, most especially one about that watery, half-cooked supper. Even the biscuits, on which I pride myself, were soggy, but Luke did not complain. Our appetites gave them flavor. So I replied to his compliment, "I thank you, sir!"

After we'd supped, we sang "Cross Over the River" and all other songs about water until far into the night. Then Husband christened this stopping place "Camp Noah."

Luke was pleased with my obvious surprise and heartfelt delight at his gift this morning, and he said slyly that he hoped I was not disappointed that I had not received a butter churn instead. I replied, in the same manner, that a butter churn had been my heart's desire, but I would make do with the gold breast pin. Then I threw my arms around him and kissed him, which he seemed to enjoy as much as I did. I shall yet bring him around to my way of affection.

31

While it is our habit to rest on Sunday, Luke proposed that we do so across the river, hoping the line at the ferry would be shorter on the Sabbath. The travelers' tents here are as thick as at a camp meeting. But many are waiting at the ferry after all. We may not cross the Missouri until midday. The waters are the color of clay, a wide river, but not so noble as our Mississippi. I think the rivers in Colorado must be more like this one than the Old Miss at home.

Luke is off talking to other emigrants, and I am left with these great dumb brutes of oxen — which Luke has named Grant, Sherman, Sheridan, and Lee — the last being the obstinate one. Luke said I might choose a name for the Alice Ann. I thought "Miss Givings" to be appropriate but prudently selected "Traveler" instead.

The oxen are more content than I am to stand in the sun and let themselves provide a feast for mosquitoes, which exceed in size any I ever saw. A few minutes ago, I took out the ugly sunbonnet and put it on. Even so, my head has begun to hurt from the sun and the glare of the white wagon covers, and I fear I will come down with one of my headaches. That worries me more than anything Luke would say about the bonnet. The wind is fierce, and I write with my little book held firmly on my writing desk in my lap while the wagon rocks back and forth in the blow.

Luke intends to inquire of the ferryman about the Red Indians. He heard warnings in St. Joe that they are bent on mischief. I observed several of them during our stay there. They are not red, but brown, not as dark as the Negro, but cursed with the same broad face. Some were vain fellows, who raced their horses back and forth on their parade ground across the river from our camp. Others are "Lo, the Poor Indian," sitting in the mud with their hands out, too lazy even to move to a dry spot. We passed one miserable beggar who looked so woebegone that I asked Luke to give him our leftover biscuits, but Luke refused because the savage was drunk. I do not think we have much to fear from Mr. Lo and his friends on our journey.

June 18, 1865. Overland Trail, Kansas. Sixty-six miles west from St. Joseph.

After crossing on the ferry, I suggested that we should wait to form a traveling party, but Luke discounted the threat of the Red Men, saying he did not believe they were "on the warpath," as the people along here say. He also did not want to get close to other emigrants for fear of catching the cholera, which had already attacked our camp at St. Joe. I saw a man doubled up with cramping, his pulsing veins engorged with purple blood. His wife halloed and prayed whilst the children cried piteously. I proposed to aid them, but Luke forbade it for fear I would contract the malady myself. Besides, there was nothing to be done beyond the mustard poultice his wife had applied, and even so, the man was dead by nightfall. So I left them fresh-baked biscuits on a rock and will remember them in my prayers.

Luke says we are likely to see more of the dreaded disease before we reach Colorado. I consulted *Dr. Chase's Recipes,* and, using the contents of the medicine chest, I mixed us a preventative tincture of spirits of camphor, ginger, and essence of peppermint. We take a spoonful each morning.

So we have left St. Joe behind but we no longer go as the wind, for the oxen travel barely a mile in an hour, plodding instead of walking.

The fifth day out, we spotted several of the savages to the rear of us, mounted on ponies. They did not specially alarm me at first, as I thought them to be indolent, like their brothers in St. Joe. Luke smartly cracked his whip over the oxen, which had no effect on the animals at all, for nothing can induce them to hurry. Then he told me to take charge of the animals whilst he made a great display of taking out his pistol, shotgun, and rifle, which is one of the new repeating kind that does not have to be reloaded after every shot. This was to show the savages we were well armed and not in the least afraid of them. They made no move to catch up with us, but neither did they disappear. I worried they would wait until dark to accost us, and perhaps Luke agreed, for in midafternoon, finding a suitable site, we stopped to make our camp.

With the shotgun in easy reach, I prepared biscuits in the Dutch oven, which I set upon the fire. Luke sat with the rifle on his knees, watching as the savages came near the wagon.

Luke let them get a hundred yards from us before he stood up. Cradling rifle in arms, he went to meet them. They were six—two braves, as the Indian men are misnamed, one of them young, and the other as old as Methuselah, a squaw with a papoose on her back, and two little boys, dressed à la Adam. When they dismounted, I took up the pan of biscuits and greeted our visitors. The younger brave reached out as if to take them all. So I snatched them away, offering them to the woman first. From the looks of her, I thought she must starve whilst her lord and master eats his fill.

When the Indians had finished the biscuits, the squaw sat, happily picking the lice from the head of her papoose and cracking them between her teeth. One of the men pointed at me and said something in Indian to Luke, but Luke only shook his head. I wondered if Husband knew a few words of Indian from his previous trip across the plains, but this was not the time for chatter. So I kept quiet, later finding out the impudent man had attempted to negotiate a trade for me!

Whilst the Indians watched us, Luke muttered for me to take hold of the shotgun, which was loaded, and to act as if I knew how to shoot it. Then Luke took a small mirror and a penknife from his pocket and tossed them to the two men, indicating with a wave of his hand that they were to be off.

One of the men saw the coffeepot next to the fire, pointed at it, and said, "Ko-fee. Ko-fee," thinking himself conversant in our language. Unlike his squaw, who was old and careworn, he was a handsome specimen, with the pronounced high cheekbones and glossy black hair of his people. He wore only a pair of Indian trousers, which do not cover him up as well as they might, and his strong legs and bare chest, which were the color of a copper penny, showed him to be a manly specimen.

The Indians walked toward our wagon until Luke called, "Halt!"—a word they seemed to know, because they did as they were ordered. The young Indian now turned to smile at Luke, pretending friendship, but knowing a member of that race would steal a dying man's shoes, Husband pointed his rifle at the Indian, motioning for him to step back. The man let loose a line of gibberish, gesticulating wildly with his arms. He captured all of Luke's attention, but fortunately, not all of mine. Out of the corner of my eye, I saw the old Indian step quickly behind Luke and raise his arm. There was not time to give warning. Instead, I raised the shotgun and fired, hitting the Indian in the hand, and he yelped. Never in my life have I seen a man whose nerves were as steady as Luke's. Instead of looking behind him, he gazed steadily at the young Indian, his rifle raised, and ordered, "Git!"

The old man cried pitifully from the wound, and he needed the aid of the squaw to mount his horse. When he was atop the animal, the others scrambled onto their ponies. Luke kept his rifle on them until they had made good their exit. Then he told me, "You saved the day. That was a lucky shot."

"It wasn't altogether luck," I told him, not without a little bragging on my part. "Father says I'm a better marksman than my brothers." My brothers say I'm as true a shot as Father, but as I know Luke is proud of his own ability with a weapon, having proved himself in the war, I said no more on that subject.

Neither of us slept much that night, but the savages did not return.

~

July 3, 1865. Fort Kearney, Nebraska Territory. Two hundred ninety-four miles west of St. Joseph.

The morning after last I wrote, we came across an empty trunk, whose contents were scattered about the prairie. Just beyond was a wagon, or what was left of it after its combustible parts were burned. Nearby was a fresh grave. As we had no way of knowing what had happened, Luke and I assured each other that the occupants of the wagon had met with a commonplace accident, such as a broken wheel or an everyday illness—measles, for instance. We checked our wheels, finding them in good condition, and each told the other of having measles as a child, but we did not fool ourselves. The sad state of the wagon was due to foul play by Indians, Perhaps those very savages we had encountered earlier, and so, anxious as we were to reach our new home, we agreed it would be prudent to wait for a wagon train before pulling out.

One arrived whilst we nooned, and its

members were pleased to add another rifle to their arsenal. Luke told the men about our visitors and said he did not think they would give us any more trouble because "we" had shot at one and hit him. The men congratulated Luke, who did not apprise them of their error, and I kept my mouth shut. It is said a true woman would rather hear even the faintest praise of her husband than hosannas to herself. The poet who wrote that, I think, was a man.

I was glad to have the companionship of others of my sex. One of them wore the "bloomer costume," which Luke said was every bit as scandalous as a man wearing a dress, but I do not agree. After dragging petticoats and skirts, even shortened ones, over many miles of prairie, I should find trousers much less incommodious.

Our decision to join the wagon train was a wise one, because Indians soon became a commonplace sight. One group followed us for two days, coming and going, sometimes disappearing for hours at a time. Foolish girl that I was, I wondered if they wanted to keep out of range of my shotgun. I fancied myself something of a legend among the Indian braves.

Shortly after we added our wagon to those of our fellow travelers, our party was joined by Mr. Benjamin Bondurant, an old prospector headed for the Colorado gold fields. He affixed himself to Luke and me, saying we were his choice because Luke had been elected by the others to be the captain of our train—the previous captain having been dismissed due to a dispute among the emigrants prior to our arrival.

Luke thought the real reason Mr. Bondurant invited himself to our campfire was that he prefers to "mess" with us instead of batching. While many of the fellows of our party live on bread and bacon, bacon and bread, we vary our meals with wild onions, prairie peas, and sweet red currants that I find as I walk along with my bag in search of buffalo chips. (Yes, I know I vowed never to stoop for them, but they are much preferred to the alternative, which is no fuel at all. The aforementioned circles of dung, also known as "meadow muffins," serve another purpose. Two men of our party got into a "snowball" fight, flinging buffalo chips at each other, until each was covered with an odoriferous gray powder.)

The cow is still fresh. So we have butter, which makes itself. I put milk into a pail of a morning, and by day's end, the movement of the wagon has churned it into butter as neat as you please, and we have refreshing buttermilk for our supper, too. We exchange butter for antelope, which is more than equal to the best beef in the world. Once we traded for buffalo so tough, it must have been the father of all buffaloes. I think the flesh to be the chef d'oeuvre of Lucifer's kitchen.

Mr. Bondurant is a bugle-bearded man with a bulbous nose the color of a plum, and but one eye, and a rheumy one at that, although it does not seem to affect his vision. He dresses in butternuts and buckskins, with a pistol strapped to one side of his belt, and a long knife, which he calls an "Arkansas toothpick," to the other. He smells strongly, but then, I smell strongly myself these days. So I do not hold it against him. He repays our hospitality by playing his Jew's harp whilst we sing, and telling us stories of his life on the Great Plains. Our first night, I told him of our experience with the Indians, and concluded that with so many of us banded together now, I, for one, was not afraid.

"Then ye not be perspicacious," said he.

I thought Luke would rebuke him, but instead, Husband asked why that was so.

"Because what you pilgrims run into was a family. Just now, we got a war party behind us. It's as plain as the nose on your face. You bet. They're all painted up, and they don't have their women and little 'uns along. They're damned rascals, bidin' their time, waitin' till us'ns get careless."

Hearing that, Luke called a parley, and Mr. Bondurant informed all that we must keep together as we travel during the day, allowing neither children nor animals to wander off. The animals are to be pastured inside the circle of wagons at night, and we were told to double the guard. In the event of an Indian attack, we are to corral our wagons as quickly as possible. The men will shoot to kill. Women and boys are to reload the guns, allowing the shooters to keep up a steady fire. If the savages get the upper hand and all is lost, Mr. Bondurant warned, the men are to shoot first wives and children, and then themselves.

One woman whimpered, her husband saying, "Here, here, Mr. Bondurant. There's no reason to scare the ladies."

"You ought not to say that, for you ain't seen what they do to white womens," said Mr. Bondurant.

"Well, I, for one, refuse to be frightened," spoke up a woman. "I'm from Gettysburg. There's nothing I haven't seen."

"Them was Christian soldiers at Gettysburg, even if they was Johnny Rebs. You ain't seen Indians at work, ma'am. Indians ain't Christian. By ginger, they ain't human," replied our Mr. Bondurant.

He guessed the savages would attack in the next day if they could catch our emigrant party unprepared. They lack patience for a sustained stalking, and like children, they allow their attention to be easily diverted. Mr. Bondurant explained that the Red Men do not work together as a fighting unit under the command of a senior officer, as do our soldiers. Instead, it is each man for himself. Here is an odd thing: They often prefer to strike the enemy with a stick than to kill him.

Some of the men complained privately to Luke that Mr. Bondurant was a freebooter seeking our protection for his journey to the mines, and that he would secure it by spreading outrageous tales. Their complaints rose as we passed a night and day, and then another night, with the Indians keeping their distance. Luke, however, kept good discipline, even threatening to thrash one man who would not take his turn at guard. Some wives grumbled to me that

Husband had become the little Napoleon, but I hotly defended Luke, saying he had crossed these plains before and had experience with the savages.

The attack came early the next morning, just after we began our day's journey. The hindmost wagon lagged behind. We do not know the reason for it. Perhaps it was carelessness. As we lost sight of it behind a hill, we heard the inhuman screams of the Red enemy, shrill and devilish enough to curdle milk. "We're in for it now. Don't crumple up!" Mr. Bondurant warned us.

Some of the men wanted to go to the aid of the helpless family, but Mr. Bondurant shouted they were lost already, and that we would be, too, if we did not make haste. All hands sprang to action. We corraled our wagons and took our places inside the circle, where the bawling animals caused so much dust, we could scarcely see across the wagons. Luke brought out the shotgun and rifle, as well as a pistol, which he handed to me. He did not say anything, but I took his meaning: I was to shoot myself if he was unable to do the deed himself. I would have, too, for Mr. Bondurant had regaled Luke and me over the campfire with stories of what happens to white captives.

We had taken our places but had not even had time to unhitch the oxen when the savages were upon us, yelling most horribly and threatening us with their lances. Most had bows and arrows, but we heard the sound of at least one rifle in the distance. I did not load for Luke, as Mr. Bondurant had instructed, but called upon a boy from the adjoining wagon to help us so that I could shoulder the shotgun.

The Indians made a sortie at us, but we repulsed them. As they retreated over the hill, one man stood up with his rifle and gave out with what Luke said was the old Rebel yell, shouting, "Victory! The day is ours! We thumped them red niggers!"

"Down, fool! Don't risk your bones!" cried Mr. Bondurant, adding several crimson oaths, but before the Rebel could follow orders, he had an arrow in his side. The Indians bore down upon us once again, more ferociously than before. Mr. Bondurant yelled for us to hold our fire until they came close, so as not to waste bullets. I strained to hear his call above the cries of children and screams of animals that were maddened from the noise and pain of the arrows and the smell of blood. The savages were nearly upon the wagons, and I was filled with a mixture of fright and exultation when Mr. Bondurant called, "Spit fire on them!" and we let loose.

Luke and I discharged our weapons at the same time and saw a warrier fall from his horse. "Got him, the old bastard!" Luke said. When the Indians made their retreat, they left behind five "good Indians," as Mr. Bondurant calls the dead ones. We hastily checked our own band and found only one wounded, and that was the Rebel, who lay on the ground in great pain, his tallow-faced wife bending over him. In her haste to remove the arrow, she had broken it off. Mr. Bondurant said we must prepare for the next sortie. He would work the arrow loose later on—if the poor man yet lived.

The savages made four more attacks, each of which we fought off. My face and hands were slick from the dust and perspiration and tears, and my shoulder ached from the recoil of the shotgun. The air smelled of rifle powder and hot blood from the wounded animals. When the savage brutes made their final charge, Mr. Bondurant called, "We're in for it now." Despite our fire, the enemy broke through our bulwark, into our circle.

One warrior snatched up a little girl and would have made off with her if the mother had not grabbed at the horse, causing it to shy. The warrior raised his hand and crushed the mother's skull with his wicked ax. Then an instant later, he was shot dead by one of our men, and he dropped the motherless child, breaking her arm. She clung to her dead parent with her good arm, the injured one hanging uselessly at her side, the tiny bone protruding from her sleeve. "O, Mama, Mama, wake up!" was her wrenching cry.

Only a moment afterward, I saw a second Indian on foot come from behind a wagon and make a dash for Mr. Bondurant. My courage did not falter, and I raised my weapon and fired, the ball hitting the Red Man in the back. Mr. Bondurant turned at the Indian's death rattle, and he saw the smoking shotgun in my hands. But at another cry, he turned again and raised his rifle, and one more savage lay dead.

Our brave fighters held the field, and at last the cowardly Indians fled for good, taking their injured with them. Mr. Bondurant thought we were safe, but he warned us to keep a sharp lookout whilst we cared for our wounded. Besides the brave mother, two others were dead—a Mr. Jamison, from Galesburg, Illinois, and his son, aged fourteen. They leave behind a grieving wife and mother and three little ones.

Our injured numbered six. The raw wound of one man looked as if he had been chewed by wild dogs, but he is recovering. The Rebel did not, and we endured his piteous moans and deathly jerks for three days, at which time, he went to the land of the hereafter. The wife blamed the death on Mr. Bondurant, whom she had begged to remove the arrow. He said he might have pulled it out, had the wife not broken it off, but in either case, he believed, the man would have died. The woman was sick with grief, saying she would rather her husband had fallen in defense of the Old South than in this godforsaken land, among his Yankee enemies. Even so, we "enemies" hitched up her wagon each day and cared for her children and passed the hat so she could return to her old home. I prevailed upon Luke to purchase her small cookstove, which we will use in our new home, and he did so, although he pointed out payment was overgenerous; she had planned to abandon it.

When Mr. Bondurant declared all was safe, several men went back to the hind wagon, where the Indians had slaughtered the family, all excepting for one small boy, the "least 'un," as Mr. Bondurant describes him, whom they had carried off, and who has not been seen since. Mr. Bondurant believes he will be raised as an Indian.

It was the Devil's own day. The sight that greeted the men was a charnel house. Even in war, Luke said, he had not seen such vicious carnage as met his eyes at that wagon. Scalps had been taken, a most gruesome practice, of which I had heard but never imagined I should witness. The Indians do not take the whole scalp, as I had supposed, but a little plug of skin the size of a pawpaw, with the hair hanging from it. The bodies were horribly abused, arms and legs slashed and mutilation about the private parts. One man had had the sinews taken from his back, for use as bowstrings, Mr. Bondurant said. Even innocent children were not spared. I wept when I saw what the heathens had done to a little girl of about three, and I hope never again to prepare such bodies for burial. They go to their eternal rest under the prairie sod, with not but rocks to mark the spot.

I thank God that Luke and I were unhurt, although I do not think I will ever again be as carefree as I was but a few days previous. In taking a human life, I, myself, broke one of God's greatest Commandments. No one knows of it, even Luke, excepting Mr. Bondurant. But my secret is safe with him.

"By ginger, I can thank your missus for saving my scalp, I'm a-telling you," Mr. Bondurant informed Luke at supper that night. "That Indian devil—" He stopped when he saw me shaking my head furiously at him, and he took my meaning.

It was too late, however, as Luke looked up, waiting for Mr. Bondurant to finish.

"I suppose I can yell as loud as any Indian," said I.

"I'm in your debt," Mr. Bondurant said, going back to his supper.

I do not understand why I misled my husband, as I am as fond of tributes as any person, but killing a man, even if he was an Indian, makes me ashamed and unwomanly, and this time I do not care for praise. I hope this land does not unsex me.

There is an irony in the events of the trail, for our lives here are the twain of both great and ordinary events: I discovered that following the Indian attack, the bread dough, which I had set in the morning, had raised nicely.

July 5, 1865. Fort Kearney, Nebraska Territory.

As Luke came back before I finished describing the events of our journey, I put away my diary and could not complete the story until now. My time had been taken up with chores here at Fort Kearney, where we have camped for two days. I have baked for the week and washed all our dirty clothes in the yellowish water of the Platte River, which is a poor stream when compared with our mighty

Mississippi. Indeed, it is not even so grand as the brackish creek that runs through our Lee County farm. Mr. Bondurant says the Platte is a mile wide and an inch deep, and I think if we had just one more team of thirsty oxen, 'twould be even shallower.

Luke is off to see if there are enough emigrants to start for Colorado. The commander here at Fort Kearney forbids our leaving until fifty wagons are assembled, although there are no reports of Indian deprivations to the west. Luke thinks the man is too lazy to send his troops to secure the area and wants the wagon trains to do his work for him. I, for one, shouldn't mind waiting until we are a hundred wagons, because I shiver each time I think of engaging in another Indian battle.

I would prefer to wait until the wind dies down, as well, although I have little hope of that, as the wind here is as constant as the prairie grasses. I had to wipe the dust from my eyes before I could prepare supper last night, and now I sit on the wagon seat, my writing desk in my lap, whilst the wind pushes the Conestoga to and fro like a rocking chair.

To our great relief, we had no further sighting of the Red enemy. We passed many graves, which increased in number the farther we were from the Missouri, and I believe they are due to Indians, though I know dysentery and accidents take their toll.

Savages were on all minds as our band continued on its journey, and each clump of bush and each skitterish antelope brought fresh cries of "Indians! Indians!" That along with the moans of the wounded kept us on edge night and day. One poor little fellow survived the attack that killed his father, only to die a few days later of the bloody flux. We came upon a body as black and shiny as charcoal, but the deceased was not a colored man; he was only a poor fellow whose remains had been in the sun too long. Our men buried him, after quick examination to determine that he had not been murdered by Red Men. We do not know how he died, or even who he was. I wonder if he has left behind in the States some poor wife who is destined to wait forever for word from her vanished mate.

Of course, the day after the attack, I had one of my sick headaches, brought on by the excitement and the dust and the sun, which is far brighter here than at home. It is my habit to walk beside the oxen, but that day, I sat on the wagon seat, a scarf tied tightly around my head. With real suffering all around me, I was ashamed to ask Luke to relieve me with the oxen, but at last, I begged him to let me rest. Even then, I got no relief from the pain. Our wagon was piled so high with goods that I lay on a makeshift bed just under the wagon cover, and I could not have been hotter had I traveled in an oven. I forgot to bring with me the vinegar and brown paper that sometimes give comfort.

It is not the first of my headaches that Luke has witnessed, but the worst so far, and he is some put out by my womanly weakness. I tried to cook supper, but I felt so faint from the smoke and dust that Mr.

Bondurant took over the chore and stirred up a stew of stringy jackrabbit.

I was ready with compliments, which so tickled Mr. Bondurant that he offered me a second helping. In reaching for the spoon, which had fallen into the grass, he was attacked by the largest rattlesnake I ever saw, which bit the end of his little finger. As Luke smashed the head of the offender with a rock, I made for the medicine chest in the wagon. But before I could prepare a poultice, Mr. Bondurant put his hand on the wagon wheel, and with the blade of his Arkansas toothpick, he cut off the tip of his finger. Then he thrust his hand into the flour barrel to stanch the bleeding. Mr. Bondurant has given his injury no further thought, and when he showed it to me this morning, I saw the finger had almost healed. I wondered how Mr. Bondurant had the nerve to do such a thing, and I took a good look at his hands, but there is no other sign of mutilation.

My travail was not yet ended. Just before morning came a horrid rainstorm, which frightened me almost as much as the Indians. There was a terrible clashing of thunder, with flashes of lightning that seemed to break the sky in half, then a clatter of hailstones nearly as big as hens' eggs. Next came an attack of rain so thick and wind so strong that I thought I would be washed overboard from our prairie schooner. The rain gave way to a sky of deepest black, no pinpoint of light from horizon to horizon. Then came a sunup such as I never saw—streaks of light, giving way to a sky of brilliant blue, and a rainbow. The raindrops on the grass appeared as a sprinkling of precious gems. What a strange land this is, with such violent contrasts. I am glad we will not live here. I should get lost with nothing to see but sky above and prairie grass below.

We reached Fort Kearney late on July third, just in time to celebrate the Day of Independence (and our own deliverance from the Indians) with much jollification. The soldiers put on a splendid demonstration for us upon their parade ground, under the banner of Old Glory, which rose to the occasion under a strong wind. We gave three times three for the glorious Union and the safe return of our gallant boys in blue, with me cheering most of all for my own soldier boy. We showed gratitude to God and country with prayer, gunshots (having brought with us no Chinese firecrackers), and hurrahs for our preserved nation. Then there were recitations, and the day ended with a reel. Since the men outnumbered the women, wallflowers were an unknown shrub, and I was in as much demand as Persia Chalmers would have been at home. One of my partners had a wooden leg, but that did not stop him from trodding on my feet with his one good. "Well, I tell you, I sure like to dance," said he.

I added to the festivities by mixing hailstones and peppermint leaves from a clump discovered by the river, to make a delicious ice cream, which was enjoyed by all who tasted it—even Mrs. Johnny Reb. A few of the sol-

51

diers participated too heartily in the revelry with a beverage that is known as Taos Lightning. Theirs is not an easy life here in this harsh land, so they will not be blamed by me.

I see Luke hurrying toward me on Traveler. As he is not frowning, I think we must now number fifty wagons. And so, good-bye, little book. I may not see you again until we are on our own land, which I have named "Prairie Home."

Chapter 2

July 24, 1865. Prairie Home, Colorado Territory, Two hundred nineteen miles west from Fort Kearney, a million miles from Fort Madison.

We are home at last, but O, what disappointment met me! There is too much sky here, sky and endless prairie. I never saw a place as ordinary as this. I counted three trees on our land, and one of them is dead. No wonder this is called the Great "Plain." What we lack in vegetation, we make up in dry weeds and rattlesnakes. Husband says to keep a stout stick at hand.

Luke has gone to Mingo, which is the nearest town, some eight miles distant, where he will buy necessities. It is the first time I have been alone since arriving here, hence the first time I have been able to sit and write in this little journal. Tomorrow, Luke will cut out strips of the prairie using a sod plow and lay them like bricks to build the walls of our home. Who would have thought myself so anxious to claim a sod hut? I think it will be a little like living in a hole in the ground, but it has one advantage: It is dirt cheap.

If the sod house is not ready in time, says Husband, we will have to live in the barn, with the animals during the bad months, since winter blizzards are fierce here. He will build the barn first, having already laid the foundation. We shall surely perish if we spend the winter in the wagon, predicts Luke, although I am told two brothers near here, having arrived Christmas before last, when the prairie was covered with snow, lived three months in their Conestoga. I looked at the backsides of our oxen for too many miles over the plains and do not relish sharing my hearth with them. Our Lord Jesus Christ may have been born in a stable, but He was not forced to spend a Colorado winter in one. I would as soon flee into Egypt.

O, I should not indulge in such blasphemy, but I will need my funny bone if I am to survive here.

My heart sank when Luke pointed out our new home, though I would not for anything let him see my disappointment, saying instead it was as pretty a picture as I ever saw. How he recognized our place, I do not know, because there are no landmarks. It looks just like the hundreds of miles of prairie recently crossed o'er by us, so repetitious and uneventful that I saw no reason to write in this book after leaving Fort Kearney. Colorado Territory is too big; it frightens me. I would like a little clump of trees or a pond to break the open space, something human-size that would make this land not so vast. I think I could get lost right out here in my front yard. The endless prairie is the loneliest place I ever saw.

Luke must have thought me a goose on our journey for going on so about the cheery brooks and flowery meadows that I expected to find in Colorado. I knew our place would not be like a farm in old Iowa, but I did think that we would pass over a hill and see a pretty green valley, and Luke would take my hand and say, "Mattie dear, here is our home."

When Luke disappeared this morning, I sat down on my little trunk and had a good cry, my first real cry since our marriage. Then I dried my eyes, for if a thing can be helped, I help it. But if it cannot, then I shall try to make the best of it. If I do not, Luke might wish he'd married someone else, like Persia. That foolish girl would not last a day out here. Of course, Luke knows that, and I hope he counts himself lucky that he fell in love with me, not her. I said at the outset that I was practical and not given to pretty phrases. So it was right that Luke did not promise me a home in a dell. I will not make Husband sorry he brought me here. I shall content myself with the blessings I have, believing, as the songwriter says, "Better times a-comin'."

Besides, Luke is happy here, and that

should be happiness enough for Wife. Last night, as we lay in our bed in the wagon, Luke pointed out the "drinking gourd" among the stars, and he said, "My cup runneth over." I did not know if he meant he was satisfied with the land or with me or both. I fancy I was at least part of that full cup, because Luke kissed me on the mouth, twice, and he hugged me some (which I enjoy), before he did what he enjoys.

I begged Luke to let me go into town with him today, in hopes I would not forget what a tree looks like, and perhaps even have a sociable visit with another woman, as I don't want to forget what a woman looks like, either. But Luke said someone must stay here or Pikers, as the Godless tramps from Pike County, Missouri, are called, will steal our things. He does not seem to care that Pikers might steal me!

~

July 28, 1865. Prairie Home.

Luke is off to town again, and though I had been hoping to go with him, I am glad for a little time to tend to Self. I have taken a bath as best I could, heating water in the teakettle and pouring it into the largest cooking pot, which I also use as laundry tub. I am adapting. I pretended the vessel was the size of a horse trough, then took a leisurely bath right out in the open, throwing modesty to the winds. The rattlesnakes were shocked! I even washed my hair in salts of tartar, which was the first time since my wedding—if I do not count the soaking it got in rainstorms on the trail.

Of course, I was not entirely wanton, because I poured the dirty bath water on the thirsty plants in my kitchen garden. Even with a well, which Luke had dug in the spring, we are careful of water and do not waste a single precious drop. I saved enough of the hot water in the kettle to brew a pot of tea from my little hoard of leaves carried from Iowa. The tea Luke brought last time he went to Mingo was so common that we use it for our daily drink and save the good for special occasions. I have declared *this* to be such an occasion and am throwing a nice tea for Self and journal, setting out my good china cup, as well as china plate for the molasses sponge cake brought to me by my neighbor, a Mrs. Smith.

I was glad for her visit on Sunday last, even if she is a queer goose. She did not present me with her calling card, because such etiquette is unknown in this land, and because she cannot read, I think.

Oh, yes, the word is out that Mr. Spenser and wife are at home, and Eban and the aforementioned Mrs. Eban Smith were our first callers. I do not know her Christian name, because after telling my own, I asked for hers, and she replied, "I am *Mrs.* Eban Smith," with the emphasis on *Mrs.* So "Missus" she will always be to me.

I am glad my "house," which is mostly fresh air, made up of the wagon cover attached to the foundation of the barn, was in good order, because Missus inspected every inch of it. "You're none like your mister described," said she, pulling out a drawer of my carved dresser to see what was inside. She clucked with disapproval at my hair wreath, which I had displayed on my trunk for the occasion, but said naught, then returned to her original subject. "I thought you'd be a bitty thing. I can see you're not. Be glad for it, I say. This land chews up and spits out the weak." To emphasize her point, she removed the little corncob pipe she had been smoking since her arrival and spat upon my earthen floor. I almost did not mind, as she tickled me so. I must remember to twit my husband for his presumption in telling his neighbors when he was here in the spring to stake his claim that he was going home for a wife ere he made known his decision to his intended. I laughed to myself when I thought what Luke would have said to them had I ~~had~~ turned him down.

The "mister," too, looked me up and down whilst he moved his quid of "tobac," as he calls it, from one cheek to the other. Then he sat down and began to pull the beggar-lice from his clothing. (They are are not real lice, but little burrs that stick to everything they touch.) I will have to get used to the manners of the country.

"He talked about you plenty. That's for sure," Mr. Smith said. I dipped my head to acknowledge the compliment, feeling inside as if I would burst with pride. To think I did not even suspect Luke was sweet on me! Mrs. Smith says they thought I might be a city girl, because Luke had hired a man to witch for water and then dug a well before going back to Iowa. The Smiths have been on their land for more than a year and still haul their water. I wanted to tell her I would not have moved west without assurances of a well, but I said nothing, as I did not want her to think me pert. Besides, 'twas not the truth. I knew so little of this land, it had not occurred to me to question Luke about water.

I set the sponge cake on my Delft plate and brought out silver forks and china plates, instead of tin ones, even though Missus sniffed and said, "Well, ain't you the fancy one. They'll be soon broke out here." While she is a friendly woman, she is large and coarse, with a face like a ham, and is none too tidy, which made me wonder about the cake. No matter how scarce water is, I intend to keep my person as clean as possible.

Still, I am not one to stand on ceremony, so I did not inspect the cake too closely, and it did taste all right. She said she "needed Sally Ann bad," and asked for the loan of a teacup of it. After some confusion, I determined "Sally Ann" was saleratus. So I gave it to her, saying it was not a loan, but a gift, for I would distrust anything she returned. As I did not want to give her the cup as well, I looked about for a container for the saleratus, but Missus came to the rescue by removing her cap, pouring the powder into it, and tying it up with the cap ribbons. She is almost bald, false hair being not so esteemed here as at home.

I was glad for the company, especially as Mr. Smith brought us a present of a clump of pieplant, which I have set out, for I do like rhubarb pie. Luke says he thinks I passed inspection.

Missus told me that earlier this year, a woman was killed east of here by Indians, and *scalped,* and she seemed surprised Luke had not mentioned it. I was vexed at Husband and told him so, but he says it was the work of renegades, who have already removed themselves to Kansas. There are too many whites in Colorado Territory this season for their liking. We are in far greater danger from the rag-tag Rebels moving west, Luke says. Besides, he added with his smile, which always makes my insides melt like jelly left on a hot stove, if he'd told me about the Indians, I might not have come. Though I shivered with the thought of savages, his answer suited me.

When we arrived here, we slept in the wagon because we did not have a tent. (Did that make us discon*tent*ed? I asked.) Then Luke decided to attach our wagon sheet to the foundation of the barn, and we have a regular fresh-air house for the summer. Luke calls it a *portal,* which is a Spaniard word, meaning "porch." He set up the stove outside, and the view from my "kitchen window" is so far off that I think I can see the earth curve.

Our crop is in the ground, and a lot of work it was, though Luke had planted most before he went to Fort Madison. For a time, we were in the field day and night. While Luke plowed the remaining furrows, in line with the North Star, I dropped in the seeds. Then I scurried to cook and clean, as much as one can clean an outdoor house. There, I knew I would find something in this living arrangement to like!

We still rest on the Sabbath. Luke reads the Bible aloud, and sometimes he gets a little preachy. I do not know if that is his nature, or if he is trying to act as he believes an old married man should. Afterward, we sing fond old hymns, always ending with "Abide with Me." It is my favorite time of the week, and Luke's, too, I think. Last Sunday, whilst we sang, Luke took my hand, and when we finished, we sat without talking, looking out over our farm. It may not be the home I had dreamed of as my bridal bower, but the husband who goes with it is first-rate!

I am having my monthly unwellness now, another reason I am glad for a day of leisure, as my back troubles me so at these times. As a married woman, I shall watch closely for signs that signal the onset of the menses. I don't want a baby yet, especially out here on the prairie, with only dirty Mrs. Smith to act the midwife. We have so much work to prepare our home, and I am just getting to know Luke. But I suppose the Lord will make that decision, with a little help from Husband.

There is a spray of dust on the horizon, like a puff of smoke. Most likely, it is Luke. I must hurry and clean up after my tea party, and put you away, my little friend, so Luke will not think I have spent the day in idleness. I hope he is hurrying because there are letters from home. We have not had a word yet.

No letters yet received from the folks, but I knew I could count on Carrie, whose letter I paste here. She is always in my thoughts. When writing in this journal, I often pretend I am having a conversation with that dearest soul mate.

Friend Mattie
 Yours of the trail, expressed from Frt. K'rny, at hand. When Will left for the post office yesterday, I said I would give ten dollars for a letter from you, and upon returning, he held out his hand for the coin. As I did not have one, he agreed upon ten kisses. Now I believe I know how to get rich.
 I am glad I may write frank. You are to do same, since Will don't read my mail either, and you know I shall reveal nothing of a personal nature to another soul. My silence is forever. I can write just a line because the hired man is saddling old Nell for a trip to town, and he won't wait but a minute for this. Men think theirs is the right to tell us what to do, even the hired hands. I want this to go today, so you know you haven't been forgotten by your friend.
 There is exciting news to tell. I am enceinte and expect to deliver in February. Don't write of it to nobody, because I want to be in society as long as I can. Will says he'll hire all the women I need at harvest, for he don't

want me to have to cook for threshers. I would have a baby every year to get out of that work! I am feeling fine, except a little tired of an evening. Will treats me as good as a china plate. I know it's bold to say, but I miss the romps that me and Will had before we knew of my condition. I hope things are better for you that way. In the beginning, when Will was in such a hurry, I found it best to put my mind to embroidery stitches, and that helped me through the act. It was then that I thought up the one we call Hen's Foot. I advise you do same. It puts that time to beneficial use.

All friends are fine. Your sister Jemima tells it about that you have a brick house and red barn, though I heard Persia say it is a lie. I asked of her, "How would you know?"

"How would I know?" she repeated in that annoying habit of hers, like she can't think fast enough to give an answer. "How would I know? Well, I know. That's all."

I saw her at the milliner's, wearing her corset laced so tight, she had to breathe like a lizard. She is keeping company with Abner, though he don't seem so happy with her as he was with you. She trifles with him, and he will be sorely disappointed if matrimony is his goal. If he should succeed on that score, he will be sorrier yet, as she must always be top hen on the roost.

I asked Will if the baby was a girl, could we name it for you. Says Will, "Name her any-thing you like, because he is sure to be a boy."

I know Luke was your heart's desire, and

once you had fallen in love, you couldn't get out. But I wish you had found a boy willing to stay at home. O, friend Mattie, I miss your company!

    Now I must put down my pen. May you be well and not forget the affectionate girl you left behind in old Fort Madison is the ardent wish of

Carrie Fritch

August 8, 1865. Prairie Home.

The dreary sunbonnet that I once vowed never to wear is my constant companion, keeping not only sun but hot wind and its cargo of dust off my face. The only shade we have is the *portal,* where I sit now, grateful to take off the hateful bonnet, which traps the heat about my face. I never saw a place so hot or so dry or so brown—or a woman the same. My hands are walnut in color, and freckled from the sun, and my face is so dried up, I must look like a snake. I don't know for sure, however. I did not put a looking glass into our wagon, and if I had, I think I would not know the woman staring from it. Still, I am a little curious to see if she has changed with marriage. The reflection in the dishpan is not a true likeness.

    I wish I could love it here as Luke does; he believes homesteading to be a noble experiment. But each time I find something to like—the cool, dry evening air is quite refreshing—I wake up to a terrifying storm that splits the heavens asunder with jagg'd flashes of white, or to another cloudless sky, where there is not a moment's relief from the yellow orb of day, as the poet calls it. Luke asked me once on the trail if I thought Colorado would be too near sunset. Not too near sunset, but it is too near the *sun* for my liking.

My plaints are only for this little book. I strive not to let Luke know my true feelings. Last evening, he asked what I would think of moving back to Fort Madison. My heart leapt up, but I was cautious and said that, like Ruth, I would follow wherever he led. Then I added, "Of course, I should miss our honeymoon cottage on the prairie, and this life in a new land." Luke put his arm around me, drew me close, and said he was glad he had chosen a woman with courage and good humor. I felt aptly rewarded for my little falsehood.

The sun's glare caused me another headache, making me feel as if a red-hot poker has been struck through my head. I am glad Luke is away today so that I can enjoy my misery in solitude. He has little sympathy for any weakness, so I must do my best to hide my pain. I enjoy these days alone when Luke goes into town, as it is a chance to spend time with my journal. I decided at the outset that this book would be mine alone, not to be shared with anyone. That means I do not record the weather and events of each day but, instead, wait until I have time to reflect upon my life. As I have not met a woman who could be my dearest friend (and will never meet one as true as Carrie), this book serves as a silent companion, a witness to my joys and sorrows and confessions.

It helps to confide to my journal the things I can confide to no one.

Well, I will have to confide them another time, as I have a more important task. Luke's birthday will be here shortly, and as there is no jewelry store where I can buy him a memento, as he did for me at St. Joe, I have put aside this day to make him a shirt out of a red-and-yellow-striped skirt that I scorched whilst cooking over a campfire. Fortunately, there is enough good material left, and as the skirt was new, the fabric will make up into a handsome garment.

Before I close this book, I must record that Husband took me with him on his last trip to "civilization," and I have no desire to return to the town of Mingo, Colorado Territory, thank you. Of course, I did not expect fine stores or even a Christian house of worship. Nor did I even hold out much hope of meeting a refined class of people. Still, I believed it would be a town of some slight substance with a dry goods, where I might have social intercourse with a woman of my class. But no sir!

Mingo, which Missus described as an "awful, sinful place," is just one shabby building, no more than a doggery inhabited by rascals. It serves as saloon and stage station, post office, lunchroom, and hospital. I saw a sign reading, "Haircuts 25 cents. Blisters removed 50 cents. Toes removed $5. Legs amputated $20." I assume the leg was removed with the toes attached, and, therefore was a bargain. Provisions, however, are very dear, and I paid twenty-five cents for a spool of thread. Others may think me as cheap as a three-legged mule, but I save and reuse my basting thread.

The food in Mingo made me long for the cold biscuits of our Overland Trail days. Luke refused to subject me to those inside the saloon (though I admit I was longing to satisfy my curiosity). So I waited on the street whilst he inquired after the mail. Two drunken men were bold enough to look me over, but I ignored them. Then one thrust his face next to mine and said, "I'll take you, Katy." I screamed, and Luke bolted out the door, and he would have thrashed the pair except that they ran as fast as they could, falling in the dirt of the street, which made me laugh. Luke announced loudly that anyone who assaulted his wife would have him to deal with. I said he should not trouble himself with such rowdies. In my heart of hearts, however, I was much pleased at this public display from my gallant defender.

I saw only one woman in Mingo, a slattern in a saffron-colored dress. She came from the barroom to see the cause of the commotion. When I mentioned her to Mrs. Smith (whose first name, I have discovered, is Elode, reason enough to call her Missus), she replied that the woman had worked in a bagnio in one of the gold camps, then in a Denver resort, before marrying Burt Connor, who keeps the Mingo saloon. She was called "Red Legs" because of her fondness for red stockings, and she is as devoid of morals as they come. I informed Mrs. Smith I assumed as much, but I had not, and when I discovered she was a "soiled dove" (the term Missus used), I wished I'd studied her better. Missus says Mrs. Connor is Southern, like many of the unnatural women in this country. The war left them little of value apart from their "virtue," and, of course, the Southern woman's morals are different from ours, for it is well known they embrace the free-love movement.

We will have to make the best of the Smiths, who aren't so bad, now we know them better. She admitted when we returned their visit, calling on her at her "poppety," as she calls it, that she was in a state when she met me. "With that well Mr. Spenser dug before you come, we figured you for some high-toned lady who'd think us common," she told me. I laughed that anybody would be afraid to meet me and assured her I'd never think *her* common. Well, what else would you call a woman who licks her plate when she is finished eating?

Missus lived on her place six months before she ever saw a tree, and when she did, she was so overcome at the sight that she hugged it. "Now, when you get to feeling like that—and mark my words, you will if you ain't already—you come to me, and we'll have us a good cry together. Men don't understand what 'tis to give up the only home you ever knew and move to hell-in-Colorado."

I hope Luke brings back letters from home. In Carrie's last (which is in my trunk, since there is not room in this book to store all), she said her secret was no more, since Will has told all. She might as well be as big as a pumpkin. There was sad news in the last mail from Mother, as she, too, is enceinte, and has been in poor health. She knew of her situation before I left but did not want to be the cause of worry, so revealed nothing. She puts the best face on it, saying a little one will be a companion in her old age, but O, I worry, because she is not strong. She has such difficulty in the last months, and I will not be there to help her. Mother says God always knows what He is doing. Well, I may blaspheme, but God is a man. If He had been a woman, He would have made other plans for childbearing.

Darling Mother was married at fifteen, a mother before a year was out, and she has had the care of little ones ever since. I do not intend to follow her example, although I am not exactly sure how I shall prevent it. Onanism is wicked, and surely must be messy, and I would never dare suggest it to Luke. I think he would not care for "French cobwebs," even if they were available at the all-purpose store in Mingo. Besides, with Luke's demands, I would have to order a gross of them, as they cannot be washed out. I may employ a small sponge soaked in a little vinegar, or a piece of fine wool, inserted into the womb, a method I have been told is so cunning that, excepting for the small ribbon attached to the sponge to remove it, even a husband doesn't know of it. Of course, I would prefer the only true method—continence.

I have spent too much time at my writing,

and now I must commence the birthday shirt, ere Luke returns and finds me at work, thus spoiling the surprise.

August 23, 1865. Prairie Home.

My Darling Boy has given _me_ a wonderful surprise.

"Would it suit you to go to church services?" he asked on Saturday before last, giving me a sly smile.

As there is no church nearby, and the sanctity of the Sabbath is disregarded by most in this region, I thought he was joking, and I replied in the same manner, "Which one should we select?"

"The one at home, in your own parlor," Husband replied. He had let it be known last time he was in town that we would be pleased to host Sabbath services for any and all who were interested. He thought to surprise me, then worried, and rightly so, that I might prefer to be forewarned.

"You should have told me. There is no time to prepare," I said.

"The other women will bring dinner. So you won't be made to cook, but I expect you'll have to sweep the floor and dust," he said, which made us both laugh, as we are still living in the _portal_. Still, one cannot expect a _husband_ to understand the many things that must be attended to before guests call.

I flew at the task, and our little "cottage" looked most festive when our fellow communicants arrived. I placed a white cloth on the table, and upon it, a bouquet of wildflowers, which tickled Missus, who called them weeds.

Nineteen were in attendance. Besides ourselves and the Smiths (who smoked and chewed throughout the day, except when eating), there were Hiram and Lucinda Osterwald, poorly dressed in faded bettermost, accompanied by the remaining member of what was once their brood of nine. The son's name is Brownie, and he is a giant of a young man, with queer ways. The mother is sickly, and at first, I thought she suffered from female debility and was in need of a tonic. Then I was told that she had taken a fall, and I observed her badly bruised arms and face. When I inquired of the husband if I could be of assistance, he asked roughly that I not take notice, since 'twould embarrass her. Since I am clumsy myself, who am I to say a thing about it?

Emily Amidon, who came with husband, Elbert, and two babes, is nearest my age, and my favorite. It is obvious another little Amidon is due soon, but that state scarcely keeps a woman out of society in this country. She did not put on airs and tell me her name was *Mrs.* Amidon, but stated at the outset that it was Emily Louise and I was to call her Emmie Lou, because she hoped we would be friends. Emmie Lou, who is tiny, with ringlets the color of corn silk, is a cultured person, having studied the piano and other instruments for ten years in Philadelphia before she was persuaded to marry Mr. Amidon and journey west.

Sallie and Fayette Garfield are about our age, but Luke says they are Southern, so he warned me not to become too friendly. I think they are not as bad as other Rebels, for Missus said they were Whigs before the war and opposed withdrawal from the Union, although, when called, Mr. Garfield gladly served the Southern cause. They have a son, a pettish boy, who remained close by the parents. Also here was a fat and jolly German couple named Himmel, well advanced in years, who put me in mind of potato bugs. They barely speak our language but seemed refined, and grateful for a chance at Christian worship.

Our little group of pilgrims was complete with the addition of three single homesteaders. Two are brothers, Thompson and Moses Earley, from Jo Daviess County, Illinois, handsome men. They are the ones who lived in the wagon one winter. Both are tall, with hair that is almost black, and dark eyes, gray, I think. Moses has a mustache like a dandy, but Tom is clean-shaven. They, too, advised us to call them by their first names, to avoid confusion.

Moses says he is fed up with this country and wants to go to the gold fields to make his fortune. Thompson is satisfied to stay at farming, having already seen enough adventure; he fought for the Union under the glorious boy general, George Armstrong Custer. When I inquired if he believed General Custer would be President one day, as some at home have talked about, Tom replied that General Custer was brave, but too impetuous for his taste. Tom prefers another heroic general by the name of Grant, a man who is a personal favorite of mine, too. I think I shall enjoy discussing politics with the brothers Earley, if Luke approves, of course.

The other homesteader is between thirty and forty, I would judge, and as big as a barn, but that is not the curious thing. She is a woman! Her name is Miss Anna Figg, and Missus says she is stronger than either of the Earley boys. This member of the fairer sex, who weighs fifteen stone and rides a horse sidesaddle, sitting it as stiff as a churn dash, does her own plowing and built her house by herself. She plans to put in a well, with but little help. Her hard work has not unsexed her. Missus says her house is as neat as a pin, and she brought with her a "prairie cake." I don't like it so much as chocolate, but it was a light and dainty cake, nonetheless.

We opened our service with prayer. Then all enjoyed the singing of hymns, and I noticed many a wet eye when "The Old Rugged Cross" was finished. There were calls for old favorites, even "Silent Night." Moses, who accompanied us on the dulcimer, suggested "The Battle Hymn of the Republic," with a glance at the Rebel couple, who stiffened. Luke replied that the selection, being a patriotic song, was not a proper Sabbath choice, thus avoiding a renewed conflict between North and South, which, due to sheer numbers, the North would have won again. Moses then proposed "Turkey in the Straw." Luke gave him a stern look, although I thought 'twas funny and nearly laughed out loud. Moses is a cheerful boy, and I think I like him better than his brother, who is a very sober fellow.

As Luke was the host and he is a general favorite, he was asked to sermonize. When he began, the women took out knitting and mending (one brought a pair of drawers that needed repair), for hands are not idle here. I picked up my piecing and was glad for it, as Luke spoke for a very long time, not pausing until the little Garfield boy said, "The preach sure comes out of that man." Even Luke had to smile at the remark, and he quickly ended his sermon.

Luke wore the shirt I made for his birthday. Mrs. Garfield, who is a true Southern woman in her flirtatiousness (though I don't mind, because jealousy is not in my nature), told him it was as handsome a shirt as she ever saw, and Luke puffed out his chest like a rooster, not stopping to think he was preening for the wife of a Rebel. I learned this about my husband that day: He is vain. But I suppose any man as handsome as Luke has the right to be.

Whilst the men talked after service, the women set the dinner upon the table, each putting out the tin plates she had brought with her, for no one here is expected to have enough dishes to serve guests. Utensils, too, being rare, were provided by the guests. Miss Figg says she has only two forks, and she prizes them so highly that she has given them names—Samuel and Little Pete.

Mrs. Himmel ran her hand over my good

Delft plate, as if it were made of solid gold, and Mrs. Osterwald whispered she could not even touch the pillow or cigar silks that Carrie made me, for fear of snagging its delicate threads with her rough hands. I was much pleased with their kind remarks over my possessions, and I had to chide myself for pridefulness on the Sabbath. I have been repaid for it with the discovery that one of my silver spoons is missing. I cannot believe any of the Sabbath worshipers would have taken it, so I conclude it fell upon the ground and will be recovered one day.

We all joined in and ate until there was nothing left. The chocolate cake that was my contribution disappeared first and was pronounced tasty by all who partook. The Earley brothers said they had not tasted chocolate since moving to Colorado Territory. All agreed it was a splendid event and that we would set aside one Sunday of each month to worship together.

September 22, 1865. Prairie Home.

Luke and I were in the field when of a sudden we saw a rider making haste toward us. Luke recognized him as Mr. Osterwald, who, as soon as he was in shouting distance, yelled, "Indians! Indians are coming!" Luke and I ran for the *portal,* where our weapons are kept, intending to make our stand there. But when he had calmed himself, Mr. Osterwald told us Indians were not following behind him but had been seen, painted for war, east of here.

He said we were to get out of the country at once and go to Mingo, where all the folks were gathering.

A farmer on his way to Mingo had spied the Red Men whilst taking his rest. He hid in a ditch until the brutes were gone, then made his way to a homestead. Whose farm it was, he did not know, only that the Indians had been there ahead of him and burnt the place, leaving only a dead man, whose face had been hacked away.

While Luke and Mr. Osterwald hitched the Osterwald horse and the buttermilk to the wagon, then saddled Traveler, I snatched up quilts and food, and in a moment we were ready. Luke helped me into the wagon, then turned and told Mr. Osterwald to get in beside me, for he would warn the neighbors farther south. Mr. Osterwald protested, but Luke said firmly, "You left your own people to come to us. Now it is my turn. Mrs. Spenser is good with a shotgun, and she's not one to lose her head." My heart swelled up with pride at this bravest and noblest of husbands, and I thought it was little wonder that with gallant soldiers like Luke Spenser, we licked the Old South.

I swore to match Luke's steadfastness, and though I desired him to carry me to Mingo himself, I would not complain. Instead, I entreated Mr. Osterwald to climb onto the seat next to me, wished Husband Godspeed, and raised my hand in a cheery good-bye. To my surprise, Luke swung Traveler next to the wagon seat and kissed me full on the mouth—

75

with Mr. Osterwald looking on! Then my brave boy took off like thunder across the prairie.

All was chaos in Mingo. The stage station is built of bricks made from earth and straw mixed together, then baked in the sun, making them as hard as stone. It is called adobe, and is thick enough to stop arrows and even bullets, and it was a far better place to make a stand than our *portal*. There was a terrible din within—women shouting, children crying, and knitting needles clacking, for nothing is so important that it keeps women's hands from work. The rooms were very crowded, and I thought we might be in greater danger of suffocation than from the arrows of savages.

Most of our fellow worshipers were there. Mr. Osterwald joined Mr. Amidon, the Earley boys, and others (including Miss Figg), who were posted about the station as lookouts. I spied Mrs. Osterwald with her son, Brownie, who, I have learned, is simple. Mrs. Smith stood guard over the cookstove with the "stumpet," Mrs. Connor. I guess Missus is not so particular about the company she keeps when there is food to be had, even if it was squirrel stew, which was never a favorite of mine.

Despite the excitement, I paid close attention to Mrs. Conner, so's I could describe her to Carrie. I confess, she seemed no different from any other woman working a hot cookstove. She is plump and pretty, with bright red cheeks, due to the heat, I think, and not to rouge. Slatterns do not wear satin and lace here, not whilst they cook squirrel stew anyway, and I could not detect even a flash of the red stockings that were her trademark. She wore a dirty apron, pinned to a slimsy dress, whose sleeves were rolled up above the elbows. Her hair was untidy, falling about her face. I was much disappointed.

I found Emmie Lou, who looked pale and frightened. "Don't worry," said I. "There are enough men out there to whip a thousand of the savages."

"It's not the Indians that scare me. I think I'm going to be sick." To my look of confusion, she explained, "My time has come. All this excitement has brought it on."

"Lordy, here?" asked I, stupidly. "Now?"

"The baby says when. I don't."

"Then you have a right smart baby, for there are a dozen women here to help," I told her, and we both laughed. Then her face twisted in pain, and not knowing what else to do, I went to Mrs. Smith for help.

"Hell's bells, why did she pick a time like this?" asked Missus, who was indeed a cross old soul that day. She held a plate of food close to her face and ate from it, using her spoon like a pitchfork. I wanted to repeat what Emmie Lou had said about the baby picking its own time, but I did not think Missus would understand our little repartee.

"You take over the cooking, Elode. You never was much help with birthing," said Mrs. Connor in a way that made me think they were better acquainted than Missus wanted it known. Then Mrs. Connor said to me, "It's all right. I've done this before. Lots of times. We'll put her to bed in the back room. You know anything about birthing?"

"I've helped with the sheep, Mrs. Connor," I said.

Missus gave a laugh of scorn, but Mrs. Connor replied, "Not much different. Sheep have a harder time of it. And you don't need to put on the airs with me. It ain't Mrs. Connor. It's just plain old Jessie."

Jessie was right. It wasn't much different from sheep, except that when it's over, the ewe and kid are turned out to pasture to rest. A woman must make up for lost time.

The baby is small and squally but appears to be in good health. She is a another girl. They are all girls. Emmie Lou said she had her heart set on a boy this time and had not picked out a name for a girl. I suggested Carrie.

Since this was the first time a baby had been born in his station, Mr. Connor thought the men should celebrate. He took out a jug and handed it around until Jessie grabbed it and held it high, saying, "Those 'at done the work gets first call." She took a swallow, then offered the jug to me, but I declined. At home, I would have let my disapproval of such an offer be known, but the manners of the country are different, and graciousness was called for.

Jessie poured some liquor into a tin cup, which she took to Emmie Lou, who was not so particular as I. Perhaps I, too, will become intemperate ere my days in Colorado Territory are over. When she returned the jug to Mr. Connor, she warned the men to go easy because "we don't need no drunken Indian fighters."

"Then best you not let Mrs. Spenser there take her a swallow. You bet," said a voice from the doorway. All turned to me as I burned from embarrassment and confusion that any chucklehead would speak ill of me. I looked to see who had made himself so bold, and caught the rheumy eye of Ben Bondurant! He is the only man I could forgive for such impertinence, and when I saw his dear misshapen face, all fear for our safety fled, as I knew we were in good hands.

"I crossed with Mrs. Spenser, and she's game," he explained to the others, without giving the particulars. When we had a few minutes to ourselves, he told me he'd found the gold fields a humbug and was cured of "quartz on the brain." He had repaired to Mingo to look about, with the hope of finding a suitable homestead.

I had put the savages out of my mind while attending the birth of the babe, but when I went outside to speak with Mr. Bondurant, worry returned. I had not expected Luke to be away so long. Mr. Bondurant and others sought to calm me as the time passed, with no sign of Husband. I put up a brave front and did not let my emotions show, because I knew Luke would not like to hear that I had dissolved into womanly tears, but, O, never have I been so frightened, even when under Indian attack on the Overland Trail. I thought if something had happened to Luke, I should not want to live, either.

At last, when night had nearly fallen, a wagon appeared in the distance, someone declaring it belonged to the German couple, the Himmels. Until then, none had remembered them, for they are newer than even I am to this country and keep to themselves. As the wagon came closer, my heart leapt into my throat because I recognized Traveler tied behind. Looking closer, I saw that Luke held the reins.

There was great commotion when he drew up, the men holding the horses and helping Mrs. Himmel from the wagon. The woman tore at her face and moaned in her guttural language, which none could understand, and fearing something untoward had befallen her husband, I directed my attention to the wagon bed, as did others.

One of the men removed a quilt, revealing the corpse of Mr. Himmel, with the top of his head torn away. That brought fresh cries of anguish from the widow, and two women rushed to her aid, drawing her inside the station. Even after the door closed, we heard the sorrowful wails in her foreign gibberish, as she had forgotten how to speak the few words of English she knows.

Those near the wagon turned as one to Luke for explanation, and even in my concern, I could not help but note with pride that the women seemed to regard him as a hero. Luke said the Indians had made a loop to the east as though to throw us off, then turned back and came upon the Himmel farm. Mr. Himmel was without, but he made it safely into the house, where he shoved his wife into a hole in the soddy floor, covering it with a rug. Then that brave husband protected his loved one by facing the savages alone until, at last, he was overcome and most horribly mutilated.

His poor wife could only listen, not knowing the outcome, until all was quiet, and she emerged from her hiding place, to discover her husband mortally wounded and scalped. Luke arrived before the man died, and he told me in private that he hoped never again to hear such pitiful cries, which were even worse than those of the wounded Rebel on the trail. As the Indians had not found the Himmel horses, which were grazing some distance away, Luke hitched them to a wagon and lifted the wounded man into it, but he died before they had gone more than a few rods.

My husband was badly shaken by his experience, because when we were at last alone, he asked me, "What have I brought you to?"

I put my arms around him, which Luke did not resist, and replied, "You did not promise me an easy life when you asked me to be your wife, Luke Spenser. I can bear anything if I am at your side."

A corpse in our midst made everyone uneasy. The men opened another jug, whilst the women and children returned to the main room of the station, staying as far as they could from the remains of Mr. Himmel. I joined Jessie, who was preparing the body, and helped her as best I could, and together, we made a shroud of an old blanket. Jessie said it was not right to keep the body in that room, where it would cause the children nightmares and turn putrid in the heat of the cookstove. Nor could we leave it outside to attract wolves. She proposed moving the remains into the bedroom with Emmie Lou. "It won't bother her. I gave her enough whiskey so's she'll sleep like sixty," said Jessie.

I sat up all night with the corpse, but I was so tired that I dozed off in my chair and did not waken until I heard Emmie Lou stir. Then I took her babe to her to nurse, and myself fed Emmie Lou a cup of the nourishing squirrel broth that Jessie had put aside. Until morning when the men came to remove the body, Emmie Lou did not know who shared her sickroom.

"There was no place else to put him," I explained. "You were never alone with him."

"No matter," Emmie Lou said. "Birth and death in the same room. Now who's the lucky one?" She laughed at that, but not entirely in mirth, I believe. She is very tired and not in her right mind. I do not envy her. She will be going home to a dugout, a hole scooped out of a hillside that is more suitable for badgers than a mother with three little ones under the age of two. It is entirely too much and will get worse, as I presume Mr. Amidon will want her to try again so's he can have a son. I count myself fortunate that Luke will not misuse me in that manner.

In the morning, the soldiers arrived, and a "buffalo soldier," as the Negro enlisted man is called, told us the renegades had run off to Kansas and would bother us no more. Being tired of the hurly-burly in the station, we hastily buried Mr. Himmel in the little Mingo graveyard. He is the first Christian to be laid to rest there, says Missus, the other occupants being gamblers, blackguards, and highwaymen.

We did not talk of it on the way, but I know Luke, as well as Self, wondered what sight would greet us when we reached our home. I admit my foolish but heartfelt fear was that the Red Men had smashed my Delft plate and taken my journal, though as they can barely speak our language, surely they cannot read it. We found no sign of the savages, however, for which I thank God.

That very afternoon, Luke took out the sod plow and began cutting strips for our little house. The plow tearing through the grasses filled the air with a sound not unlike that of ripping yard goods. On our ride home, I had insisted he start the work immediately, for the *portal* is no protection against the savages. Luke gave me no trouble on that score. I helped him lay the strips, staggered like bricks and sod side down so that the prickly grass grips the dirt on the layer of prairie grass beneath.

Within three days, our house was finished. It has a window frame of lumber (which awaits its glass), for when Luke sets his mind to a thing, he does it proper. We will make do with the dirt floor until there is time (and money) for boards. Packed hard and swept each morning, a dirt floor is every bit as nice as a carpet. And it won't wear out! I am glad that Husband has already fashioned us a bedstead, for I do not relish making up my bed with rake.

I asked Luke what would become of Mrs. Himmel. The poor woman is a foreigner, with none of her own people in this country. Mr. Amidon had asked her to go home with them to help his wife with the babies, but the grieving widow refused, and so remained at the station, where Jessie said she could give a hand with the work there. I think Jessie is softhearted, and a good woman, despite her unsavory past.

"Oh, I shouldn't worry about Mrs. Himmel. There are plenty of old bachelors about. She'll be married within the month," replied Luke. I was shocked, and told him so, but Husband said gruffly, "This isn't a land for weaklings. It's root hog or die. If you can't understand that, you shouldn't have come."

My eyes stung at the reproof, especially after his loving words of a few days before, but I said nothing, blaming Luke's ill temper on his own emotions at the danger we had just passed through.

October 4, 1865. Prairie Home.
Luke was wrong about Mrs. Himmel. She did not marry an old bachelor as was expected. The Earley boys have just brought the news. A week after her husband's death, Mrs. Himmel went into the stable in Mingo and hanged herself from the cross beam.

84

November 10, 1865. Prairie Home.

Luke has taken the horses to help Mr. Smith pull a stump, though why anybody would care about moving such an item, I cannot understand. Out here, the remains of a tree is a landmark to be ranked with the the United States Capitol. Mr. Smith asked to borrow our horses, as his are poor, and Luke said he would go along to help. He feared Mr. Smith had something more in mind than stump pulling, and Luke did not trust him not to overwork our animals. Since observing the Smiths at Mingo, I am not so fond of them. Borrow, borrow, borrow, and never repay—that is the Smiths. With so few neighbors, we dare not refuse, however, and we hold our tongues. Luke said I might go with him, but I did not care to spend a day gossiping with meddlesome Missus in her soddy with no window. She does not wash her teeth, and she smokes and spits the day long.

Helping each other is the way of the country, as none can afford to hire workers except, perhaps, the Amidons. Emmie Lou confided her people are well-off, and they had sent her funds to build a proper house, which was begun right after the latest babe was born. Both her mother and father said a dugout was not a proper house, though whether they would consider her new home to be "proper," I do not know.

It is a soddy, but it has two stories, and Mr. Amidon ordered doors from Denver, made to his specifications. What is more, there are six glass windows, and one of them opens! O, we are becoming first-rate on this prairie. Included are a large parlor and kitchen with buttery on the first floor, four bedrooms up, wooden floors on both levels, windows on all sides, and muslin pinned to walls and kitchen ceiling to keep the dirt from falling into the soup. That makes quite a mansion for Colorado Territory! A sod house is as snug as brick, though I discovered one drawback. Last evening as we ate our supper, I looked up, to see a rattler making his way through our wall. Luke struck it with a griddle, and Mr. Snake was no more.

Before the Amidons moved into their sod castle, they held a roof raising, and all were present. Luke and others brought tools, and the roof was done in short order. Miss Figg, our lady homesteader, was longing to join them, I think, but she stayed on the ground with the women and helped set out dinner. The repast was presided over by Missus, who tasted each and every dish before heaping her plate. Along with a vegetable stew, I brought my chess pie, which all pronounced tasty, especially Mrs. Garfield, for it is a Southern recipe.

Emmie Lou says Sallie Garfield came from a family in Georgia that owned Negroes to do all their work, and Mrs. Garfield even had a darky to fan her when she got hot. She has no one to help her now, however, and must be a trial to Mr. Garfield. She does a pretty job with fancywork, and indeed, she is rarely without her tatting, but she cannot do plain sewing, nor does she know anything of keeping a house or working a farm. Emmie Lou reports Mrs. Garfield could not cook anything but mush with milk before she left Georgia, and I say she cannot cook now. She made a mess of a pan of fried sage hen, burning it badly, though I told her that Luke preferred it well cooked, as he didn't like a chicken that was too raw. I was sorry for the falsehood, because Mrs. Garfield pestered Luke throughout the meal to take another piece, and nothing would do but that he must oblige her. She is a terrible flirt, but I do not think he will be tempted. After all, I won Luke from Persia Chalmers, the worst trifler I ever saw, so I need not fear the Rebel girl.

I had hoped for a chance to know Mrs. Osterwald, as she seems in need of friends. The poor woman fell again, this time against a table, and her eye is blackened. At least, that is what she said, but I studied her closer, and I think it is something else. I believe she has fits. I would like to ask Emmie Lou but do not want to start the gossip. Mrs. Osterwald is too timid for society, and she keeps close to son and husband, so we had little chance for a chat. I mean for Luke to take me to call on them, because I think she would enjoy a visit if she does not have to put herself out too much. Her contribution to the meal was little meat pies, which she called pasties, and they were much commented upon.

As it is a pleasant day despite a hard frost last night, I sit outside, where I can look out across the prairie, which dons a golden cloak in fall, not at all like the brilliant red mantle of maples at home. I am wrapped up snug in my paisley shawl, with my little confidante in hand. Instead of writing the past hour, I have been reading this book. The events of these months have changed me from a silly girl into a woman, and one who is able to handle the trials Providence chooses to give her, I think. Pray God, it shall always be so. If Luke is not aware of my change for the better, well, I am. And I am just a little proud of myself.

I am aware in rereading my journal that I write too much. Luke would think so, too. One evening whilst talking of enjoyable pursuits, I said many thought a diary to be a pleasant pastime, as well as an efficient way to remember events of note. Luke said if one had to write down such happenings, they weren't worth remembering, and that diary keeping, like writing poetry, used up time that might be put to better use. So now I know I was right in keeping this little book from him. I don't agree with Husband, of course. I think a journal causes one to reexamine the events of one's life and find ways to improve oneself. Still, I am sure I spend entirely too many hours with my pen, and I vow to be more judicious in the use of my time. That means I shall write less often.

First, however, I must put down the events since my last entry.

We have got us in a poor crop. I never worked as hard as I did helping Luke in the fields. Luke believes a woman should not unsex herself by doing a man's work, but he could not finish the harvest without my help, and as I have a good arm with a sickle, I told him there was nothing wrong with a woman performing honest labor. Whilst I aided him in "bringing in the sheaves," Luke did not unsex himself to help in my domain, but what man does? I was as weary as I have ever been.

The wheat crop was not good, the corn even worse. Luke was told 'twas folly to plant corn in this country, but he does as he pleases. So he put in a field of it, thinking he knew more than the naysayers. For a time, he appeared to be right. One morning, he called me to come for a stroll to see how tall and green and fine our corn was. In the forenoon, a hot wind came, and by nightfall, all that was left was a field of withered stalks.

I said he had no cause to reproach himself, because a man must take risks if he wishes to progress, but Luke refused to be comforted, and for several days he acted almost as if the charred crop was my fault. When things do not work out for Luke, he wishes to place blame, and as I am convenient, I come in for more than my share. I do not think that is right—after all, I scarcely control the wind—but it seems to be the role of the wife. I have learned to ignore his strange moods, which cause Luke to stand off by himself, staring at nothing. If I ask the reason, he replies in anger, whose cause I do not understand. I wish I knew more about men.

Well, despite my promise to write less, I have filled up several pages. Now, surely, I must put you away, little friend, and hope you understand if I do not see you soon again. My bread has raised well above the pan and now calls to me.

~

December 31, 1865. Prairie Home.

Now that the winter storms keep Luke inside our snug home, I have little privacy in which to write. Just now, I am alone, however, the only sound, the scratch, scratch of my pen as it scribbles on the paper. I never saw such snow. At first, I thought 'twas cozy, as the flakes looked as if someone were shaking a feather tick. But I quickly tired of the howling winds and swirling snow outside my window, and I do not look forward to many months of white ahead.

Luke has tied a rope twixt house and barn so he will not become lost in a blizzard. When he feeds the animals in bad weather, I place a light in the window as beacon, in case he should let go the rope and lose his way. Although Luke complained at the cost of the pane, I am glad we spent the money, and Luke is, too, for he has remarked at how cheery the light seems, shining through the snowflakes. He is in the barn, caring for the animals now, so this entry will be short.

As the year ends, I count myself specially blessed. I have both Husband and Prairie Home, and in the summer, we will welcome a little stranger! I have known for several weeks but wanted to make sure of the blessed event, so I did not inform Luke until Christmas Day. He is much pleased!

We had no tree for Christmas, as we did not care to chop down one of our precious two, but I piled together several Russian thistle, which the Earley boys, who shared our Christmas feast, call "tumbleweeds." Decorated with ribbons and scraps of yard goods, the result was said by all to be far more dazzling than the standard item. Our brilliant company dubbed it a "Christmas bush" and declared that, henceforth, it would be part of our traditional festivities. I placed the presents from home around it, including the pen wiper Carrie made for Luke and the slipper tops of plush that she embroidered in Hen's Foot for me. I wrote her that they are too elegant for a dirt floor and that I shall save them for my confinement.

Dinner was served on our humble table, which is made of four posts driven into the earthen floor, with a very large provision box turned upside down and set upon them. It is a sturdy piece of furniture indeed. Luke and I sat on bed and washtub, giving our only two chairs to our guests. I had prepared a hearty holiday meal of sage hen, but as I had not had the fixin's for a plum pudding, we finished off with a cake made from the last of the precious chocolate brought from Iowa. I mourned to see the end of it, as I have a passion for chocolate, favoring it above all things. Just when we thought we could not eat another morsel, the Earleys presented us with a jar of pickled walnuts, which we agreed must be sampled instantly.

Our gift to the boys, as we call them, was a

box of divinity, made with black walnuts I gathered in the spring when we passed through Missouri. I gave Luke a tie that I had made from a silk waist of mine, which looked specially nice when he put it on with the embroidered vest I had made as his wedding present. Luke gave me a fine stirring stick, fashioned with his own hands from a pole that had been part of the head frame of our Conestoga wagon. Made of the best hickory, the stick has one end flattened just enough to allow me to beat the cake batter properly. It is as well-designed a stirrer as I have ever seen.

That evening, after the Earleys left, Luke and I finished the Christmas syllabub, which I had prepared from wine and sugar, without benefit of eggs. (Nonetheless, it was as tasty as the authentic item.) I am an abstainer, but I do not believe Our Lord would disapprove of a taste of wine at Christmas to celebrate the birth of His Son, and the anticipation of our own.

Luke and Self talked of all that had happened to us in the year just ending, and we sang together several favorite Christmas songs. Then I told him his most important Christmas gift was yet to come—an heir, who is due late in the spring, early June, if I have figured it correctly.

Luke hugged me hard, then drew back, asking if he had hurt me. I laughed and told him both baby and I enjoyed hugs. I find Carrie was right, and I am not quite so adverse to the matrimonial bed as I once was. Still, I shall be glad enough to dispense with it until after Baby's arrival. My condition only intensifies my feelings for Luke. On impulse, as we sat talking, I took Luke's hand between mine and told him how glad I was we had joined our lives together, that I loved him dearly and considered myself the luckiest girl in the world. Luke squeezed my hand in way of reply. I had expected to be fond of my husband, but I did not know that love of him would give me such a terrible ache in my heart. Perhaps I love him too well, too passionately. Luke does not talk of such things, so I can only wonder if he returns my ardor.

Husband is stamping his feet outside, and so I must bid adieu to the old year and its many blessings and welcome 1866, wondering if it will hold as many joys and surprises as did its predecessor.

Chapter 3

February 17, 1866. Prairie Home.

It is white outside as far as the eye can see, the ground covered in snow, and the sky above so close to it in shade that I discern no horizon. Neither sagebrush nor buckbush stands out as landmark. Little wonder that Mr. Bondurant (who has spent this winter in Mingo and talks of taking up a homestead), calls our snowstorms "whiteouts." I think this must be a little like living inside a snowball. I would record the temperature, but our thermometer froze and burst last month. The Earley boys call when the storms abate, lifting our spirits with their amusing stories of the weather. Moses recalled a man who went to sleep while soaking his feet in water and awoke to find them encased in a block of ice. Tom told of another man lost in the storm, who dug himself a hole in the side of a stream bank for shelter. He was found, frozen in a ball, and had to be buried in a square coffin, as his family did not want to wait until he thawed.

When Luke goes to Mingo now, he paints dark lines under his eyes with soot to keep the glare of sun on snow from blinding him. So marked, he looks like a raccoon, though I keep that humorous thought to myself. Husband is vain, and he does not take kindly to jokes about his person. I fear for him during his trips to town now. He could become lost in the fierce blizzards, which are the worst I ever saw. I keep my concerns to myself, however, because Luke grumbles so when there is no activity to occupy him.

I take the time to enter a few words on this disagreeable day as I wait for the bath-water to warm. All available pans are filled with snow and sit on the stove to melt. I shall bathe at leisure, knowing I need not worry about Husband coming into the house and finding me stark.

There is much to tell. First, in order of the events, my own Self. I am well, with none of the sickness that others in this state complain of. Were I able to button my dress, I would not even know I was enceinte. Luke is the best of husbands and offers his assistance so that I may rest. This morning, he rose early, ground the coffee, brewed it, and brought me a cup, whilst I stayed abed, a true shirker. Emmie Lou, the first here to whom I confided my state, says I must let Luke do whatever he will now, for husbands do not offer their aid in further pregnancies.

My condition is no longer a secret, here or in Fort Madison. After I announced the coming event to Luke, I wrote of it to Mother, who was not well, and she asked Mary to read the letter aloud. There was much whooping among the sisters, and although Mother cautioned them to keep the letter's contents to themselves, she might have easier asked the sun not to rise. Carrie wrote that even Persia Chalmers was aware of it and straight away demanded the truth. Carrie was pleased to mimic her, repeating the question, as is Persia's way, saying, "Is Mattie with child? Why, I wonder at your propriety in asking such a thing, Persia," thereby giving her no answer. Little wonder Persia was quite out of sorts. Poor girl! Does she yet pine for Luke? Well, he is my Darling Boy, not hers.

Husband's last trip to Mingo brought a letter with the good news that Carrie is now the proud mama of a healthy eight-pound boy. Well done, my dearest friend! He is named William for his father and called Billy, but I think of him as Wee Willie.

Carrie told me all about her confinement,

as we keep no secrets from each other. Thanks be to God that her pains lasted but six hours. Will was half-crazed looking for the doctor, who was found at last in a billiard hall and arrived after the deed 'twas done, although he took the credit and demanded payment. It was Carrie's mother and sisters who did the honors.

Childbirth is painful, but bearable, Carrie writes. It hurts less than a broken arm, and the discomfort ends once the birth is over, when, instead of a splinted limb, there is a dear little babe for all the trouble. The way Carrie describes them, I think the pains must be like those we felt as girls, when we ate green corn and paid for it with bowel complaint. I shall know all these things myself soon enough.

I have given thought to whom I shall call upon for assistance with my confinement. Missus made it clear that she has experience, but as she failed to be of much help with Emmie Lou at Mingo and has proved herself to be more than common, I do not trust her. Emmie Lou could not leave her little ones (and is, herself, once more in this condition). Miss Figg is clean and matter-of-fact, and I would put my faith in her, but she has not expressed interest, and I could not take her away from her homestead, where she is responsible for all the work. Mr. Bondurant is a first-rate doctor, although I do not know if he has performed in this particular capacity. I do not think Luke would approve of him anyway, and I myself fear he might staunch any cuts by dropping me into a barrel of flour! If no other opportunities present themselves, I shall send for Jessie. She is a worker and saved the day for Emmie Lou. Besides, she washed her hands before aiding in that birth, and I prize cleanliness. What care I for Jessie's unsavory past when the safety of my own little stranger is at stake?

The same mail brought sad news from home. Sister Mary wrote that Mother lost the little one she carried, and while I think the Lord knew what He was doing on that account and do not grieve for the babe that never was, I cannot but wonder why He started the business in the first place. Mother has had enough burden placed upon her in this life. Sister wrote she was still in bed, three weeks after the event. The girls give her loving care, but as firstborn, I suffer, knowing that I cannot be there. My first memory in this life is toddling into her room with daisies after brother Randolph was born. Out here, so far from home and family, I feel as if I were living on the Moon—or in Oregon, which is not much different. When will I ever see my mother's dear face again? I pray that Luke brings home a letter telling of her complete recovery.

All this thought of childbirth makes me wonder why women are made to suffer so. Why must new life be paid for with pain? The preachers say it is because we are the daughters of Eve and must be punished for her sin, but in my Bible, Adam, too, fell from grace, and I do not see that his sons suffer for it. Would it not be better to pluck a babe from off the ground, just as we do cabbages? Of course, it would be my luck to select one that was green and wormy.

~

February 18, 1866. Prairie Home.

Luke has not returned, and I am on pins with worry. I barely slept a wink last night, due to Baby's quickening and my fear for Luke's safety. I turned up the lamp in the window as high as I dared, less afraid of burning down the house (does a soddy burn? I wonder) than of Luke's missing the light in the storm and passing on by. Whenever I heard a sound, I threw off the coverlets (we sleep under eight of them to keep warm) and opened the door in hopes of seeing my husband, but all I got for my trouble was a swirl of sharp, stinging snow. I turned blue as a pigeon from the frigid air. Our old friend Mr. Bondurant says it is cold enough in Colorado to freeze the smoke in the chimney, and one must open the door to let it out.

Now that it is daylight (or what passes for daylight in a whiteout), I know that Luke likely stopped for the night in Mingo, or took shelter with a neighbor. When I went out to feed the animals, holding fast to the rope twixt house and barn whilst the storm's cold and angry breath pushed me about, I prayed that was so, since one can scarce see more than a yard in any direction. Luke knows I value his safety over my own peace of mind, and he would not have hurried home on my account.

But what if he started off before the storm's fury? I stir the soup, then go to window and door, and in such fashion have I spent the day. It has taken several hours to record just these lines, as I keep running to look outside, believing I hear Traveler.

I shall never understand why Luke loves this place with its burning summers and icy winters. What I would not give for the gentle snows of home and the sounds of sleigh bells announcing the arrival of friends.

As I was feeding the animals, my eye caught a place where the barn's sod wall had fallen away, revealing a paper object. I am not a snoop and did not stop to think the hidden item might be of a private nature, but I reached for it and found myself holding a photograph of Persia Chalmers. I cannot guess why Luke placed it there. Perhaps it fell out of his photograph album and he set it on the sod, then forgot it. Though it is not my nature, I was a trifle jealous when I compared Persia's glossy curls, cascading like a silken waterfall, and corseted form with my own dry hair and bloated shape. I wondered if Luke saw the difference and found me wanting. I thought of replacing Persia's likeness with one of Abner, but I do not have Abner's photograph. So Luke is spared an unpleasant discovery.

After dwelling on the matter of the picture, I have concluded I was a little cross at finding it. I will not question Luke, however, for I do not want to be among that piteous group of women who consider their husbands unworthy of trust. So, resolving to confide the discovery only to my journal, I opened my trunk and reached inside for the little book. My hand touched a crumb of chocolate, which must have fallen there during our wedding journey. As there is no chocolate stocked in Mingo, I had not tasted it since Christmas, and I thought it a reward for my steadfastness. So I gobbled the morsel right up, with not a thought for Luke, who cares for chocolate, too. Then I cried and cried for my greediness. This wretched country!

I have just returned from looking out the door for the hundredth time, and I have smudged the page with the snow that attached itself to my sleeve. Rereading this entry, I am ashamed at my lack of faith in my husband, and I fear my fretfulness will result in a peevish child. The wind has died and the snow is stopped, and a tiny bit of blue shows through the white. Like the weather, I have found calm and shall reward Self (and babe) with a cup of the good tea and a dish of snow ice cream, made with sugar, a drop of vanilla, and snow, whilst I wait for my "white" knight.

February 19, 1866. Prairie Home.
Well, of course, Luke is safe! My thanks to Divine Providence for his return. Having been caught in the storm, he took refuge in an abandoned adobe house not far from Mingo and waited there until the blizzard had passed. Luke knew I would worry and left the

instant the last flakes fell. I was so glad to see Husband that I threw my arms around him and shed a few tears.

He was stiff from the chill air, and, fearing he would take cold, I quickly removed his boots and filled a basin with tepid water for his feet, which were frostbitten. Luke shook so as he sat there that I warmed his flannel night-shirt and woolen stockings by the stove and put him to bed, where he ate his supper. Then I did his chores for him.

I think the cold affected his head just a little, for he said he had been frightened (the first time I ever heard Luke admit a fear), not knowing if he would reach safety. When I got into bed beside him, Luke said he was never so glad to see a sight in his life as the smoke curling up from our Prairie Home and that he never tasted a thing as good as my soup. Then he hugged me hard, and so forth.

March 13, 1866. Prairie Home.

Does winter in this country never end? At home, the crocuses are blooming and the tulips are sending up their pretty heads, but here in Colorado Territory, there is snow, snow, and more snow. Just when I think spring is ready to show her face, why there comes another storm, turning the sky and earth the color of lead. A few days ago, we had a chinook wind, as Mr. Bondurant calls it, that melted so much snow that I could see bare patches of ground. But after a few days of teasing, winter returned. How can anyone call such a country home? Husband, that is who. He has already begun the spring plowing.

I blame my condition for my black moods, because cheerfulness has always been my nature. When things seem darkest, I put aside my work and go to piecing, since the bright colors rouse me. I saved the blue paper that comes wrapped around the cones of sugar, and last week, I soaked it in water, producing a beautiful indigo dye that I used to color a piece of muslin. Combined with the tiniest scraps from my piece bag, my new blue material will be turned into a Postage Stamp quilt for Baby. In Carrie's last letter, she included a snippet of lawn with an odd design of squares. She had fashioned it into a Sunday dress for her first outing since the birth of Billy, only to discover Persia wearing a garment made from the same goods! Though Carrie laughed aloud, Persia was quite put out.

Carrie said to use the scrap for a crazy quilt, which is all the rage back home. The scrap looks much like the dress that Persia wore in the picture Luke had secreted in the barn, but why would Luke have a picture of Persia taken so recently? Even Persia would not be bold enough to send her likeness to a married man. I looked for the photograph to compare to the piece of lawn, but it is no longer there, and I believe Luke has thrown it away.

There is little to do day after day in a house that measures just eighteen by fifteen feet, so I spend some of my time reading *Dr. Chase's Recipes*. He will be of little aid in parturition but is indispensable in other matters, and will be a great help after Baby arrives. Little did I know when I put the good doctor into my trunk that we would become such intimate friends.

～

March 15, 1866. Prairie Home.

At last, I made up my mind to have Jessie attend me when the time comes, and I told Luke as much. He asked wouldn't I rather have Missus, but I replied that I had concluded she would be as much use as singing hymns to a dead mule. Luke gave me no argument, suggesting I write Jessie a note, which he will deliver to her directly. He even proposed making a special trip to town for that purpose. I asked could Jessie read, and Luke replied she could indeed, since it is she who sorts the mail.

I was surprised when Luke agreed so quickly about Jessie, but I discovered the reason a short time later when he asked, "What would you think of my going back to Fort Madison?" To which I replied, "Not much." I supposed he thought that, tit for tat, I would favor the idea, but I do not, and it is now the subject of much disagreement between us.

The purpose of such a journey, says Luke, is to investigate a new type of wheat seed that may be suited for our dry prairie climate. Little else seems to grow here, with the exception of potatoes. But I think there is another reason. I believe his mama is demanding his presence. I think a letter arrives from her in every mail, though Luke does not share them with me. (That does not hurt my feelings, because I do not share Carrie's letters with him, at least not until read by Self to determine whether there is a private message, as there 'most always is.)

Luke's plan is to go as soon as he finishes the planting and return before Baby is due, which by my best reckoning is early June, and he wants to leave me behind! I protested vigorously, but Luke was firm, saying that going alone, he could make the trip in half the time. Besides, said he, the journey was too strenuous for a woman in my condition, as if thousands of women in the same circumstance have not already crossed these plains! When I suggested waiting until after the babe's arrival, Luke argued that delaying the trip until the harvest meant we would take our chances with blizzards. He knows how I fear storms.

When I brought up the subject of the Indians, Luke said not one of the Red Men has been seen in our vicinity this year, and it is the general opinion in Mingo that they had been chased to the north. Then Luke remarked he had chosen me for a wife because I was levelheaded and had said as much in his proposal. He had not expected me to turn into an example of frail femininity, of a sudden.

Luke believed with that argument he had turned aside all objections, but he could not counter one. I told him I refused to let him go. It was the first time I have refused Luke a thing, and he was much upset. He tried to change my mind again this morning at breakfast, and when he could not, he stomped out, thinking his displeasure would influence me. On this one thing, however, I stand firm. Luke's duty is to me, not to his mama.

~

March 20, 1866. Prairie Home.

Luke talks of nothing but the trip to Fort Madison, trying to persuade me, first with compliments and a bouquet of prairie blossoms, then with sulks and ill temper. Sometimes, I am so weary from his arguments that I am tempted to give in. Then I think of spending weeks alone in this country in my state, and I refuse once again. I do not understand why he has his heart set on the trip when I need him beside me. Luke promises to be home well before Baby's arrival, would not attempt the trip otherwise, says he, but I do not want him to leave at all.

At last Sabbath service, Luke enlisted the aid of our neighbors to persuade me, and I think I came out the poorer.

Missus was no help, as she volunteered to take charge of me whilst he was away, saying there was no need to worry even if he was delayed, since I was built to "calve." Emmie Lou says I ought to make him wait until the baby is two months old, because that is the time she always becomes pregnant again. (I was shocked at such language, especially Emmie Lou's, as she is highborn, but coarseness passes for good humor in this country, and I expect that someday I shall adjust.) Ben Bondurant, who has decided to "stay a-put" by filing for a homestead not a mile from us, offered to oversee our crops while Luke is away, as he won't plant but a few acres himself this year. He would even sleep in our barn, because he is tired of his own cooking. I think Mr. Bondurant is not much of an agrarian, because he told me he can recognize only two trees. "One is cottonwood," said he. "The other is not."

Moses Earley promised to help with the out chores if I will name the babe for him. I replied pertly that Moses was a poor choice for a girl.

My only allies are unwelcome ones—Sallie Garfield, who announced that she would be deathly afraid of Indians were she to be left alone, but that she did not have to worry, for Mr. Garfield would never leave *her* to go skylarking. Then, having gotten an audience, Mrs. Garfield tossed her head and gave a lengthy account of how she lost her babe, and nearly perished herself, for lack of proper care after her wartime confinement.

Lucinda Osterwald, who clings more than ever to her "Old Pap," whispered to me that she would die if left alone, thus confirming my earlier suspicion that she has fits or some other condition of which she cannot speak. Mr. Osterwald said their son, Brownie, would hire out cheap to stay with me, but I declined the offer. This nugatory young man is feebleminded, and I do not care for him, as he has strange ways and can be fractious. I think Tom Earley disapproved of Luke's plan to return home, which made me wish he had spoken his mind, because Luke values his opinion, but Tom keeps his own counsel.

In Colorado Territory, women are expected to endure hardship, and the consensus is that I will change my mind. Lordy, we shall see about that.

～

March 25, 1866. Prairie Home.
The naysayers were right, and I have indeed changed my mind, but, O, God, not willingly! I had no choice. Luke announced he would leave within the week for Fort Madison, with my approval or without it. As I want there to be harmony between us, I said that his mind being made up, he would have my blessing. It is bad enough that he should carry with him an image of his helpmate in her swollen state. I do not want him to remember a mutton-headed wife, as well. The journey is a long and arduous one, although Luke expects to make the round-trip in about the same time it took us to travel one way. He will be on Traveler instead of behind a team of oxen, and he will take a direct route, not going through St. Joseph, which we have been told was greatly out of our way. So I shall wish him Godspeed and not let him see that there is bitterness in my heart at his choosing Mama and wheat seed over Wife.

Luke toils in the fields now from first light until the setting sun, to finish the planting. He has replaced the sod on house and barn that was torn away by winter winds, and in every way he is making sure that I will be comfortable during his absence. I am grateful for that. Myself, I am busy preparing food for the journey, the most wholesome edibles I can make with our limited stores. Mr. Bondurant taught me to make jerked antelope in the Indian manner, by cutting the meat into strips and pounding them flat, then hanging them on a rack to dry, outside in the sun or next to the cookstove. Luke will take the remainder of our dried apples, which I am happy to be rid of, having, indeed, grown to "loath, abhore, detest, and despise dried apple pies."

Luke requested that I pack the embroidered vest I made him, for he says he intends to greet our friends in style. I have written letters for him to deliver to my loved ones. O, that they might be presented with my own hand, but in that case, there would be no need for letters, would there?

Despite all the preparations he is undertaking for the journey, Luke found time to make me a surprise, a bench to place on the sunny side of the house. He teased me by saying I was to sit there and remember him. As if Baby's quickening doesn't remind me I have a husband! Still, I am grateful for his thoughtfulness, and I sit there now as I write. A minute ago, I looked up and saw the queerest thing. Our sod roof is in bloom. Weeds grow in its dirt, making our soddy appear to be dressed in a green bonnet. I shall ask Carrie to send me dandelion seeds to plant upon it.

April 4, 1866. Prairie Home.

I begged Luke to stay just one more day, but he said every day's delay added another day to his return. I could not argue with the logic of that, but in my heart, I cried, And what if the trail claims you, and you don't return at all?

Of course, I did not admit my fears to him. This morning, long before sunup, Luke left me. He rides Traveler and leads a mule, borrowed from Mr. Bondurant. This mule is packed with provisions and will carry seed on the return trip. As the Indians in these parts have been quiet since the scare last fall, Luke will go by himself to Fort Kearney, then inquire there about conditions to the east. He promises to join a train if told the Indians are on the warpath.

Luke was anxious to be off. Even so, after he was in the saddle, he dismounted to give me one more hug, and as he looked back to wave from the far side of the barn, I fancy he was tempted to return a final time. I waved long after he had disappeared into the dark, then stared after him until daylight, before turning to Luke's morning chores, which I had insisted he leave for me.

I had barely begun when Mr. Bondurant rode up, and nothing would do but that he should finish them. He stayed and talked so long that I invited him for dinner, and just as we sat down, why, there came the Earley boys, Moses carrying his dulcimer. They, too, were persuaded to join at table. Afterward, we sang many fine songs, accompanied by both dulcimer and Mr. Bondurant's Jew's harp. I requested "Lorena," it being a favorite of Luke's.

I think the three men have decided among themselves that they will not allow me time to be lonely, for they talked of which one would come on the morrow to check on the animals; what they mean, I believe, is check on *me*. God and Husband may have forsaken me in Colorado Territory, but my good neighbors have not.

April 18, 1866. Prairie Home.

With Luke away (two weeks today!), I am able to write at leisure, but what is there to tell? I miss him, but the days pass quickly, since there is much work to be done, my own and Luke's, although Mr. Bondurant or one of the Earley boys always seems to be about so's to help with our chores.

No woman on her "at home" day entertains as much as I. One of the three men and sometimes all of them visit each day. I am alone only after dark, which is when I miss Luke most. It was our time of leisure together, when we discussed the day's labors or Luke read aloud while I sewed. But then Baby thrashes about so that I know I am not alone. I feel quite heavy and weary of an evening now, and I will be grateful when Husband returns, and Baby can make his appearance. I wonder if I have miscalculated the date. I think the day may be sooner than I had expected.

There is not a trace of snow anywhere, and the prairie is thick with many grasses. Mr. Bondurant is teaching me their names — bluestem, buffalo, big gama, and so on. There are wildflowers, too. I never saw the Great Plains with so many bright colors. If it looked as pretty all year-round, I think I might even come to like this country.

May 1, 1866. Prairie Home.

Moses returned from Mingo with a letter Luke posted with an emigrant headed west. It tells me all is well with Husband. Traveler lost his footing whilst fording the Platte, which was swift and cold from melted snow. The misstep caused Luke to drop the mule's lead rope, and that animal panicked and went under. But Luke kept *his* head, and by the most difficult exercise was able to claim the mule. Luke is making good time and says he will return before I have a chance to miss him. This is the first letter I ever received from Luke. It is not a love letter, but it satisfies me.

May 2, 1866. Prairie Home.

This morning, as I sat on the bench outside, rereading Luke's letter, paying no attention to the world around me, something intruded upon my thoughts, suggesting I was not alone. I looked up and caught sight of a naked chest and a flash of feathers tied to hair. Frightened almost unto death, I jumped up and ran, dropping the precious piece of paper.

Before I could reach the door, a powerful hand gripped my arm and spun me around, and I expected next to be scalped. But instead of an Indian, the half-naked man was Brownie Osterwald, pretending to be a savage.

I suppose I should have felt relief, but I did not, because Brownie has always scared me. It is not just his childish mind, for I have known simpletons at home, but a feeling that his brain was twisted in some way and his soul warped.

"Fooled you," Brownie said, twitching and jerking as if he had the Saint Vitus' dance.

I did not know whether to agree that it had been a fine prank or to let him know I was displeased. I decided on the latter course, thinking it would send him on his way, and so I stamped my foot and said slowly, as if speaking to a child, "Yes, you did, Brownie, and it was wrong of you. Remove your hand, and go home."

Brownie dropped his hand, but he showed no signs of leaving, and he replaced the grin with a frown. He studied me for a moment, his eyes slipping down over me like greasy water, until he was staring at my protruding belly. Before I could make out his intention, he put his hand over the baby.

I jumped back and ordered, "Don't you do that."

"Baby in there. Like Ma," he said, obviously pleased with his deduction.

For just a second, I supposed Lucinda Osterwald had lost babies after Brownie's birth, because he is her youngest child, but

I did not dwell on the thought, for Brownie came even closer, placing his hand on me a second time. I was greatly alarmed, for I was alone with him on the prairie, with no one in hailing distance and no way to reach the safety of the house. I prayed Brownie was merely curious and, that being feeble, he didn't know enough to restrain himself. So I stood quietly, my heart beating just as it had during the Indian attack. Then, before I could prevent it, Brownie's hand was upon my breast.

"Bubby," he said with a wicked leer.

I snatched his hand away and slapped him smartly.

Brownie's dark eyes glistened with beastly lust and darted about. He leaned toward me, his hair like moldy hay against my face, and his breath so foul that I was forced to turn away. That angered the dunce, who took my head between his huge hands and wrenched it back so that I faced him again. I knew he could crush my skull as easily as I would a walnut, and a chill came over me, as I feared for Baby's life, as well as my own.

"Good Brownie. Now let me go," I said, summoning a calm I did not feel. His licentious nature had put him beyond reason. So I concluded to treat him as I would an animal, showing neither anger nor fear, as that would have let him know he had the upper hand.

At first, I thought my ploy had worked. Brownie smiled uncertainly, and the pressure on my head lessened. But instead of letting go of me altogether, he put his filthy mouth against mine and, at the same instant, ripped my bodice from neck to waist. I screamed and wrenched free, but Brownie, his face purple with rage, hit me across the brow with the back of his hand, knocking me to the ground, where he kicked me in stomach and ribs. By instinct, because I do not remember thinking to do it, I rolled into a ball to protect Baby, while I braced for further blows.

Brownie circled me, then drew back his boot, but instead of kicking me in the head, as I think was his intention, he made a bellow like that of an enraged ox. I looked up—into the angry face of Ben Bondurant, a bullwhip in his hand. When Brownie turned to Mr. Bondurant, I saw a wicked red streak on his back where the whip had cut through his shirt and lacerated the flesh. Mr. Bondurant drew back the whip and struck Brownie across the face with the lash. Brownie screamed again, but he stood there dumbly, making no move to defend himself, as if he was used to being whipped and knew protest was of no use.

Mr. Bondurant swung the whip again, but this time it flailed harmlessly above Brownie's head. Then, for good measure, Mr. Bondurant cracked the lash twice more, letting it come within inches of Brownie before saying, "You come around Mrs. Spenser again, I'll whip your eyes out. You understand, dummy?"

Brownie protested that he had done nothing, but Mr. Bondurant cut him off. "Aw, shut up, will you. You even look at Mrs. Spenser again, and I'll tell your Pa. You know what he'll do to you."

Brownie was so filled with alarm that he shook and whispered piteously, "Don't. Don't tell. Don't tell Pa."

"You remember. I'll be hanged if I ever let you near Mrs. Spenser again. Don't you never come back here. Never. Now git!"

Brownie did not need to be told twice. He set out across the field at a run, glancing back from time to time in terror. Mr. Bondurant watched him until he disappeared, then helped me up. I tried hard to control myself but could not, and I clung to him, weeping.

Mr. Bondurant let me cry myself out, and when I had finished, he said, "You don't need to worry now. Brownie won't be back. He's a mean dog. You can't cure him, but you can put a scare into him. He fears his pa more than anything."

"If you hadn't come..." I said, but Mr. Bondurant shushed me.

"Now, now, Mrs. Spenser, with all in this world you got to fret over, there ain't no cause to add somethin' that didn't happen. It's me you ought to blame and not yourself, for I did not know what Brownie was up to when I seen him come this way. I thought nothing of it till I chanced to mention it to the Earley boys, and they said it's known about that Brownie's not to be left alone with a lady. I come here as fast as I could. The boys'll be along directly."

"You won't tell them!" I said. "O, Mr. Bondurant, surely you will keep this quiet. I would be so ashamed if they knew, or Luke.

115

He must never find out! What would he think of me!"

Mr. Bondurant studied me with his one good eye. "It's your business," he said, but before I could extract a promise, I saw dust to the east and fled into the house to change my dress. When I returned, Mr. Bondurant was deep in conversation with Tom and Moses, then turned to me. "I told them Brownie Osterwald crept up on you like a wild Indian and scared you."

Tom said hotly that Brownie ought to be run out of the country, but I shook my head, telling him that such a thing would kill poor Mrs. Osterwald. Now I know the reason for her timorousness: It is worry over Brownie's outbursts.

After the three men talked it over, Mr. Bondurant announced that henceforth he would sleep in our barn and the others would relieve him during the day. They insisted that I was not to be left alone, not even for an hour.

I protested, but Mr. Bondurant drew me aside and whispered that he thought it would be a "jim-dandy bargain" if, along with cooking for him, I would "learn" him to read. Then he asked me not to shame him by mentioning the agreement in front of the boys, for they were not aware of his ignorance. That seemed to be a fair exchange of secrets, and I agreed to the arrangement, for, despite Mr. Bondurant's assurances, I feared Brownie's return.

The three stayed to supper, entertaining

me so heartily that all thoughts of Brownie fled. Not until the boys were gone and Mr. Bondurant comfortably settled in the barn was I allowed time to dwell on the terrible incident. Is it not unfair that I am alone in my condition, without a husband or female companionship *and* must encounter Brownie Osterwald? I do not know whether to hate this country for the trials it gives me or to take satisfaction in knowing I encountered its challenges and was not found wanting—not yet, anyway.

Just now, I remembered Luke's note, which flew out of my hand when Brownie frightened me, and I grieve that the only letter I ever received from Husband has blown many miles across the prairie.

May 7, 1866. Prairie Home.

What would I do without Mr. Bondurant and the boys? Brownie appears in my dreams each night, and when I awake, I fancy I see his eyes gleaming at me in the dark, like a rat's. I can scarce believe any man would behave in such a brutal way and blame it on Brownie's weakened mind. O, that my husband were by my side! I would not get the slightest rest if not for the care of my good friends.

Today, Tom Earley arrived just after breakfast, relieving Mr. Bondurant for work on his own homestead. Tom brought with him a copy of the *New-York Weekly Times* that is only two months old, and he read parts of it aloud. The steamer *Lockwood* exploded her boilers whilst on the Mississippi and was wholly destroyed, with great loss of life. Musicians in New Orleans, who dared to play "Bonnie Blue Flag" and other Secession airs, were arrested.

Perhaps I do not miss civilization as much as I had thought.

Still, there is good news in the *Times*. In Mississippi, a newspaper editor gives cheering information about the state of the freedman: "As a general thing, they have gone to work, and seem disposed to faithfully comply with their contracts." I guess we Northerners had greater faith in the darkies than their former masters did, for I am not at all surprised at that intelligence.

The paper also brings news of the Mormons, who, under the leadership of a son of their infamous polygamous leader, Brigham Young, are in St. Louis, laying in a supply of goods to be transported to Utah. I joked to Tom that we should request them to make their way through Colorado Territory, for I should pay a pretty penny for their wares. Tom said he should not encourage them, as one of their band might offer a pretty penny for me to add to his harem of wives. He would be lonesome without me, Tom says, and what is more, how ever would he explain my disappearance to Luke?

After discussing the events of the world, I do not feel so far from society after all.

I have been unwell since Brownie's attack, knowing not whether it is the natural state of my condition or the result of Brownie's blows. At times, I am cold with fear that Brownie has injured Baby. I would like to question Emmie Lou about my symptoms, but Mr. Bondurant would not allow me to visit her alone, and I cannot ask him to deliver me.

Mr. Bondurant's bargain is not so jim-dandy for him, as I can scarcely stand up long enough to cook, and he takes my place at the stewpot. I endeavor to make up for my shortcomings by being a willing teacher, and Mr. Bondurant is the best of students. When I complimented him on how quickly he learned all twenty-six letters of the alphabet, he said slyly, "It's twenty-five I learnt. I'm well posted with *X*."

I am grateful for his company, but I long for Luke's return, which I hope will be within the month. I have not had a second letter nor any news from home since his leaving.

May 14, 1866. Prairie Home.

My time now is spent lying in bed or sitting on the bench in the sun. The men are concerned with my poor health. Yesterday, Tom rode for Jessie, who came and recommended rest and more rest. She studied my face but did not remark on it. I think it must be bruised from Brownie's attack, but I do not know, since the dishpan does not reflect a clear likeness. Jessie offered to stay on to tend me, but I think Mr. Bondurant was jealous, for he insisted there was nothing she could do that he could not. So she returned to Mingo, promising to come again when called for. Mr. Bondurant does most of the cooking now. He writes his name and asked me to write mine so that he could copy it. It came out "Mutt." I said 'twas close enough.

⌒

May 17, 1866. Prairie Home.

This morning at breakfast, a tooth popped out of my mouth. Distressed as I was, I was grateful it came from the back, where its vacant place will not be noticed. Lordy, I hope this loss is due to Brownie's blows and not my condition. If 'twere the latter, I should be toothless ere my family is complete. I suppose I am vain after all.

⌒

May 21, 1866. Prairie Home.

I felt poorly all last night, taken with cramping and sleeplessness. When the boys arrived today, I could not keep up with their jolly talk, thinking instead about the pains. I was frying doughnuts when I realized the contractions were coming with some regularity, and I said with a calm I did not feel that I thought we might be five for dinner.

At first, the men did not get my little sally, but at last, Moses grinned and said, "Hellfire and brimstone!"

There was hurried discussion amongst the three about which should ride for Jessie, at length deciding on Moses, since both Mr. Bondurant and Tom have some familiarity with doctoring, the one having aided in emergencies on the Overland Trail and the other having learned a little of medicine in the war. Mr. Bondurant said from what he knew about the subject, Moses would have ample time to reach Mingo and return before Jessie's services were required.

Moses was scarcely gone, however, when there came a great pain, the worst I ever felt, and I did not need to be told that Baby had chosen this time to greet us. For a moment, I was distressed that two gentlemen who were not doctors would see me in a state of nakedness unknown even to my husband, but as there was nothing to be done apart from delivering the babe myself, I put thoughts of modesty aside and have since refused to think of it.

Whilst they went to the well to draw water, I changed into my nightdress. Then, at my direction, the men arranged things first-rate, spreading a clean sheet upon the table, heating the water, and setting the bellyband and other tiny garments I had made for this occasion near the stove to warm. I was gratified to see that before making the preparations, Mr. Bondurant poured water into a basin, and both men washed their hands thoroughly with soap, although Mr. Bondurant did not remove the shirt he has worn each day that he has been with me.

When Tom inquired, "Do you have knowledge of what we are about?" Mr. Bondurant replied, "I know everything there is to know about medicine. That is, keep in fear of the Lord, and keep your bowels open."

The remark did not inspire my confidence. Still, no woman at home, not even sisters,

Mother, or Carrie, could have given me better and more loving care through my ordeal than those two faithful friends. They strained and sweat as hard as I, and I fancy they even felt a little of my pain.

Once all was in readiness, we sat down to wait, the two men helping themselves to doughnuts, although I abstained. Each time the pains came, Tom grasped my hands for support, and Mr. Bondurant rubbed my lower back, which seemed ready to break in half. At their cessation, however, I was inclined to walk about the room.

We continued on in this manner for more than an hour, when the sac of waters broke, and shortly afterward, I felt a great pushing. When the thrust was over, I got upon the table (having been told beforehand by Jessie that a hard surface was preferable to a tick, and made for easier cleanup). Mr. Bondurant remembered an Indian trick, and, "be as you was needing it," he scrubbed a piece of kindling for me to bite down on. I have it now, prettily decorated with teeth marks.

The pains came harder and harder, one scarcely stopping before the next began. And each time, I thought surely Baby would force itself into this world. Indeed, when Mr. Bondurant examined me, he agreed the little stranger would be there momentarily.

Then came a great cramping, and I pushed with all my might whilst Tom held my hands, telling me what a good girl I was. Mr. Bondurant remained in position to "catch" the baby, as he put it, but Baby had other ideas and refused to emerge without more work. There were two more pains, and I thought I would not live to see the end. My body was covered with perspiration, but still I shook as if chilled, and I am ashamed that I cried out more than once, letting the stick fall out of my mouth. Of a sudden, I felt a great stretching and pain so bad that I feared I would be split asunder. Then Mr. Bondurant shouted that the head was out. Another pain or two or three—I did not count—and Mr. Bondurant shouted that I had delivered a "biggity boy."

The tears ran down Mr. Bondurant's face whilst he presented Baby for inspection, muttering, "By ginger. By ginger." Tom turned aside, but not before I saw that his eyes, too, were moist. O, Carrie was right when she said after Wee Willie was born that a baby is worth its price of pain, and I would gladly suffer it again—but not just yet.

Boykins is small but perfect in every way. He has Luke's cheekbones and serious eyes (and his strangely shaped earlobes and two of Luke's curious brown spots on his body; I consider all to be marks of distinction, not imperfections). He has my impatience, however, arriving as he did before he was expected. Mr. Bondurant wrapped him in warm flannel before giving him to me, and I never saw a man handle a thing as gently as he did that babe, saying over and over again, "Well, I swan!"

Both Baby and I were resting when Moses returned with Jessie, who inspected all and said she could not have done a better job herself. That pleased Tom and Mr. Bondurant enormously. She will stay a few days to make sure I am all right, perhaps even until Luke returns. O, that he were here to make this happy day complete!

Whilst Jessie fussed about the sickroom, the three men presented me with their own surprise—a "rocky chair," as Mr. Bondurant calls it. I prize it more than anything I ever owned and do not care if they used the wood of a precious tree in its manufacture. I am grateful they did not make it out of sod!

Baby sleeps in the cunning cradle that Luke fashioned during the winter, under the Postage Stamp quilt made by my hands, whilst I rock back and forth in my handsome new chair. The others are outside just now, having given me orders to rest, but I will not until I have recorded the events of this momentous day. A great happiness and feeling of calm came over me when Mr. Bondurant handed Baby to me, and I felt I must be the first woman in the history of the world to produce such a wonderful creature. As I look through the tiny glass pane beside me, at the marblelike streaks of purple and bright pink that make up our sunset on the Great Plains, I cannot help but think that Baby will grow to manhood in this country. He is a child of the prairie, not of the great Mississippi, as I am. We are bound together, he and Luke and I, in this place. His presence means that henceforth, Colorado Territory, not Fort Madison, is "home." I hope I am up to this challenge.

In honor of these dearest friends, I have decided to name my firstborn Benjamin Earley Spenser—with Luke's approval, of course.

～

May 23, 1866. Prairie Home.

Jessie says Little Ben, as we call him, looks less like a drowned rabbit than some she has seen. I am glad to have one of my own sex around, and she is good company, sitting by my side as she sews on a sunbonnet whose pattern she borrowed from me. Yesterday, Jessie baked a vinegar pie, and Moses Earley made short work of it, so she was required to bake another. Our Moses is quite taken with Jessie, and I think, were she not already married, she might think of him for a husband. Of course, in Colorado Territory, where women are as scarce as trees and valued almost as highly, I have heard it said that a wedding ring is no impediment to taking a new husband. I had hoped that Moses or Tom would be interested in Miss Figg, who is a charming lady, despite her girth, but neither cares for her, and she does not seem interested in men.

Now, I must say a thing about Jessie. She confesses she is grateful that I requested her to aid in the birth of Baby, for amongst our neighbors, it raises her standing, which had been greatly hurt by gossip. She inquired whether Missus had told me of her background, and I mumbled I had heard a thing or two about it.

"She's a meddlesome old soul and shouldn't have said it, for I'm not what she claims. La! A lie travels a hundred miles while truth is putting on its boots. I have many times had my chances, but I never worked the line," Jessie told me hotly. "Elode, now there's a cheeky old 'hoor' for you. I'll bet she didn't tell you about the place she ran on Holladay Street in Denver. Smith—he was her 'mac,' as the men who live on the earnings of women are called—he gambled it all away. Then there was trouble, but I won't tell it. So they came out here, where they pretend they're good Christian people."

Now, I do not know for sure who is telling the truth, but I put my trust in Jessie. In Colorado Territory, not so much attention is paid to a man's past. I think the same consideration should be applied to a woman's.

Babykins is as healthy as can be, and my strength is returning, thanks to Jessie's care and good beef tea—beef tea made from antelope, that is. Jessie tells the men I am "smartly better."

⌒

May 31, 1866. Prairie Home.

As I am now as good as new, Jessie said at midmorning that it was time to return to Mingo and she asked Moses to deliver her. It is a long trip. So I insisted they go immediately, although it meant I would be alone until Mr. Bondurant returned from chores on his homestead. I promised to stay within the house, but I disobeyed and went to the well to draw water. While there, I spied a horseman galloping across the countryside from the direction of the Early place. Alarmed, for I knew he was not Tom, I shaded my eyes for a better look, then, recognizing a familiar form, I dropped the bucket and ran as fast as I could in his direction.

In an instant, Traveler was beside me and I was swept into the arms of my husband. Right joyful we were, I to look into his dear face and he into mine, inquiring if I was well. I nodded, the lump in my throat so big that I could not reply.

"I stopped at Earleys'. Tom said to get here quick, so I left the mule. He'll bring it directly. He didn't say..." At that, Luke realized that my belly no longer came between us, and he asked with alarm, "The baby?"

I did not keep him in suspense. "The baby," I replied, "is a fine boy, who is ten days old today."

At that, Luke grinned broadly and said, "A boy! I'm damned. A boy!"

With a mother's love bursting inside me, I led Luke to the cradle where his son napped, and nothing would do but that the proud papa should awaken him. Baby yawned and fussed, which pleased Luke, who picked him up and sat down in the rocking chair, singing a lullaby to his boy. Were I not already convinced Baby was the finest child in the world, I should have been jealous that, upon his return, Luke was more taken with Son than Wife. But as I am quite taken with Baby myself, I understood.

Tom arrived shortly, bringing the mule as

promised. He had thought it was not right for him to tell Luke of the birth of our boy, so he had said only that Husband should make haste for home. Tom refused my invitation for supper, and Mr. Bondurant, upon his return a few minutes later, withdrew with his mule to his own homestead, leaving our little family alone.

This afternoon, Luke left to inspect the fields. So I take the time to record his safe return in my journal, knowing that in future, I shall have less time to write as I attend to responsibilities for my two men—Husband and Baby, whom Luke has named John Shiloh Spenser.

Chapter 4

July 14, 1866. Prairie Home.
I knew there would be little time to attend to my journal. Still, I had not meant to neglect it for so many weeks. There is no leisure for Self these days. When Baby is asleep, Luke is underfoot, and when Luke is busy elsewhere, why then Baby demands attention. He frets a great deal, due to the heat, I believe. When he finishes nursing, his face must be pulled from my breast, making a great sucking sound, as his little mouth is glued to my skin with his perspiration.

It is so hot in the soddy that I think my milk

must sour, but I am loath to go outside with Johnnie for fear of rattlesnakes, more numerous even than last year. Mr. Bondurant brought me a stout buffalo-hair rope to lay on the ground in a circle about the cradle, saying the snakes will not cross it. Perhaps not, but they come close, and I have killed seven this summer. I fancy that by chopping off their heads with a hoe, I even the score a little for Mother Eve!

I suffer much this summer with headaches and lack of sleep, and I think back on my wedding trip to Colorado Territory, with all its dangers, as a carefree time. Last summer, Emmie Lou confessed she was so weary, she could sell her soul to the Devil for a night's sleep. I thought the remark blasphemous, but now that I am awake much of the night with Johnnie, I believe it a passable bargain. If Lucifer would agree to give me a real bath in the bargain, then my soul would indeed be in jeopardy.

Of course, no one suspects my despair, for I endeavor to keep a cheerful countenance around Luke and friends and tell my real thoughts only to my journal. Confiding them renews my strength, even if the listener is only a blank page.

There is much for which I am grateful. With Baby to keep me busy, I am not so lonely for the dear ones in Fort Madison. Like Luke, I enjoy the violent sunsets of an evening, although they do not thrill my soul as they do his. After a year, they still frighten me because they set the sky on fire, and I think they will consume me. Perhaps someday I shall come to love Colorado, but not yet.

Luke works harder than any man I ever saw, and I have no complaints on that score. He is quieter, more critical, since his return. Perhaps the reason is that he is now an old family man with responsibilities for Son, as well as Wife, but sometimes, I think I understand Luke even less today than I did when we were wed. I have learnt little about men in fourteen months of marriage.

Luke is the most indulgent of papas, playing with Baby in the evenings and showing him off to all who visit. Luke is right pleased with his "seed."

He is pleased, as well, with the turkey red seed for hard winter wheat that he brought back from Fort Madison. (Luke would be shocked with this little joke, but I intend to write it to Carrie, who will find it funny. I wonder, do men know we women talk about such things, just as they do?) It not only resists drought but also thrives under the hot winds. Our wheat does better than any in the neighborhood, and I believe my husband will leave his mark as an agrarian.

Mr. Bondurant's pack mule was loaded down with farm necessities when Luke returned from Fort Madison. Still, knowing my sweet tooth, he found room for a little gift of chocolate. I am not so wanton with it as I was last year, using small amounts now, and only on special occasions. Luke brought other favors, including photographs of loved ones. Carrie's precious Wee Willie is every bit as splendid as my own Johnnie, which means he is very handsome indeed. Carrie also sent a purse she embroidered with ferns and heartsease, which is displayed upon the wall, as the neighbors would accuse me of putting on airs were I to carry such a fine item. I shall save it for the day I am in *real* society again.

I have resumed my marital duties. At first, I held off, for *Dr. Chase's Recipes* warns about too quick a resumption of relations. Besides, I do not care to follow Emmie Lou's example and pop out babies as if I were shelling peas in a pod. But as a nursing mother, I believe I am safe from conception, and since Luke was so insistent, I gave in. I am rewarded each time with his kind attentions for a day. I think men benefit from the act, and women from their husbands' gratitude.

All loved ones are well except for Mother. Luke says she was in good spirits when he visited, but you can always count on Mother to rise to the occasion. The girls reveal so little about her in their letters that I wrote Carrie and *ordered* her to tell me plain how things stood. Carrie wrote that Mother is bedridden, and my faithful friend believes that she will live out her life in that condition. Now that I know, I shall write Mother letters that will cheer her and not expect much in return. Mother begged Carrie not to let on to me her true state, as it would cause worry on my part, and Carrie would not have done so, except that she had given her promise to me. Mother does not want for good care, but O, it is painful to think I am not there to bring her comfort or that I might never see her dear face again. If Luke returns to Fort Madison in the spring, he shall do so only if he takes along Baby and Wife.

Persia Chalmers is now a married woman, but Abner was not her choice! Carrie wrote it was all the scandal, as Persia began keeping company with Henry Talmadge only four weeks before they tied the knot. But, Lordy, I cannot be too critical on that score, because Luke never courted me at all. He simply arrived on my doorstep one evening and threw himself on my mercy, as the poet says.

It is no surprise that Persia was attracted to Mr. Talmadge, for he owns a bank and a sawmill and is as rich as a Pikes Peak nugget. She has always longed for a redbrick house on Third Street, and his is kept with such style. But here is the thing of it: He is *old,* two or three times Persia's age, I should judge. And she is older than I! The marriage, coming so soon after the death of the first Mrs. Talmadge, certainly stirs the gossips' tongues.

Carrie writes, "That don't bother Persia. What does bother her is gaining a daughter at least as old as herself." Well, I think that must be a great trial to Persia. An even greater trial is that Abner, rejected twice in a year (by Self and Persia), has taken up with old banker Talmadge's daughter. Persia must be in a state, fearing that Abner could become her son-in-law and perhaps make her a grandmother! Well, I think that our Persia will be a grandmother before a mother, since Mr.

Talmadge resembles nothing so much as the prune, above the neck as well as below the waist buttons, is my guess. When an old man marries a young girl, you may be sure she is after gold and he is after sex. But if that is his goal, Mr. Talmadge will be sorely disappointed, for Persia does not keep her bargains.

I informed Luke of Persia's marriage as soon as I learnt of it. He was greatly surprised, then displeased at the idea of Persia being "an old man's darling." Well, did he think she would spend her days an old maid because my Darling Boy had thrown her over for me?

We see little of our neighbors now that all labor in the fields during daylight hours. We put aside our toil on Sunday last, however, and gathered for Sabbath services at the Garfields'. I had not been inside the Garfield soddy before and found it a charming place, if a little ridiculous. There is a Persian carpet on the floor and several large portraits in heavy gilt frames. When I remember how little space we had in our wagon for any but necessities, I wonder how Sallie Garfield got them here. Missus said she never saw things so useless, but I spoke up and defended Mrs. Garfield, saying her pretty treasures made the day festive. Others do not care for Mrs. Garfield, believing she is stuck up and spoilt, but she is gently bred, and I prefer her silliness to Missus's grumbling. Besides, in this place, one cannot be particular about one's friends, for fear of having none. Luke has all but forgotten they are Rebels, because he no longer tells me to keep my distance.

The service was Baby's first outing, and he received many compliments. Right proud was his papa, acting as if he alone had produced this son, with no help from the mother. Tom and Moses took a fatherly interest in our boy, both asking to hold him, and Mr. Bondurant fairly danced around him with pride, telling each and every one the story of his birth. At Fort Madison, I would have pretended not to hear, but one does not take offense so easily in this country.

Emmie Lou whispered that I was lucky to have a boy and hopes the babe she carries will be of that sex so that Johnnie will have a playmate. I hope so, too, not just for Johnnie's sake but also because a boy may give her a respite from her pregnancies. Surely if he has a male heir, Mr. Amidon will practice continence. Emmie Lou dreads this birth more than the others, since each one takes a greater toll. When I tried to lighten the mood by recommending Ben Bondurant and Tom Early for her confinement, she said she was afraid she would have time to summon only Lucinda Osterwald, as the Osterwalds are her nearest neighbors.

"You won't let Brownie come with her?" I asked with alarm. I have told no one of my encounter with him, but Emmie Lou gave me such a piercing look that I wondered if Mr. Bondurant had betrayed my confidence. "My husband has given Brownie Osterwald orders not to set foot on our land unless he is accompanied by another, and I advise you to do the same," Emmie Lou replied.

When the Osterwald wagon arrived, I feared that Brownie was in it, and I sent a frightened glance to Mr. Bondurant, who came quickly to my side. But it was just the old couple. Mrs. Osterwald looked very pale, and I wished to let her know she had my sympathy for the cross she bears. But I concluded silence was the kinder course.

We did not tarry as long at services as I would have liked, for after a quiet spring hereabouts with little sign of savages, there are reports that renegades, those hostile outcasts who are greatly to be feared, are making sorties into the neighborhood from the north. After last year's dreadful encounter, none care to be surprised by them again. So all were anxious to be safely home.

When Mr. Bondurant informed us of the reports, Mrs. Garfield turned to her husband and cried out, "Oh, Mr. Garfield, why ever did you bring me to this place?" I was shocked at her outburst, for I cannot abide a scold. Does she think she is the only one who suffers? These burdens were not sought by us, but they are borne by all other women here, and in silence.

⌒

July 18, 1866. Prairie Home.
I had scarcely finished writing in my journal four days ago, when the sky blackened and a hot wind began to blow so hard that it pushed clouds of dust, tumbleweeds, and even jackrabbits ahead of it. Johnnie was safely inside, so I ran to the barn, the wind

pushing me forward, to make sure the door was latched tight. As I tested the door, the wind wrenched it out of my hand, pushing me inside, where I saw the cow was greatly agitated. (Luke was to Amidons' with the horses.) I did not take the time to calm Bossie, because I feared the noise of the wind had awakened Johnnie. It took all my strength to secure the door. Then I pushed into the wind, seeming to take a step backward for each two I took toward the house. The sky was as black as I have seen it in daytime, but an eerie light was cast upon the prairie, and there was a prickly sensation, as if a loathesome lightning storm was about to burst upon us.

At last, I reached the safety of the soddy and pushed inside, where Baby was crying loudly and would not be soothed, for he is as frightened of thunderstorms as his mother. I could hear the moans of the wind outside, and I felt its force as it blew against the side of our little house. With Baby safely in my arms, I went to the window, where I watched a herd of antelope rush blindly toward the barn. They were almost upon it when they turned as one and raced into the distance. By now, I could feel the soddy brace itself against the wind, which was roaring as loudly as the Mississippi's angry waters when they tear into the riverbank at flood time.

Far in the distance, I saw a black cloud that looked a little like a funnel. It moved quickly across the prairie, its strange black shape whirling about in the wind as it came toward me. The air prickled me all over, and I held Baby tight, expecting him to comfort me as much as I did him, for I was taken with a great gloomy sense. As the misshapen cloud came nearer, I turned, intending to hide us both under the quilt, but I changed my mind, and, pushing Baby ahead of me, I crawled under the bed. The soddy around me shook so fiercely, I thought it would blow away, taking Baby and me with it, and I began to shake just as hard, as if Armageddon were being fought in my barnyard.

Then, as quickly as it had begun, the wind died out, and I emerged from my place of safety, to find all in the house was just as it had been. I was ashamed of my cowardice, and vowed I would not even tell Luke of the wind, for surely he would say I had imagined its intensity. Then I opened the door and looked out onto a desolate landscape. The prairie grasses were flattened, as if trampled by a giant steamroller. The barn roof had blown off, and pieces of the implements stored therein were scattered about the yard. The cow was safe but bawling loudly. My washtub, which hangs on the wall of the house, was inside the barn, and the bench Luke made before returning to Fort Madison was nowhere to be seen. Saddest of all, one of our precious trees was uprooted.

As I picked through the wreckage, Tom Early arrived at a tear, his horse badly lathered. "I saw the twister head for you and feared the worst," he said.

I replied 'twas not the worst, but close to

it, that if there had been rain, I would have called the storm a hurricane. Of a sudden, I burst into tears, putting my head against Tom's chest, while he, poor fellow, tried to comfort me. When I had cried myself out, I begged him not to tell Luke.

"Where is Luke?" he asked.

I am ashamed to say that until that minute, I had not thought of the danger to Husband, and I cried, "He is at Amidons'. Pray God that he is safe."

"He is. That was a tornado. It doesn't cover such a wide area as a hurricane, but it's just as deadly, for it takes everything in its path. You were lucky it veered off before it reached the soddy. A whirlwind is so powerful that it can pick up a house and set it down a hundred feet away." I must have appeared ready to cry again, for Tom said slyly, "Why, it's been said a twister can suck the milk right out of a cow and churn it into butter, which drops from the sky like gold coins."

Tom's little sally brought me to my senses, and when Luke returned from Mingo, he found us both in good spirits, cleaning up the mess. He had not seen the tornado, but he feared something was amiss, for on the way home, he had come across our little bench, sitting upright in the middle of the road, as if someone had placed it there for a friendly chat. He took it out of the wagon and returned it to its proper place, none the worse for its journey.

August 8, 1866. Amidons'.

At the last Sabbath services, Mr. Garfield solicited Luke's opinion on how well the Fort Madison seed would perform on his land, which is on the river. Luke had planned to visit earlier but then delayed his plans, due to the damage caused by the whirlwind.

So not until yesterday did Luke issue an invitation to Baby and me to return with him to Garfields', where the two men could discuss agriculture at their leisure. I did not worry so much about encountering another twister, for I am told they are rare and the season for them is over. But I did express fear of running into savages. Luke retorted that when he married me, he thought I was game. He said it was his belief that Mr. Bondurant was making mischief with his latest remarks about the Red Men. I am inclined to put more trust in Mr. Bondurant, but as there have been no other reports, and Husband seemed anxious for us to go along, I threw concern aside and replied that Baby and I would be pleased to accept his kind invitation for an outing.

The Garfields being our farthest neighbors, and knowing the trip would be a long one, I packed a picnic, which we enjoyed under the branches of a tree. The tree was dead, but we are not particular about such details in Colorado. Luke was in the best of humor and even paid me the compliment of saying that it was his opinion I "might be" the finest cook in Colorado Territory.

"And just who 'might be' finer?" I inquired, which brought a laugh and a rare hug from Luke. As he held me a moment longer, I could feel that private part of him stiffen and, without thinking, I laughed gaily, which shocked me every bit as much as it did Luke. I thought my response would draw a rebuke, but instead, a strange look came over his face, such as I had never seen, but perhaps that is because, heretofore, Luke has been aroused only in the dark of night, and so I have not observed his face. I think Husband would have demanded his marital rights under that dead tree had not Baby awakened and saved the day by demanding *his* rights to lunch.

The Garfields welcomed us with all the natural hospitality for which the Southerner is famous. Mrs. Garfield put her arms around me and kissed me on the cheek, and though I am not fond of such displays of affection from those I do not know well, I did not take offense, concluding this was the way of her people. As she did not know when we would visit, Mrs. Garfield had no refreshments but water, which we said would suit us fine. In this dry country, water is the most precious of all liquids.

Sallie (as Mrs. Garfield insisted I call her) made a great fuss over Johnnie, saying he was the best-behaved baby she had ever seen. When I responded that her own little Frederick must have been a fine baby, she said she did not know, as he was her husband's nephew, given to them to raise as their own. His pa was killed in the war, and the sorrowing mother lost her wits and starved herself to death. Little Freddie nearly died, too, "for the niggers turned on him and did unspeakable things," Sallie said. Such treatment weakened his mind and brought about strange outbursts. The three Garfields are all that is left of two large families, the rest being dead from effects of the War of Southern Rebellion. They came here to mend their broken fortune.

"I do not know why the Yankees could not leave us alone. They are vile meddlers," Sallie said, not stopping to think Luke and I were members of that meddlling class. "O, I hate them. If it weren't for the War of Northern Aggression and the price the North extracted for peace, we would be safely at home instead of in this hateful place."

As one who had lost friends from childhood in that awful war, which was instigated by the Southerners, I found the President's treatment of the treasonous Rebels not only generous but lenient. But it was not polite for a guest to respond in such a manner, so I sought a new subject. Looking about me, I remarked that the view from her door was as pretty as any I had seen since arriving in Colorado Territory.

"And how lucky we are that there is not a tree to spoil it," she said, causing us both to burst into giggles. That brought us closer, and Sallie impulsively took my hand and said there was a place along the stream bank that reminded her a little of home. Nothing would do but that she should show it to me. Since the men were already in the field, sifting dirt between their fingers, as is their way, we did not ask permission, but took the two little ones and set off. Sallie's spirits improved with the prospect of visiting her "secret dell," and she fairly skipped along.

We two laughed about the hardships in this place, Sallie saying the women had to put up with everything the men did, and with the men, as well. I scarcely noticed how far we had gone, until I realized we were no longer in sight of the soddy. Just then, Sallie called out, "Here we are," and she led me down a steep bank to the stream, which is as crooked at that point as a "Sherman necktie," which is what the Southerners called their railroad tracks after the Yankees tore them up. The sight was indeed a pretty one, with scrub brush and wildflowers and a tasteful rock garden that Sallie had fashioned.

"Now, here is what I like best," she said, removing her shoes and putting her toe into the water. I followed, and soon, we two, along with Frederick and Johnnie, were bathing our feet. Before I knew what she was about, Sallie splashed water on me, and I replied in kind, feeling carefree for the first time since arriving in Colorado Territory. Sallie was affability itself, and the day promised to be one of the pleasantest I had spent in this place.

As I wondered if Sallie would prove to be the friend for whom I have longed, a sound came from above, and, believing Luke and Mr. Garfield were searching for us, I proposed to play a game of hide-and-seek with them, putting a finger over my lips and pointing to a hollow in the riverbank. Sallie and Frederick took my meaning, and we hastened into our hiding place. I raised my head to ascertain whether the men had seen us, and there came a sight that chilled my blood—a long, deadly lance decorated with feathers. I grasped Sallie's arm and pointed. We held the children close and pressed into the safety of the stream bank. The Red Men had not seen us, and I think they were making ready to leave when, of a sudden, Frederick darted up the bank and rushed them, hollering abuses. I do not know what caused him to do that—possibly his enfeebled mind thought they were the darkies who had harmed him. With not a thought for her own safety, Sallie followed. I started after her, but something—perhaps it was Providence—told me I would be of no aid and called me back to protect my own little one.

From that hiding place, I heard the shouts of Frederick and the pleas of Sallie, mixed with angry grunts from the rude children of nature, sounds so terrifying that I was unable to restrain myself, and I peeked out, to see six braves, their faces hideously smeared with paint.

Mr. Bondurant had told me that savages do not allow their children to cry, and these heathens seemed greatly displeased with Frederick's outburst. One prodded the poor boy with his lance, while another struck him a blow. Such acts do not quiet a white boy, and Frederick only cried harder. One fiend raised his weapon as if to tomahawk the boy, but before he could do so, his companion grabbed Frederick by the feet and smashed his head against a boulder. I gasped aloud as the blood and gore rushed from the poor broken head, but the Red Men made such a racket, they did not hear me. Knowing what was in store for my own blessed babe should he awaken and cry, and that I could be of no assistance to Sallie, I crept back under the bank. Just then, Johnnie awakened, but unaware of the danger, he yawned and stretched out his little arms, and, mercifully, he fell asleep again.

For what seemed like hours but I know was only a few minutes, there was a great commotion above me, and I heard Sallie's pleas for mercy. Then all was silent. The Indians mounted their ponies and were off. I scrambled up the bank, leaving Baby behind for his safety, in case the savages discovered me.

I was met by the grim sight of little Freddie's broken body, covered with arrow wounds, for the Indians had not been content with bashing out his brains, but had added further insult. Mercifully, they had not taken his scalp. Perhaps it was too small. I looked for Sallie, calling her name, although I despaired of finding her alive. She was nowhere to be found, and with horror, I realized my poor friend had been snatched up and carried off, to be murdered or subjected to acts too vile to contemplate.

I removed Johnnie from his hiding place and keeping as low to the ground as possible to avoid detection (though how a woman in a red dress could not be seen in this terrible open prairie, I do not know), I ran toward the Garfield soddy. When it came into view, I opened my mouth to call for help, but I was too exhausted to make a sound. I dropped to the ground, gasping for breath. I lay there, face-down, for some minutes, until I heard a noise and was seized with fear that the savages had raided the soddy, killing Luke and Mr. Garfield, and that now they would aim their flying arrows at Baby and me.

Then I heard my name called and recognized the dear voice of my husband. Baby must have recognized it, too, for he set up a loud wail, and in a few seconds, we were safely in Luke's arms, whilst I blurted out the details of the fatal outing.

Mr. Garfield was crazed with fear for Sallie and would have gone to her aid instantly had not Luke prevailed. "Six Indians against one white man? You'll only get yourself killed, and Sallie, too," Luke said in a harsh manner, which was intended to bring Mr. Garfield to his senses. "She's safe for now. They wouldn't have taken the trouble to carry her off if they'd planned to kill her. The best course is to form a rescue party."

Mr. Garfield saw the wisdom of Luke's words, and while he ran for his horse and weapons, Luke and I set off at once, Luke whipping the horses until we reached the Earley place, where, to my relief, I saw the welcome form of Mr. Bondurant. He knew by our speed that something untoward had happened, and he was beside the wagon before Luke brought it to a stop.

"Indians. They killed the Garfield boy and took Mrs. Garfield captive. Mattie saw it," Luke told him. "Hurry, man. They may be on their way here."

But Mr. Bondurant stood quietly, taking my hand between both of his. "Think you, Mrs. Spenser. What direction taken they? Did they cross the river?"

I thought a minute. "Why, yes. They must have. I heard horses splashing in the water."

"I thought so. Did you get a good look at them?"

I shook my head. "When you have seen one, you have seen the whole. I could not tell them apart, and their faces were painted."

"Was there a big one with a white stripe in his hair and a hooked nose, pushed to the side?"

I nodded, amazed that Mr. Bondurant could draw from me a memory I did not know I had. "His arm was drawn up, as if he'd been injured, and the wound hadn't healed properly," I added. "He had on a necklace of bones."

"Boiled finger bones, they are." Mr. Bondurant sighed. "Red Thunder. He's a savage brute. His own people don't have no more use for him than a damned cur dog. The army chased him halfway to the Missou, but he sneaked back through 'em. Him and his band of hostiles is cowards, and now that they've got a white woman, they'll stay away from the settlements, prob'ly go back north. You ought not to worry, Mrs. Spenser. You'll be safe here. Pay it no mind."

Having barely made my escape from the

146

Indians, I did give it mind, however, and told Luke that Baby and I would not stay on our homestead alone. By now, the boys had joined us, and Mr. Garfield was in sight, so it was agreed the Earleys would alert the neighborhood, sending all to the Amidon house, which is the nearest thing on our prairie to a fortress. The rescue party would leave from there.

Before nightfall, the women and children were safely sequestered at Emmie Lou's, and the men were off, leaving to defend us only Mr. Amidon, who is too sick with the ague to mount a horse, and Mr. Smith, who is too sick with fear to leave this safe refuge. Nevertheless, Mr. Smith struts about and pronounces himself our "protector," believing such work entitles him to sample all the provisions the women brought with them. He has the appetite of a poor relation and the greed of a rich one, and he complained that there was not more to eat.

"We don't need more," Emmie Lou said. "Our men will rescue Sallie tonight when the Indians camp. Why, she'll be home before morning."

"Ha!" replied Smith. "That goes to show, you don't know the fiends. They'll ride all night and tomorrow and the day after that, with the lady tied to her horse; that is, if they ain't already tortured her to death. What an Indian'll do to a white lady ain't human."

Missus said, "Do be quiet, Old Smith," although she seemed a little proud of him, and confided, "Don't he have a good time, though?"

I quickly tired of his recital of unspeakable acts and was glad when Johnnie announced it was time for his supper. Emmie Lou invited me to make use of her bedroom, insisting that I should rest myself when finished. I tried, but my mind is too taken up with fear to sleep. So as I do not care to be further terrorized by Mr. Smith, I am recording the day's events in my journal, which I snatched up during our brief stop at home.

As I pen these sad lines, I go back over my part in the terrible tragedy of this day and wonder if I chose the right course in seeking safety instead of going to Sallie's aid. I know that such a rash act would only have given the Indians two more victims, Baby and Self. Still, is it fair that Sallie has no one of her own kind to share her ordeal? When I broached the subject to Mr. Bondurant and Tom, they said I had acted wisely. But myself, I am torn with doubt. Is life more important than principle? Are Self (and Baby) of more value than a friend? I am haunted with fear that I was called and found wanting, tested and proven a coward.

~

August 17, 1866. Prairie Home.

Sallie is alive!

Our men returned the morning after the abduction, having followed the hostiles some distance before losing their trail. Many were willing to continue the search, but Mr. Bondurant warned that the renegades might join with a larger force of their brethern, and the men were ill-equipped to fight an Indian war. Besides, they had the care of families and farms. So, reluctantly, they retraced their steps and are now back on their homesteads. Several men went for the soldiers, who left in pursuit, accompanied by Mr. Garfield and Moses, who will do most anything that isn't farming. Brownie went with them, too, though I do not know what earthly good he can be.

Mr. Bondurant, who accompanied the soldiers for several days, reported to Luke and Self, immediately he returned. He relayed the intelligence that Sallie was alive and as well as could be expected under the dreadful circumstances. She had been seen more than 150 miles from here, some three or four days after her abduction. Mr. Bondurant did not give the particulars, and, thinking he wanted to spare me, I excused myself. But I wanted to know her state, and so I lurked in the neighborhood to listen.

The man who had seen Sallie was hiding in the bushes not more than a hundred yards away and concluded she was more dead than alive. Indian women do not protect their heads, even in the most inhospitable weather, and Sallie was not allowed her sunbonnet. So her face was blistered from the sun. She was clothed with shocking indecency, the Indians having taken her shoes and other apparel and forced her to wear a filthy dress made from animal skins. She appeared so much like an Indian that only when she fell from the horse and cried out did the man hear his own language spoken and recognize her as a white woman. He told the soldiers he would have given his life to rescue her, though that was merely a pretty speech, as he did not trouble himself to go to her aid. But how can I condemn another for following the path I took?

The Indians stopped but a few minutes to water their horses, drinking their fill but refusing Sallie a single drop. Nor would they allow her a morsel of food. Instead of showing her the least bit of human decency, they taunted her with obscene threats. One bravado dealt Sallie a sharp blow to the head to silence her pleas, then fell upon her and ravished her. Poor Sallie! How can I forget the terror I felt when Brownie showed his detestable disposition. And he is a white man!

"She'd be better off if the Indians had killed her with the boy," Luke told Mr. Bondurant, who heartily agreed. I am not so sure. As terrible as Sallie's plight is, she wants to live, or else she would have done the deed herself. There is something in the human spirit that forces us onward, even under the most trying circumstances. After losing home and family in the War of the Rebellion, Sallie, in her weakened state, may not find the behavior of the savages so much worse than that of her hateful Yankees.

"I don't suppose they'll let her live much longer," Luke ventured.

"If the men don't kill her, their squaws will torture her or work her to death. Ain't that nearly hell? If Mrs. Garfield's lucky, some buck-'ll protect her by taking her for wife."

Luke's head jerked up at that, and Mr. Bondurant added, "Or maybe if she's unlucky. You think Garfield would take her back if she's carrying an Indian's brat? There's not many that would. I heard of a white woman living two years of pure hell with the Comanches before she got rescued. Nothing she put up with from the Indians was as bad as the way her own kinfolk treated her when she come back to 'em. O, her own husband said how he was grateful and all, but he wouldn't live with her as man and wife no more. He said mixtry of the races was agin the Lord, and he made it continual severe misery for her. So she drowned herself. Folks said it was an accident. It weren't."

I gave a gasp, and the two men discovered me.

"Don't worry yourself about the heathens coming back," Mr. Bondurant said, explaining it was his belief that they had gone east through Nebraska and were on their way to Dakota Territory, where they would meet up with the main branch of their tribe.

"Why then, perhaps their brethren will force them to return Sallie. Surely there are some among them who would want to prevent war with the soldiers," I said, joining the men.

"It ain't up to the tribe. They believe her to be the prop'ty of the buck that took her," Mr. Bondurant said. "Maybe he'll sell her."

"How barbaric!" interjected Luke.

I thoroughly agreed. Still, here is the irony of it: The Garfields went to war to defend that

151

very thing, the right to buy and sell human beings.

Despite our concern for Sallie, our lives return to normal, for with hardship afresh each day, we do not dwell on what is past and cannot be helped. Sallie and the frailty of our lives are always on my mind, however. One moment, I was enjoying the pleasure of her company. The next, her boy was murdered and she a prisoner of his killers. I am much troubled in my dreams, hearing Sallie call to me. By daylight, my mind tells me the course I followed to protect Johnnie was the wise one, but I am not so sure at midnight.

Luke rode to Mingo early this morning. I begged to go so that I might pay my respects to Jessie, but Luke said he would make better time on horseback than in the wagon. So I take advantage of my time alone, thoroughly bathing both Boykins and Self. He lies in the cradle now, making his pretty baby sounds, whilst I sit in the sun in my clean dress, drying my hair.

The day is cool yet, due to a nice rain last night that turned the fields a brilliant green, sending up the rich odor of the soil. But there are great black clouds in the sky that spread their blotchy shadows over the earth like spilled grease, and I fear we are in for it. I hope it does not thunder, for that noise frightens me so, a weakness in Self that does not please Husband.

Just now, a wagon appeared on the horizon, heading in my direction. Distances deceive the eye here, and the wheat can grow an inch by the time the wagon reaches me, so I do not need to rush inside and bolt the door. I check my pocket for the box of cayenne pepper now kept there to throw into the eyes of Brownie or any who would try to accost me, and I sit on the bench to await the visitor.

～

August 18, 1866. Amidons'.

The caller was Tom Barley, come straight from the Amidons' to tell me Emmie Lou was delivered of not one but two babies within the hour and required my presence.

"Did you do the honors?" I asked, making hasty preparations for the trip.

"It was Mrs. Osterwald," Tom said, taking Johnnie into his arms so I could write a note to Luke informing him of my whereabouts. "I happened by just as it was over."

"I think I should be jealous if you had officiated."

Tom, who now has uncommon expertise for a man in the subject, said Emmie Lou was doing poorly, "not like you, who we could scarce force to rest." It was Tom's opinion that the babies, a girl and a boy (to Emmie Lou's great relief, I am sure), are small. Mr. Amidon had gone to fetch Jessie, and Emmie Lou requested that Tom carry me to her.

When I arrived, I went directly to the patient, not even pausing to remove my sunbonnet. Emmie Lou was in a dreadful state, and I feared she had slipped into melancholia.

"The boy is dead," said she. "Oh, if it'd

153

been the girl, I wouldn't have minded so, but a boy! That means Elbert will demand indulgence of me before I am ready. I love my wee ones, but I think I would rather die than have another."

I was in complete sympathy with her remarks. She was greatly agitated, and she begged me to promise I would look out for her little ones if she were to follow the boy in death. I replied I did not think she was in danger, but she grasped my arm and said that she was sick with worry that something would happen to her and that Mr. Amidon would marry a woman who would mistreat the girls.

Just as I gave my promise, Jessie arrived, and her cheerful disposition calmed Emmie Lou. As is her way, Jessie quickly took over the sickroom, spreading good cheer and making my appearance unnecessary. So now I enjoy the coolness of the only parlor between St. Joe and Denver City to write in my book. I slipped it into my pocket when I saw Tom's wagon and was pleased to discover a few minutes ago that I had forgotten to return it to the trunk.

Knowing I would be here, Jessie brought our mail with her. After riding all the way to Mingo, Luke will be disappointed to find the cupboard bare, as they say. There is a letter for me from Carrie and another from Mother, which I am anxious to read but put off in order to record the events of the week in my diary. After all, precious as they are, letters may be read at any time, but journal writing must be done whilst alone. There are letters for Luke, as well—one from his father and another, I think, from his precious mother, because it is in a childishly feminine hand. I am grateful he does not share Mother Spenser's letters with me, for I suspect they contain complaints about me and suggestions for my improvement, which, thank you, I do not care to hear. If Luke is not satisfied, he may lodge his own complaints.

O, such wonderful news from Carrie that since Luke was at Fort Madison, Will talks of nothing else but Colorado Territory and would like to see it for himself. Carrie will not allow him to come here without taking her along. "What would you think if you heard a knock at the screen door and opened it, only to find your old friend on the porch?" she writes. I shall reply that I would be much surprised, and so will she if she thinks we have screen door and porch. She will find a humble prairie home, but a welcome grand enough for Mrs. President Johnson. I may even share parts of this journal with her, for sometimes when I write in it, I pretend I am writing to Carrie.

There is more exciting news, though I should have wished it could wait. Jessie confirms my suspicions that I am once again enceinte. I have thought so for some weeks but felt I should discuss the symptoms with her before telling even my journal. I had been of the opinion that nursing mothers were "safe," as we women put it, but we are not. So "that's what's the matter," as the songwriter says.

After assuring me my conclusion about pregnancy was correct and that the babe should arrive early in the spring, probably March or April, Jessie looked at me closely and said, "There's things I can do for you if it's not wanted. Rhubarb compound and pepper."

I quickly silenced her, saying she should save her knowledge for Emmie Lou, who may have greater need of it in future.

I had intended to stay with the Amidons to help, so that Mrs. Osterwald might return home, and I told Jessie as much.

"Lucinda don't want to go home any sooner than she has to. Can't you see the way of it?" Jessie replied.

"Her son is a trial, and I understand her desire to be rid of him for a few days," I agreed, hoping Jessie would not inquire as to the reasons for my feelings against Brownie.

Jessie snorted. "Brownie's no good. It's a fact. But the old man is a hundred times worse. The way he beats her, and her being such a little thing that can't fight back, it's a wonder she's alive. He does it every chance he gets, not just when he's drunk, like Connor does. La! Haven't you seen the bruises she wears?"

I had never heard of a man acting in such a beastly manner toward his wife, and I protested that Mrs. Osterwald's wounds were the result of her own clumsiness. Jessie shook

156

her head. "I could tell you things about the Osterwalds. You know Brownie...." Of a sudden, Jessie stopped and put her arms around me, saying, "This is a hard place, Mattie. Women have to be hard, too, to make it here, but maybe *you* don't. You're a lady. I hope the land don't do to you what it's done to the rest of us." She stopped then, as if she had said too much.

Just as Tom was to carry me home, Mr. Garfield and Moses returned from their mission, accompanied by Brownie, even though he is not welcome at the Amidons'. His presence was allowed only because of his mother. They report no sign of Sallie, which I interpret as good news, for it means she may yet be alive. If she is returned to us, I vow to do whatever is necessary to restore her to sanity, for Sallie's sake as well as my own troubled mind.

The soldiers encountered hostiles and engaged them in a lively battle, killing two. Moses took a pair of moccasins as a souvenir, presenting them to Jessie, who was much pleased, as they are soft and nicely made. Brownie himself took a memento, a foul trophy, which he displayed to all, including the ladies, whose disgust he enjoyed. It is the scrotum of an Indian, which Brownie hacked off the fallen enemy and says he will tan and use for a tobacco pouch. The Red Enemy are not the only savages in this place.

August 30, 1866. Prairie Home.

Luke at Mingo, and came a thunderstorm at noon with lightning and so much noise that I took Baby to bed and held him tight. By the time the dreadful event was over, I had one of my headaches. I fixed tea to soothe myself, and I felt right proud of my return to calm, when I opened the door and discovered 'twas not just rain but also hail. The house and outbuildings are safe, but I fear the crops from the good Fort Madison seed are ruined. Nothing seems to grow in this country — excepting potatoes and me. Luke is much pleased that Johnnie is to have a sister or brother. When I told him of the impending arrival, I said I wondered if I could love another as much as I do him and Johnnie. Well, of course, I will, because love is not limited.

September 4, 1866. Prairie Home.

The hail was meant for us alone. Luke saw no sign of it until he reached our fields, and he discovered much of our crop is gone. For a time, he was furious, seeming to blame me for my failure to stop it.

"Did you expect me to sew an umbrella big enough to cover forty acres?" I asked, trying to lighten the situation. Luke did not find the remark funny, however. Sometimes, he is a hard man to keep in good humor. After a few days, his anger is gone, and though Luke does not say he is sorry for his outbursts (marriage has taught me that women are the only ones who apologize), he acts contrite and is once again my Darling Boy.

He brought word from Mingo that a Nebraska man who trades with the Indians heard of a white woman living with them, although he did not see her. He waited two weeks to report to the soldiers and by then, the savages had decamped.

Mr. Garfield has returned to his soddy, but Luke says he pays no attention to the crops. He is drunk from morning to night, then night to morning from the liquor that Mr. Bondurant makes. I did not know until now that John Barleycorn is the principal source of that old sinner's income and the reason he farms but little. If at home, I would not approve. Here, I do not consider it such a serious stain on the old scapegrace's character, but instead, I hope that he will offer me a dram or two for my Christmas cakes.

~

September 24, 1866. Prairie Home.
Our little group pretends now that Sallie was never one of us, so seldom do we make reference to her. I do not speak of her either, but she is always in my thoughts. I asked Luke if he thinks life is of less value on the frontier. After giving the matter thought, he replied it is sentiment that is less precious. Our own lives have value, so we must live them as best we can, not wasting time on mourn-

ing and other niceties. I do not disagree, though I find the conventions he dismisses are what make us civilized.

Still, I have changed, too, and now find humorous many actions that I would not have laughed at even a year ago. Among them is the deportment of a woman in Kansas, whose husband was attacked and killed by Indians. When the tragedy was related to her along with the news that the Indians were nearby and she must flee, she bid her rescuers wait whilst she changed into black mourning dress, black silk cap, and jet earrings.

Mr. Garfield hangs about the saloon in Mingo now, leaving his farm in ruins. He lost everything in the war, excepting Sallie and little Freddie, and now they, too, are gone. I think Sallie must be dead by now, because a woman of her sensitivity could not live indefinitely with brutes. Still, Mr. Garfield told Mr. Bondurant that after what she had put up with from the "Yankee pigs," she would be able to tolerate savages.

We remain safe but endure troubles of our own. What the hail did not kill, the insects ate, and Luke is again in ill humor. He is the best of farmers, but he does not have the farmer's forbearance or belief that Providence brings both good years and bad.

Because we had so little left of our crops, Luke hired out to Mr. Amidon, not as a bindle stiff, but to oversee the construction of a large barn, as Mr. Amidon is still troubled by the shakes and needed a trustworthy lieutenant. I helped Emmie Lou with the cooking, which I enjoyed enormously, despite my physical state, which fatigues me. It was almost like home when Mother, sisters, and I cooked for the threshing crews—hard work, of course, but what did that matter when we women could be together in the kitchen? I have not seen so many pies in one place since I left home. But there is the difference: Here, they were all dried apple pies!

Mr. Amidon is the only one of us with money (perhaps I should say the only one whose wife has money), and he hired five men for three days' work. Emmie Lou said Mr. Osterwald showed up with Brownie, whom Mr. Amidon refused to employ. When Mr. Osterwald said he would not work without his son, there were ugly words, and Mr. Amidon ordered both off his land.

On our first night, one man begged Emmie Lou to play the piano, requesting "Tenting Tonight on the Old Camp Ground." Emmie Lou, who takes great pleasure in the instrument sent to her by her parents as a housewarming present, did not need to be asked twice. We sang many old favorites until the men retired to their blankets, which were spread upon the ground. Instead of going to bed herself, Emmie Lou sat at the piano and continued her performance. I had retired, but I crept back into the room, listening quietly in a dark corner. Emmie Lou was transfixed until startled by a sound at the window. Turning, she beheld the hired men, tears upon their faces. Emmie Lou shed a few tears herself while continuing to play, and before long, there came upon her face a look of rapture. I had never before seen her so happy.

Of a sudden, Mr. Amidon came down from the bedroom above and ordered her to stop, for fear of waking the little ones. Emmie Lou protested that if the girls could sleep through the noise of barn building, the sounds of music would not awaken them. But Mr. Amidon said harshly, "I won't have bummers paying attention to my wife."

"It's the music. They're only homesick boys. It doesn't mean anything," Emmie Lou protested.

Mr. Amidon was not to be moved. "You will never do this again. Do you hear?"

As neither of them knew I was in the room, I sat silently until they had gone upstairs. Then rising, I saw the men, still at the window. They, too, had heard, and they did not ask for a repeat performance the next evening.

The second babe I carry is not as content as Johnnie was at this stage, which is between two and three months, and I suffer from ill health.

October 2, 1866. Prairie Home.
We have long known that Moses Earley was not of a farming nature. He is charming and fun-loving but leaves the toil to his brother and would rather find a gold mine than work for a living. Now, he has gone off to discover one, and taken Jessie with him! In this place where all prize freedom so highly, there

is still room for scandal! Of course, that is because it involves a woman. I am not altogether surprised, for I had observed Jessie and Moses enjoyed sparking.

All blame Jessie, of course, and express sympathy for her husband that was. I am told he is heartbroken, and why not, as Jessie ran store, saloon, and post office, and now he must work to make his way. Mr. Connor disappeared for a few days, and all thought he had gone after the two miscreants, but he returned with another woman, whom he introduced as Mrs. Connor. Without her, he was in danger of losing the post office, since he cannot read. Missus declared she recognized Jessie's replacement as a prostitute from one of the houses in Denver, which prompted Emmie Lou to ask Missus if she was acquainted with every woman in Colorado of shipwrecked virtue.

I remember the kindness of both Jessie and Moses when Johnnie was born, and I cannot help but wish them well in the gold fields.

Now that it is cooler, Johnnie no longer has the croup. He grows every day and already has a tooth, which I discovered when he bit my breast. Luke said last evening that he is glad we are to have a second child in the spring, as he hopes for a large family, perhaps ten — the first I knew of it, as I had not thought it proper to discuss the number of our children before we were wed. Luke's is not the last word on the subject, however.

October 8, 1866. Prairie Home.

I came near to losing the babe and have spent two days in bed, something I never did before in my life. I think the Lord, suspecting I was tentative about the arrival of this child, sent me this trial so I would know how precious the little one is to me. If it is a girl, I hope to name her Sallie, and Luke agrees that would be a satisfactory name. Sallie still occupies my thoughts.

October 18, 1866. Prairie Home.

Just before Luke rode off to Mingo this morning, he called out, "What would you think if I brought some guests for supper?"

"Mr. Bondurant or Tom? Or both?" I inquired.

He merely smiled, and 'twas then I noticed that he was in the wagon instead of on horseback, and I recalled that he had swept it out yesterday. What's more, he had taken greater care than usual with his toilette. "I'll bring back a surprise," he called.

O, Carrie! Dare I hope it is she? Was that feminine hand on the letter to Luke really Carrie's, disguised to fool me? She and my dear husband have cooked this up between them, and her visit was to be a secret. How like her not to let me know ahead of time so that I would not wear myself out with preparations. I have the best friend and dearest husband in the world. O, I shall *act* surprised, but

164

here is a note for you, Carrie: I shall let you read this page so that you will know you were not as sly as you thought!

There are a million things to be done before you arrive. I shall even make you one of our famous dried apple pies. I take the time to write this brief entry only so that I can show it to you upon your arrival, and you will know how welcome you are. O, my friend, you bring me such pleasure.

~

October 22, 1866. Prairie Home.

I flew about my chores, wishing for at least two pairs of hands so that all would be in readiness for Carrie's visit. There was much to do. Still, the hours dragged by until I saw the cloud of dust on the horizon that meant Luke was returning. I quickly changed my dress and surveyed my little home with much pride, knowing my little improvements, such as the linen tablecloth, which is folded in half to fit our humble table, and the bitters bottle filled with pretty weeds would both please and amuse Carrie.

I was not disappointed when I made out a parasol and a member of my own sex, dressed in traveling attire, sitting beside Luke on the wagon seat. I took up Johnnie from his cradle and said, "See, Baby, it is your aunt Carrie come to admire you." I fancied he was as anxious as I to meet his playmate Wee Willie, who I thought must be sleeping in the wagon bed.

The wagon drew near, and when I made out

the faces, I could scarcely believe my eyes. There, clinging to Luke's arm, was not my darling Carrie, but Persia Chalmers, now Mrs. Talmadge! Behind her sat the banker, his face red and wet from sun and perspiration and looking more than ever like a prune. My heart sank, and Johnnie felt the disappointment so keenly that he let out a loud wail. I would have joined him, but social responsibility required that I hide my true feelings.

'Twas a cruel joke on Luke's part, I thought, then realized that in deference to his past affection for her, I had never told Luke my lack of regard for Persia. For all Luke knew, she was my dearest friend but one. He truly believed he had brought me a pleasurable surprise. So I vowed he would not know my disappointment.

I was determined to be pleased with any visitors from home, even the new Mrs. Talmadge, and, for a moment, I surmised she felt the same way, because she put her hands (she wore the first mitts ever seen here!) on her breastbone and proclaimed with great drama that she had missed me dreadfully. She pronounced our little place "charming," although I saw on her face a look of disgust when she entered our soddy and surveyed its single room. She inquired where Luke and I would sleep during their stay.

"Right here, unless you want to get up in the night and nurse the baby. Do you?" I replied, as sweet as I could be.

"Nurse the baby? Do you expect me to nurse the baby?" Persia was confused, but Luke and Mr. Talmadge laughed at my little sally.

166

Then Persia understood and put her nose into the air, saying, "Do you expect us to sleep in the barn with the animals?"

I was tempted to retort that Mr. Talmadge must be used to sleeping with an ass by now, but, fortunately, Luke spoke up and said the two men would make use of the wagon, leaving the bed to Persia and me. It was not the best arrangement, but at least Luke did not offer to let Mr. Talmadge share my bed with me! (Persia is not much more desirable as a bedfellow, however, for she thrashes around terribly. She complains she is used to goose down, and the "prairie feathers," which is what we call the grass used to stuff the tick, cause her to itch. Never again will I complain about sleeping on a grass mattress.)

One sees vain girls like Persia in every town along the Mississippi, but they are not to be found in such quantity here, as they cannot make the grade. I shall not here relate all Persia had to say. I know Miss Persia right well and was not surprised by her immodesty, her high opinion of herself, her smart remarks. Suffice it to say, she was not above finding fault with me at every turn. I have studied her, and I conclude it is because Persia is a flatterer that each man believes himself to be her protector. Such deportment is beyond my ability, and I think, should I act in that fashion, a man would think me a donkey.

Persia found many ways to show her superiority to me, stroking her long ringlets while viewing my untidy braid and placing her milk white hand next to my sunburned one.

She said she could not bear to have common calico next to her skin, that only silk would do. I need not put down here what each of us was wearing. I am a true member of my sex and wish that I, too, had lotions and fine clothes, but I would not take all the gold of the Queen of Sheba to trade my husband for Persia's. That was a comparison Persia did not make.

Mr. Talmadge has come west to investigate the gold fields, where he hopes to place his money, of which he has a good deal, according to Mrs. Banker Talmadge. She persuaded him to look over the "Great American Desert," as they call our part of the country, for investment, but Luke says that while capital is in short supply here, a man must farm his own land to make it pay. This is no place for an aristocrat.

Luke is out now, as Mr. Talmadge wanted to survey the country, and Luke wished to invite the neighbors for a reception honoring our guests. Mr. Talmadge is not such a bad man, though too grim and humorless for my taste. He dotes on Persia, always addressing her as "Persia, dear," but "the light of his household" shows him not the least affection, removing her hand from his if he should be so bold as to take it.

I am glad that Persia accompanies the men, since it gives me a few minutes with my journal. I do not believe she would be much help to me in preparing for the party.

October 27, 1866. Prairie Home.

Here is a funny thing that happened when Luke, Persia, and Mr. Talmadge stopped at the Smiths'. Those neighbors have taken to raising pigs, and as the three callers entered the door, Missus was pelting a piglet with her broomstick. The poor creature had wandered into the house and caught fast his head in a cream can, then gave way to panic and ran about the room, upsetting the food safe and spilling crockery, making a terrible racket. At last, Missus chased the pig outside, where it ran off, the bucket on its head like a bonnet. Missus was not the least bit ruffled when caught thus, and she took both cake and plate from the floor and offered refreshments. Persia calls the Smith place "Dirty Woman Ranche."

We have had our reception. The neighbors, excepting Missus, treated Persia as if she were a bisque dolly, all staring at her in frank admiration, the men vying among themselves to do Persia's bidding. I found it unseemly that they do not care if their wives carry heavy buckets of water or till the fields in the fierce heat, even when in the family way, but they could not let Persia so much as fetch a piece of pie, and insisted she sit at table whilst they held her parasol to protect her from the sun. Among the admirers she had caught in her web, I am ashamed to admit, was Luke. It is said that women are deceivers ever. Well, I think men are fools ever—most of them, anyway.

Only Tom was not to be taken in by Persia's helpless ways and told me she was as useless on these plains as a conservatory lily. "Give me the wild rose or the sunflower. They are prettier by far, and can go the distance."

"And what of the dandelion? That is what I feel like next to Persia," I said with so much self-pity that I was immediately ashamed.

"It flourishes best of all. I prefer it above the others," Tom replied, then looked me full in the face and said "Luke is the luckiest man in the territory. I wonder if he knows it." O, it was wrong of me to let Tom make love to me like that. I should have pretended not to hear. But I was in need of a compliment, and after Luke's own behavior around Persia, I do not think I was so wicked.

The men all fought for slices of Persia's cake after she announced it was her contribution to the dinner. What she contributed was all of my chocolate, every crumb. We shall not have chocolate for our Thanksgiving or Christmas, and if Luke asks the reason, I shall tell him. As she passed out slices, Persia sought congratulations from one and all. I suppose she has never heard that modesty in all things is the best guardian of virtue.

I found the cake too heavy, and the little stranger, who is now nearly four months along, protested it all night long.

⌒

October 29, 1866. Prairie Home.

Last evening came a night sky of indigo blue, with stars as big and bright as pigeon eggs against a dinner-plate moon. I thought it the loveliest sight I have seen since arriving here. Even the men paused in their talk of farming to admire it.

Mr. Talmadge is keenly interested in the question of agriculture, believing if there was some way to bring water to our dry land, it could be made to produce. Luke takes the opposing view: that we must find crops that will flourish with but little moisture. In these past few days, I have changed my opinion of Mr. Talmadge and find much to admire in him. He is well mannered, interested in everything about him, and has a fine mind. Like Luke, he sees great possibilities in this country. He is blind when it comes to his wife, however. I had to hold my tongue, when he told me his "Persia dear" was a mere child. You might as well call the mutton lamb, for she is older even than I. His is a jealous nature, which does not bode well for the marriage, because Persia will ever be the flirt.

But I do not turn to my book this day to write about Mr. Talmadge and the future of farming in Colorado Territory.

After viewing the sky, the two men returned to the house, leaving Persia and Self under the stars. The sky seemed to be the only thing that had won Persia's approval since her arrival here.

"If the days were as fine as the nights, I think I might reconsider my decision to come to Colorado," murmured she.

"But you did come," I said. At that moment, my heart was so filled with the beauty of the evening and the sight of the little soddy in the moonlight, with Husband and Baby safely inside, that I felt charitable enough toward Persia to tell her I was glad that she had come.

Before I could speak further, however, she said, "I mean permanently. You were Luke's second choice. I turned him down. Don't you know that?"

I was no less thunderstruck than if she had slapped me across the face. "Don't I know that?" I replied in that stupid way Persia has of repeating every question.

Persia laughed at me. "He begged me to marry him. Begged me on his knees. He said he'd dug a well out here just for me. 'Well, well, well, that won't do for me,' I told him."

It was just light enough so that I could see Persia's eyes narrow as she searched my face, looking for the wounds her barbs had caused.

"He was so sure of himself. He brought me that brooch you wear, thinking I'd accept it as an engagement present. I always wore garnets, but no more." Persia touched the heavy gold watch with its design of diamonds, which she wore pinned to her waist. "Mr. Talmadge gave me this. Of course, Mr. Talmadge goes with it. Luke is furious that I married him. You know I speak the truth, don't you?"

Persia enjoyed herself immensely at my discomfort. Though I strove mightily to keep my feelings to myself, Persia saw and gloated at my pain, as in my mind I reviewed instances that seemed to prove the truth of her words. Luke had never shown any feelings for me before asking for my hand, and his proposal was better suited to buying a pig than declaring his love for a life's companion. I remember the shock of our Colorado neighbors when Luke introduced me as his wife. Had he described Persia to them? But I would not admit any of this to Persia. "Why do you say such things?" I asked at last.

"O, I thought you knew. Everybody in Fort Madison does." Persia started for the door, then turned back. "When he came home last spring, he spent his time with me. It was almost a scandal. He still wants me, you know."

I would not reply. Instead, I preceded her to the house. "Baby needs me," I said. "Luke's baby."

Now, Persia is gone. Luke is carrying the Talmadges to Mingo, and from there, they will make their way to the gold fields, and I hope I shall never see them again! I put this down because I have no one in whom to confide. Perhaps writing of it will help me to understand the truth. My pride prevents me from inquiring of Carrie if those at home laugh at me. Does the one I care for most laugh at me, too? I have told him of my love for him and confided in him my hopes and dreams for us. Now, I am forced to wonder if he listened with the wish that another was speaking.

Did Luke marry me only because *she* rejected him? I thought of little else as I lay awake through the night, next to Persia, whose wagging tongue did not keep her from sleeping well. My mind will not be still. I vow to be the best wife I can, so that if Persia did indeed speak the truth, Luke will conclude that while I was not his first choice, I am the better choice.

My head aches so, almost as if there were a terrible fury inside pounding on my temples to get out. I can barely see to write. But I think it is an easier pain to live with than the ache in my heart.

~

November 20, 1866. Prairie Home.

Mr. Bondurant arrived at midday with the news. A large troop of soldiers came upon an Indian encampment, startling the Red Men. The savages made for their weapons, and in the melee, a woman ran in the direction of the soldiers. Thinking her an Indian, they did nothing. Then she called out, "Help me! I am Sallie Garfield, a white woman!" The cavalry sprang to their rifles and rushed forward as she raced toward them in hopes of rescue.

Sallie had nearly accomplished her desire when Red Thunder—for he was the evil savage who had held her prisoner all this time—let fly an arrow, which struck her in the back. She staggered a few steps and fell, mortally wounded, into the arms of a brave soldier. His comrades let loose with such a barrage of shot that her cowardly captor and his brutish fellows were killed instantly. Mr. Bondurant says it is the Indian way to murder captives rather than to allow them to be returned to their loved ones.

Poor Sallie survived months of inhuman treatment, only to die within an arm's reach of freedom, but perhaps there was some mercy in this; Sallie was enceinte.

———

December 27, 1866. Prairie Home.

On Christmas night, I lost the baby, a boy more than five months along. The birth was easy, and I was not aware I was in labor until it was over. The year that began with such hope ends in sorrow. There are too many deaths in this country. Still, I count it a good year, for it brought Husband and me our beloved Johnnie.

Chapter 5

January 22, 1867. Prairie Home.

Luke has gone to Mingo, and I have gone to quilting, as I am good for little else. Came a headache last night so painful that I went outside and pressed snow against my temples in hopes the cold would drive it away. It seemed as if tiny men were inside my forehead, pounding upon the flesh with their hammers. When the snow failed to do the desired job, I built up the fire and brewed a cup of tea from the spearmint leaves Carrie dried for me. It soothed the head a little, and the soul, as well, freeing me of self-pity. After an hour or so, I was able to creep back into bed and sleep until Luke brought my hungry babe to me for his breakfast. What kind of mother is she who does not hear the cries of her wee one?

Now I sit here quietly with a handkerchief tied around my head to keep the tiny miscreants from returning with their tools and resuming their mischief. These headaches always leave me drained, with a feeling that I am sitting elsewhere in the room, watching my poor self.

The quilt with its Flying Geese pattern brings happy memories of home, as it is made with so many scraps from my piece bag. I had been stitching around a triangle made of goods left over from Carrie's graduation dress. But due to the aftermath of the headache, my hands are stiff, and the needle picks at the material. I might just as well quilt a cracker. So I set aside the work and turn to my journal.

I give a great deal of thought to Persia's cruel words of last year, but I keep them locked inside my bosom, for I refuse to attach unnecessary importance to them by discussing the truth of the matter with Luke. I know he cared for Persia once, having kept company with her for many years, and all (including Self) believed the two of them would wed one day. Even though Luke was her lover once, I have concluded that upon returning to Fort Madison two years ago, he found her unsuitable for his life's companion on a Colorado homestead, so sought a better candidate. That was when he came "a-courtin' " to our farm.

Persia spoke to me out of spite, being jealous of our happy Prairie Home. I am persuaded that no matter what Luke's feelings were for her in the past, he loves me, else why would he have resumed the marital act just two weeks after I lost the babe at Christmas, and with such frequency? No, Luke is mine alone, to be shared only with Johnnie. Luke loves Baby almost as much as I do, and that is very much indeed. I believe he is more than satisfied with his little family, and I am determined to put Persia's claims out of my mind.

Luke and I are settled in this winter like an old married couple. After the day's work is done and the supper dishes put away, Luke reads aloud from the Bible, a newspaper when we have one, or from *Oliver Twist,* which is our passion this winter. At such times, I sometimes tell Luke about my hopes and dreams for us. Yesterday, I said I want him to build a big white house right here on our homestead, with large veranda and rosebushes growing over the railing. "When we are a hundred, dear, we can sit on a swing in the evening and enjoy their fragrance," said I.

"I do not believe I'll last that long," replied Luke.

"Than neither shall I, for if something happened to you, I do not think my heart would continue to beat," I said, taking his hand and holding it against my breast. I think Luke was surprised at my boldness, but I am determined to open up my heart to him.

The weather, being as harsh as last year's, with much snow, keeps me from my little bench in the sunshine. As a good farm wife, I am glad for the moisture, which will ensure a better crop, and for myself, I do not mind the poor weather that forces me to remain indoors, now that Babykins keeps me company. We chat together, he and I, believing each understands the other. After Luke left this morning, Johnnie attempted to soothe the ache in my brow by playing his baby fingers across my face. The little taps are as soft and as welcome as raindrops.

Because of the weather, our only guests these days are our two lonely bachelors, Tom and Mr. Bondurant. The latter came two days ago to tell us that Lucinda Osterwald had broken her arm in a "fall."

"You mean, her husband beat her again," I corrected him pertly. Luke and Mr. Bondurant exchanged glances, telling me they knew the truth of the matter.

"If a man beats his wife, it's his business. She may bring it on herself," said Luke. "We must not interfere."

"No woman is responsible for such beastly treatment," I replied, for I would defend any of Eve's daughters against that kind of brutality.

Luke did not reprimand me, but inquired instead, "Does she require Mrs. Spenser's help?"

His question shamed me, for I myself should have offered my aid. Nonetheless, I was alarmed, lest I should go to her and find Brownie about.

"Mrs. Smith is there. I guess that's punishment enough for old Osterwald. She took 'em a funeral pie. Them things taste worse than death," Mr. Bondurant said. When I did not understand his meaning, he explained, "Funeral pie's raisin. That's what women's always takin' to buryings."

"Then I shall take the cake I've just baked," I said. "And if you care to accompany us there, Mr. Bondurant, I'll fix you a fine supper upon our return."

Even with Mr. Bondurant and Luke to protect me against Brownie, I was grateful to find the Osterwald men gone and Missus returned to "Dirty Woman Ranche," as we all now call her place, for the afternoon. Mrs. Osterwald was alone. I had not been in the Osterwald dugout before, and I found it to be a hovel, so shoddily constructed that it was not even as tight as a woodpile. An animal stench assaulted me as I entered, and I think I should have backed out had I not seen Mrs. Osterwald lying on a rough wooden bench, a dirty quilt pulled up to her chin. The once-gay fabric was the only bit of color in that room.

Mrs. Osterwald's eyes were frightened at the intrusion, then confused, but when she comprehended who had come to call, her eyes showed a spark of joy.

"I have brought you a cake," I said with a cheerfulness I did not feel. I looked for a place to set it on the table, which was littered with bones and scraps of food on battered and bent tin plates. I brushed off the cleanest of the plates and cut Mrs. Osterwald a large piece, for I feared her greedy men would not save her a crumb if I left the cake for them to serve her. Then I fed it to her with my own hand. Despite Mrs. Osterwald's feeble state, she ate every bit, and in her eagerness, she spilled crumbs on her much-mended night-sack. When I took out my handkerchief to wipe them off, Mrs. Osterwald grabbed my hand and examined the little square of cloth.

"Pretty," she said, uttering the first words since I had entered the squalid house. On impulse, I presented to her the fine square of linen that Carrie had embroidered for my twenty-first birthday. I think Carrie would not begrudge my giving it away if she knew how much pleasure it brought to one who has nothing.

Just then, I heard Brownie's voice without and saw a look of terror cross Mrs. Osterwald's face, which I did not altogether understand. Surely she had reason to fear the husband, but a mother loves even the most flawed child. Perhaps she confused the one with the other.

As I wanted to spend no time with the Osterwald men, I was anxious to leave, and I quickly laid out the loaves of bread I had brought. I sought to tuck a sack of molasses candy under Mrs. Osterwald's pillow, allowing her alone to enjoy it, but there was no pillow. So I placed it in Mrs. Osterwald's hand and pressed her fingers together. Instead of removing the cake to a tin plate, as was my intention, I left the china plate (not one of my best ones) for Mrs. Osterwald's enjoyment, though I knew I was unlikely ever to see it again.

Looking into the cupboard for a cloth to cover

the cake, I found one hidden in the back, wadded into a ball, and opening it, I discovered my own silver spoon, which had disappeared after our first Sabbath service. How can I blame one who is devoid of all that is beautiful for her impulse in taking a single pretty thing? Still, the spoon is an heirloom, inherited from my grandmother, and is precious to me. So I slipped it into my pocket. Perhaps it was not Mrs. Osterwald but Brownie who was the thief, and the mother was too shamed to return the object to its rightful owner. Mrs. Osterwald had fallen asleep, so I did not say good-bye, but gathered my things and went without, where the two Osterwald men looked up at me sullenly, without greeting. Brownie took a step or two backward.

"Mrs. Osterwald needs bed rest," I said. When neither responded, I ordered, "She must get it." I knew, however, that neither would pay the least attention to my instructions.

With no further word, I took Baby from Luke's arms and climbed into the wagon, the men joining me, and in an instant we were off. "Lordy, that dugout to them is as a mud hole to a pig," I observed when we were out of earshot.

" 'Tis a lick-skillet place," Mr. Bondurant agreed. "And they is pigs themselves, by ginger! I don't take to a man that lives in his own filth or treats animals like Osterwald's done."

"I think I should have spoken to them. Perhaps I will yet," Luke agreed, then turned to me in explanation. "It is a crime what they have done. The Osterwald animals are beaten and starved."

"And so is Lucinda Osterwald," I replied.

～

February 2, 1867. Prairie Home.

I was about to blacken the stove when I was relieved of the chore by the arrival of my favorite conversationalist—Tom Earley. I accused him of spying on us, for he always seems to call when Luke is away. The two men are great friends, and the only ones in this place who are keen on trying out the latest farming techniques. When they are together, agriculture is always the subject. So I am glad for the opportunity to have Tom to myself and discuss the affairs of the day, and, I am not ashamed to admit, to indulge in a good gossip. If Tom were only a woman, he should be the boon companion I have sought in Colorado Territory.

After a lively discussion about the state of the Negro, now that he is likely to be enfranchised, we turned to the subject of women's suffrage. I asked if an ignorant darky can vote, then why not I, a woman who has the advantage of an education at Oberlin College? Tom says it is the belief of most men that the responsibilities of the ballot box would coarsen women. I argued that casting a ballot was no more harmful to a feminine nature than gathering buffalo chips and living in a dirt house. When Tom prudently inquired about Luke's belief in the matter, I told him Husband thought women should vote in matters of concern to them, such as school elections.

"Well, then, he agrees with the majority, since in this place, that means no vote at all, for we haven't any schools."

Having exhausted ourselves on such weighty matters, we turned to pleasanter affairs, Tom telling me that he had heard from Jessie and Moses. Upon fleeing Mingo, they went directly to the gold fields at Central City but discovered all the claims there were taken, and so they established themselves for the winter in Denver, where Moses has found work at a place called the Mozart. I said any establishment with such a name would be pleased to have an employee with Moses's fine voice and skill on the dulcimer. Moses is well paid, but he finds prices almost double what they are in Mingo, which makes them very dear indeed, as Mingo prices are double those in Fort Madison.

Jessie, too, is employed, which does not surprise us, as she is a hard worker and not one to remain idle. She conveys her regards to me through Moses, being afraid to send me a letter, since Mr. Connor might recognize the writing and follow her to Denver. Could an illiterate person spot a familiar hand? asked Tom. I replied that one could recognize the unsigned work of an artist. So why not handwriting? We agreed the subject needed further consideration and that we should discuss it upon his next visit.

Before he left, Tom gave me the loan of Mr. Whitman's new volume, *Drum-Taps,* which is all the rage back in the States. Good friend that he is, Tom said he was too busy to read it now. Tom is ever anxious to read, so this is a kind favor indeed.

❦

February 4, 1867. Prairie Home.

Luke presented me with a single letter upon his return from Mingo. At first, the hand was unfamiliar. Then I recognized the dear penmanship and knew at once that it contained unhappy news, for Father has ever left correspondence to others. With a heart already heavy, I ripped open the envelope and read the tear-stained sheet, which I paste here:

Dear Daughter Mattie

Sorrowful duty requires relating to you sad news. Beloved Wife and Mother was called beyond on Thursday last. We put her into the ground, with many mourners present. Mother had suffered poor health since your removal to Colorado, and crossing over was God's will for her. Your sisters will write the particulars when time permits, but it is my duty to inform you of the event at once. Hers was the kindest, most affectionate, and simplest heart that ever beat in a woman. She often talked of you and young John in far-off Colorado, and her fondest wish was to see her firstborn again. Now, you'll meet her in a better place, as shall we all. Dear daughter, your father, sisters, and brothers console you in your grief and ask you to pray for us in ours.

Your Loving Father
Jeremiah C. McCauley

I had scarcely read the terrible news when I dropped senseless to the floor, and Luke gathered me up in his arms and carried me to the bed. When I revived, I saw a look of great compassion on his face. The letter was held in his hand, and he did not have to tell me that he had read its contents. Luke understands the love of a child for its mother, and he treated me with great tenderness, helping me into my nightgown and cooking the evening meal himself. After I fed Baby, Luke tucked him in for the night. Then he held me whilst I cried for the loss of my dear parent, and when I was finished, he gave great care in kissing and hugging me, and talking in soothing words, until I fairly melted, and he sought his gratification with great ease.

February 9, 1867. Prairie Home.

I try to keep my tears from Luke, as he does not care to see me with the blues. So I cry during the day when only Baby is here to see. Johnnie eases the ache for a time by distracting me with his merry laugh, but then I think again of Mother, who was never privileged to hold this only grandchild, and once more the tears scald my cheeks.

Sister Mary has written the particulars of Mother's death, which was not unexpected, for she scarcely moved from her bed after the loss of the last baby. She asked the girls to keep her illness from me, as there was nothing I could do for her, and she did not want me to take sick with worry. While Mother's body wasted, her mind was as keen as ever, and she knew I would press Carrie for her true state. So on Carrie's visit, the girls endeavored to show Mother in the best light. Mary begs me to forgive their deception, as it was Mother's wish that I not know. Besides, Mother enjoyed the game, believing her efforts kept me from fretting. Had I known of her illness, Mother believed, I would have insisted on returning to Fort Madison last spring, and that would have been a trial for both Self and Johnnie.

She was right, of course, since I would have given birth on the prairie, but would that have been such a bad thing? With the ease of my parturition, Johnnie could have made his appearance in the morning, we would have been on the trail after noon, and Mother would have had the satisfaction of beholding both her daughter and grandson.

<hr>

February 12, 1867. Prairie Home.

I sorrow for Mother so, and when I give way to grief, I cry not only for her but for Sallie and the German settlers and those poor emigrants who were killed in the Indian attack. The tears run afresh when I think of Father, who was so devoted to the noblest of life's companions. I am unable to do my work and so neglect both Husband and Son. Luke rebuked me yesterday for forgetting to bathe Johnnie. I have been disagreeable of late and replied harshly for the first time in our marriage, saying if we did not live in a sod house with a dirt floor, Johnnie would not need to be bathed so frequently. I regretted my outburst instantly, knowing I had wounded Luke, for he does the best he can for us. He fears I shall sink into melancholia, and at times, I, too, fear for my mental state. Then I rouse myself for the sake of the little family that needs me. When Luke returned from chores, he found a jelly cake for his supper.

~

February 18, 1867. Prairie Home.

Necessity forced Luke to go to Mingo today, but my dearest husband made a detour by the Earley place and asked Tom to call, as Tom's visits cheer me. Tom brought with him a cunning eggshell, which is mottled and as finely colored as if it were made of marble. I roused myself from self-pity to take part in our old bantering ways, saying I did not know if I could accept a gift from a gentleman who had not first asked permission of my husband to give it to me. Tom replied, that being the case, he would take it back along with Mr. Whitman's capital book, and the next shell he found would go to Johnnie. We laughed at the idea of Johnnie's little hands making quick work of the fragile present. I think it is the first time I have laughed since the news of Mother's crossing.

~

February 24, 1867. Prairie Home.

We are to go to Denver City! Luke returned from Mingo last week with the news that he had made plans to attend an agricultural conference in Denver and that Baby and I might go along. Luke is the most generous of husbands, and I vow to put sorrow behind me and be the gayest possible companion so that he will not regret his invitation. Already the excitement has lifted my spirits, and I go an hour or more without giving way to sadness. I know Mother would approve, as she believed grieving was an unbecoming state. I cannot help but think that she has had a hand in this turn of events.

There are so many decisions to be made, since Luke will allow me to take only my small wedding trunk, the one in which I hide this journal. At first, I laid out several dresses, but as there is no room for them, I will limit my costumes to two—a sensible suit for traveling and the navy China silk that was my wedding dress; it will make an appropriate mourning gown. I can enhance its plainness with my breast pin and purchase a lace collar in Denver to dress it up. I wish I had paid more attention to the way Persia trimmed her hats, since she is always in the latest style. Do the ladies today wear their hats wide or close to their faces, lavishly trimmed or simple? Luke would not want to be accompanied by a woman who is out of fashion, but I suppose that in Denver, so far from civilization, few women are dressed with much style. I shall pack Luke's wedding vest, and when he puts it on, he will be the handsomest man in Denver. But he would be that on any account.

March 4, 1867. Denver City.

O, I shall be glad when the transcontinental railroad is completed, though it has been so long since I have seen an engine, I think I should run from it in fright. We left Mingo for our great adventure in a stage. Lordy, it was the dirtiest and most uncomfortable conveyance I have ever seen. The cushions on the board seats were ripped to shreds. The floor was covered with mud and tobacco stains, and the side curtains were so tattered that they kept out neither wind nor rain. But I was not to be deterred from enjoyment of the trip, and so upon entering, I overlooked the state of the vehicle, turning my attention to our companions instead. Alas, this brilliant group appeared to be little better than the coach.

Three men sat across from us. At one end was a gambler from the Southern states, judging from his manner of speaking. He was dressed in a dirty white shirt, and while his coat was expensive, it was as ragged as our traveling compartment, the velvet collar shiny with wear. He proffered a deck of cards, but upon discovering there were no suckers amongst us, he rested his head against the window and slept.

Next to the other window, opposite Luke, sat a large, fierce man with yellow teeth, and not many of them, who told us his name was Wilson. This giant of a man wore a buffalo coat, and with his shaggy beard and windy stomach, he resembled a bison in more than dress. He had a familiar manner, which I have not gotten used to in this country, and he informed me the coat weighed more than I did. From its depths, he drew a bottle, which he cheerfully held out to all, and he was not offended when it was greeted with no more enthusiasm than his neighbor's cards.

Squeezed between these two unsavory characters was a young man with clean features and mild manner. He informed us he was a professor from Maine on his way to Denver to seek a position. It was his belief that with so many giving up their professions to prospect for gold, he would encounter a great shortage of teachers, and, therefore, he was confident he would be well compensated for his work.

I enjoyed talking with the young man, whose name was Slade, as he was familiar with the news from the States, and his intelligent conversation helped pass the time as well as divert me from the unsavory sounds and smells coming from the others. Without asking my permission, Mr. Wilson lit an enormous cigar, which was offensive to both Johnnie and Self, and I hoped Luke would request that he put it out. As I did not know the manners of a Colorado omnibus, however, I dared not ask Luke to intervene, and so I reached into my purse (the dear little bag Carrie embroidered for me) for my handkerchief, intending to fan the foul air away from Baby.

It was then that I discovered the theft of my breast pin. Prior to entering the carriage, I had checked to make sure it was pinned to the lining of my purse. So I knew it had not fallen out of its own accord. Immediately, I announced the disappearance of the precious object, looking at Mr. Wilson as I did so, for I knew him to be the culprit.

Instead of producing the object, however, the "buffalo" turned to Mr. Slade and said, "Best to empty your pockets, hoss." I thought this to be a diversion, for I knew Mr. Slade to be innocent, but Luke touched my arm in a manner that silenced me. With great protestations, Mr. Slade did as he was told, revealing a great many interesting objects, but none of them belonged to me. Satisfied that he had proved himself guiltless, Mr. Slade gathered up the items, but Mr. Wilson was not to be satisfied. He reached inside the accused's coat, ripped out the breast pocket, and my precious brooch fell onto the floor. Then shouting a command to the driver to stop the coach, Mr. Wilson ordered the miscreant out of the carriage and told him he could walk to Denver—or to perdition. When last seen, he was trudging along the road behind us.

We learnt then that my protector was a confectioner who hoped to set up shop in Denver. Mr. Wilson hails from Wapello, just up the Mississippi from Fort Madison, and we spent several pleasant hours discussing the old home state, even discovering we had mutual friends. O, when shall I learn not to judge the book by the cover?

We have made our arrival in Denver, but as Baby demands to be fed and Luke is due back here at our hotel room at any moment, I shall write of that later.

March 6, 1867. Denver City.

Denver is the rawest and ugliest town I ever saw, but I am much taken with its bustle and sense of purpose. One cannot step outside without having the senses assaulted. The streets are filled with inebriated men, who sleep where they fall after their nightly rounds. When they awake, why, they begin again, and are drunk by breakfast. Denverites pay them not the least attention.

Tradespeople yell their wares as loud as fishmongers. So do proprietors of theaters and magic-lantern shows. The wind carries sounds from the saloons in every direction. There are shouts of teamsters and exhortations by fire-eating street preachers. I even heard the squeal of a pig as a butcher chased it down the street. Shortly after our arrival, when Luke, Johnnie, and I strolled the main street, which is called Larimer, we saw a minstrel show right out in the open. The darkies sang the new favorite, "Michael, Row the Boat Ashore," and passed the hat. I myself contributed a two-cent piece, others giving more, until the performers had collected over a dollar for a few minutes' entertainment. No wonder no one works in this place.

All are after easy riches. We passed a man who had set bars of soap on a box and was asking a dollar for each one. "Come and try your luck. One in three has a five-dollar bill," he called. Easy ciphering would have told the crowd that the claim could not be, for that meant the hawker lost two dollars for every three bars sold, not to mention his cost of the soap. I was the only doubter, however, for the man did a brisk business.

After a time, when none of the buyers discovered themselves to be the recipients of large bills, the crowd held back. Then a man who had been watching stepped forward and put down his coin, unwrapped the soap, and held up a five-dollar note, loudly proclaiming his easy winnings. At that, the rabble surged forward, demanding to be allowed to try their luck again. Luke says the fortunate man was a confederate of the soap-selling blackleg and bought a marked bar to tempt the crowd.

The cry all about is "Gold!" Every second store offers prospecting outfits for such outrageous sums that one would have to find a rich strike just to pay for the provisioning. A man approached us with an offer to sell us the map to a lost gold mine.

"If you know its location, why don't you mine it yourself?" asked Luke. Knowing logic was not in his favor, the seller did not even answer, but turned to another, who, in short order, took out his pocketbook and handed over a sum of money.

At every corner, there is talk of which mine is a "bonanza" and which a "borrasca." Even women discuss nothing but gold, chattering like magpies about whether a camp is promising or "played out" with as much familiarity as if they were talking of hat pins.

I had thought to get away from the subject at our hotel, but no, the first woman whose acquaintance I made, a Mrs. Chubb, told me her husband was touring the mining towns in search of investment, and that as he represented a wealthy syndicate, it would be worth my while to pass along to her any intelligence I had of a promising "play." Despite that unseemly introduction, I have become very fond of Mrs. Chubb. She is a jolly, fleshy woman who spends her time reading romantic novels. She said she had been unable to cure herself of the vice and feared it would excite her passions unduly, but I replied I thought the greater harm in novels was exciting the purse.

We are stopping at the West Lindell, a large plain building with verandas. It is not so nice as the Kaston House in Fort Madison, but it suits us, even if the price does not. The clerk attempted to extort $1.50 per day (and that without our meals!), acting as if it were a trifle. Luke offered him five dollars for four days, which amount the usurer was happy to accept. I think even that is excessive. The hotel is famous for its third-floor roof garden, which Mrs. Chubb had heard was very fine. She herself had not seen it, however, as she feared she would faint at the height and fall into the street. I made the journey up the flights of stairs so I could get a clearer view of the mountains, which first I glimpsed from the stagecoach. They appeared then a little like a fringe of dirty lace on a petticoat, to my great disappointment, as I had thought they would be grand as the pictures I have seen of the Alps. The view from the West Lindell did not change my first impression of these peaks, and I find them to be greatly overrated. As they are a considerable impediment to travel, I believe Colorado Territory would be better off if it were entirely flat.

Our room is well appointed and clean, which Mrs. Chubb says was a rarity in Denver just a few years ago. When first she visited the city, she stayed in the Eldorado, a log hut operated by a French count, a near relative of the Emperor Napoléon, it was claimed. Notwithstanding that, the place was a hovel, distinguished only by a flag made from "Mrs. Count's" red petticoat.

Our accommodations at the West Lindell are far finer than that. Still, the room contains one object that causes me distress, and that is a large mirror. I thought I recognized the face that stared back at me from its depths but could not be sure, for I have not seen her in two years, and though familiar, she is much changed. When Luke was away, I took time to study her at leisure, not from vanity but curiosity, as I want to see what Colorado and the birth of a son have done to her form. She appears far more than two years older than when last seen. She is still much too gaunt for my taste, though she is wider in hips and waist. Her face, to put the best light on it, has more purpose than youth. The cheekbones are still too prominent, and despite her concession to the sunbonnet, her skin is no longer rosy, but a pale brown. I suppose none of that surprises me, but I was horrified to discover a streak of gray the width of my little fingernail in her hair. Before I came to Colorado, I never had a single gray hair. Now, I think I shall be white at thirty.

After taking advantage of the looking glass to primp, I have spent the day waiting in the hotel for Luke's return, but I think he intends to spend all his time at the conference. So tomorrow, Baby and I will venture out on our own. Since Denver is the first "city" I have visited in the West, I intend to see all I can of it.

Luke was greatly pleased with his meeting last night, as there was much discussion of crops that could survive with but little moisture. He believes finding such crops is the salvation of our part of Colorado Territory, although some contend nothing at all will ever be grown there. Tomorrow's agricultural subject is wheat. A man in Denver discovered it growing in his backyard, although he did not plant it and does not know how it got there. But it thrives in this climate, and many believe Colorado offers a promise for cultivation of cereal grains.

March 7, 1867. Denver City.
Johnnie and I did not ask Luke's permission to go skylarking, for fear he would forbid us from leaving the hotel. So, waiting until Husband was safely away, I bundled up Johnnie for protection from the fierce wind, and we two set out upon the grand Larimer Street boulevard, which is laid with logs to keep wayfarers from slipping into the

muddy ooze and sinking out of sight. We crossed over the Cherry Creek, which is not an impressive river, as it has but a trickle of water. I am told it swells during storms, however, and in 1863, it overflowed, sweeping away all in its path. That does not deter Denverites from building right up to its banks once more.

Just a year before the flood, the city had a fire that blackened the town. Merchants rebuilt their stores with brick, but the homes are yet log or raw clapboard, each with a backhouse behind, and none with either paint or planting to soften the ugly lines. Perhaps that is because Denver is viewed as a temporary residence. All say they will stay here no longer than is necessary to make a fortune. I believe the city itself will sink into the mud and disappear one day.

The sidewalks are choked with people, and one must be fleet-footed not to be overrun. I never saw people hurry so. When Johnnie and I stopped to admire a bracelet in the window of J. Joslin, Jeweler, we were nearly run over by a man who did not break stride, but merely offered his apology on the run, so to speak. At home, he would be thrashed for his impudence, but here, any apology at all is considered gallantry.

There are many foreigners in Denver. Spaniards come from Mexico to do menial labor. These descendants of the Alhambra, wrapped in serapes as colorful as Joseph's coat, compete with the manumitted members of the African race. Neither is much respected, although they are ignored rather than mal-treated. Such conventions as color and class are less important here than in civilization.

There are Chinamen, too, who prefer the city to living in the gold camps, for they are not allowed to own claims there. So they operate laundries here. I had thought to leave my good petticoat with one, for it was spoilt from the mud, but Mrs. Chubb told me the Chinamen iron the laundry by filling their mouths with water, then spitting it upon the garment to be pressed.

I have seen Indians, as well. Just after Johnnie and Self were nearly knocked down by the impudent man, we passed an Indian lying senseless in the mud and slush of the street, a victim of intemperance. Naughty boys pelted him with rocks, and I thought to admonish them. Then I remembered Sallie and wondered if the savage was one of the braves who had stolen her away and treated her with such indecency. So I did not speak out.

I laugh at my concern that I would look the country bumpkin, for people dress in all manner of apparel, from coats made of blankets, favored by those who live in the mountains, to sackcloth and ashes, worn by one poor soul, who stood on a corner and prophesied Armageddon, arriving one week hence. The multitudes did not worry themselves with impending doom, but cheerfully wished him well. Men are not the only ones who are strangely dressed. From the window of the hotel, I saw a woman wearing rainment so gaudy, I thought her to be a harlot, but Mrs.

Chubb told me she was a social leader of the city. And when I witnessed a funeral procession made up of carriages filled with the most fashionable women and dignified gentlemen, why, I was told the caisson bore the body of a strumpet who had been a favorite of the town.

We saw many tempting items in the shop windows, but I had vowed to be prudent, and so I passed them by on my way to W. Graham Drugstore, which Mrs. Chubb had recommended for items indispensable for a lady's toilette. She herself has found it a reliable source of the Indian hemp she takes for nerves.

I located the store with no trouble, finding it complete in every way, except that it lacked a soda-water fountain. I was explaining to Mr. Graham how to concoct the mixture of rosewater, oil of nutmeg, oil of lavender, and tincture of cantharides that would return my hair to its normal hue, remarking such items were not available in Mingo. But before he could prepare it, an attractive woman rushed into the establishment and demanded his immediate attention.

"You'll have to wait your turn. As you can see, I am busy," he told her. I was in no hurry and happy to look about, so I offered to let her precede me, which she did without the slightest acknowledgment or thanks.

"You must help me," she said in a whisper to Mr. Graham that was just loud enough for me to hear.

"I have done so before, Lila Kate, and I am

not inclined to again," he said.

"But you must. I am in the worst kind of pickle. Nigger Mag's gone, and who else is there?"

"Do you not know of the new woman on upper Holladay Street? She will perform the operation."

"Yes, for ten dollars. Now where's a poor girl like me to get ten dollars? Shoot, I'd as easy get a hundred."

I believe Mr. Graham glanced my way, but I was studying the directions on a packet of tea (the directions being written in Chinese, which language he must have supposed I could read) and pretended not to be listening.

"You can get it the way you always do," Mr. Graham said.

At that, the woman broke into tears, and Mr. Graham agreed to sell her what she desired, leaving us alone whilst he went into the back of the store.

When he could not be seen, I gave her a friendly glance, as one woman does to another, but she mistook my meaning and put her nose into the air.

Returning, Mr. Graham caught her look of disdain. "Don't you bother the customers," he told her sternly, setting a blue envelope on the counter. I moved farther away but continued to observe the woman as she took a coin from her purse and handed it to him. Mr. Graham shook his head. "No, Lila Kate, you keep it, but don't you come back here again. This is the last time."

The woman muttered a reply, which I could not hear, for I had moved away and was studying a packet of opium powder.

"I expect you'll come out well ahead this time. Knowing you, you'll tell as many men as possible they're responsible for your condition. You'll likely get ten dollars from each one," he said as the wretched woman left the store.

I was not so green that I did not know about cyprians, but I was innocent of a woman's attempt to extort money from her distressing condition. The matter did not appear to disturb Mr. Graham, who clapped his hands a few times to make Johnnie laugh, then hummed under his breath as he readied my hair preparation. He charged me $1.50 for it, his generosity, apparently, extending only to soiled doves.

Johnnie and I walked along the street until we came to Greenleaf & Company, which we entered to purchase a tin of spiced oysters and a dozen of the best cigars for Luke. Husband does not use tobacco as a habit, but he enjoyed a cigar with Mr. Talmadge and told Tom he wished he could offer him one. Luke spends but little money on himself, and I have a small amount put away from my teaching days, so I thought to surprise him with the purchase. My little "bank" is known to me alone, for Luke did not inquire when we married whether I was a woman of fortune, and I did not offer the intelligence, for I believe a woman should have a little cash of her own. It is not fair that both husband and wife work together and yet the money belongs to the man and the woman must ask for an allowance. Since "our" money is Luke's, my money remains mine, and I shall spend it as I see fit.

I am judicious with it, however, and, having purchased the items for Luke, a few necessities (including chocolate), and a toy for Johnnie's Christmas, I was satisfied that I had finished my shopping. But I had not counted on the establishment of Mrs. Bertha Ermerins, Millinery, and was drawn to it as a bee to honey.

I went inside, believing I would purchase only ribbons to restore my poor old hat. But I spied a most wonderful silk bonnet, the inside white, the outer portion just the deep purple of lilacs near our porch at Fort Madison. It reminded me of Mother, for lilacs were her favorite. Mrs. Ermerins insisted I should put it on, then exclaimed that the color turned my eyes lavender and the cut of the brim covered up the gray streak in my hair. As if that was not enough to turn my head, she added that many had tried on the bonnet but that none looked better in it. So being Eve's vain daughter, I fell victim to her flattery. When I emerged from the shop, I had the bonnet in hand, and Mrs. Ermerins had my five-dollar coin in hers. Each of us feels she got the better of the other. I do not think the price too dear for something that makes my eyes lavender.

Poor Baby was nearly spent from his busy morning, so we made just one more stop, and that at Mr. W. G. Chamberlain,

Photographist, where we sat for tintypes. The likenesses will go to Luke at Christmas, to my family, and to Carrie. All will find Johnnie a handsome boy, and I hope they kindly overlook the old woman who holds him.

At last, we two weary sojourners returned to our hotel, where Johnnie was greeted with much pleasure, as he has been everywhere in the city. Mrs. Chubb says if we had been in Denver only five years previous, I should have made my "strike" by charging homesick men just to hold him. She holds Johnnie for free, and she enjoys it greatly because she misses her grandchildren at home. As Mrs. Chubb reluctantly returned Johnnie, she inquired whether she might tend him for the afternoon, freeing me to go about on my own. I have not left Johnnie with another before, but as Baby likes her and is a good judge of character (having selected Luke and Self as parents), I agreed.

Mrs. Chubb will come to me as soon as she has had her dinner, and I intend to call on Moses at the Mozart concert hall. I am sure he will be pleased to have a visitor in such an attractive lilac bonnet.

Johnnie was asleep when Mrs. Chubb arrived at our room, which disappointed her, for she had hoped to take him to the reception room, where she would be the center of attention. Instead, she settled onto a chair and picked up the copy of Tom Earley's *Drum-Taps*, which I had brought with me.

I left at once, for I did not want to be away

from Boykins any longer than necessary. I was some distance from the West Lindell when I remembered that I had not inquired of the clerk the location of the concert hall. So stopping a woman, I asked the way to the Mozart. She looked at me sharply, and at first, I thought she would not reply, but she answered curtly, "Up Larimer. Next block," and hurried on her way.

Following her instructions, I reached a small white building with the name Mozart displayed across it and plunged inside. To my dismay, I found I had entered one of Denver's infamous gambling halls, and I stopped, intending to back out. But others pushed in from behind, and I was propelled into its very midst and deposited next to a large wheel with a sign reading "Chuck a Luck." I heard the click of dice and a loud "Damn it to hell," then grunts and sighs from a table where sat four men with cards in their hands. One aimed a stream of tobacco juice in my direction, missed the spittoon behind me, and landed the foul wad on my skirt instead.

"Sir!" cried I.

He glanced up but did not offer an apology. "Move yourself, lady," he said as he returned to his cards.

I made ready to follow his suggestion when I heard my name called. Coming toward me was the familiar form of Moses Earley.

"Fancy you in this place." He laughed as if I had just played a huge joke on him.

"I did not know the Mozart was a gambling hall," I replied, grasping his hand. In fact, it is what is known here as a "gambling hell."

"Thought it was a concert hall, did you? Well, I guess you have gotten into the 'wrong pew.' " Moses laughed loudly at this sally, and I joined in so he would not think he had hit the nail on its head. "Well, the Mozart isn't so bad. It sure beats the Connor place in Mingo." He looked about. "Say, where's Luke? You didn't come here alone, did you? Aw, you're a brave woman."

I explained the nature of Luke's conference and said that as I had an afternoon free of Johnnie's care, I had decided to pay him a call.

"With all there is to do in Denver, your husband's attending an agriculture meeting? Don't that beat all! Well, it suits Luke. Him and Tom never could stop talking about how wide to make the furrows and what crop soaked up the littlest water. It wasn't the life for me. I guess you know I'm not for farming. Hell, the only good thing I got out of Mingo was Jessie."

A man entered the room, shoving me aside. Moses did not reprimand him, but said, "We are impeding progress," and led me to a vacant table in a corner, where he removed a cigar butt from a chair, and I sat down. A waiter approached, but Moses brushed him aside. "I do not think you'd care for anything that is served in this place," he said with a laugh. "Now, what is the news from home?"

I told him of Sallie's unsuccessful rescue.

"We heard about it here. Denver's full of soldiers from the war, with plenty of fight left in them. What they wouldn't give to kill

Indians, and I guess I wouldn't mind it myself. Old Ben Bondurant's right: The only good Indian has a bullet through his back. I guess you feel that way, too, Sallie being your friend and all."

I did not care to dwell on Sallie, so I changed the subject. "Tom is well, but he's lonely, I think. I have suggested that he call on Miss Figg."

"He'd have to be plenty lonely to court her. Tell him to come to Denver, and Jessie will introduce him to more pretty girls than he ever saw in his life."

"Where is Jessie?"

"O..." Moses looked down at his hands, which I observed were as smooth and finely manicured as Persia's. He caught my glance and flexed the fingers with pride. "You don't see a farmer with hands like these. In my profession, I need them." To my quizzical look, he explained, "I'm a dealer. Cards, that is. O, it's not what I came here to do, but I've got the knack for it, and it's better than panning a mountain stream in winter. Jessie's got her heart set on going to Buckskin Joe—that's south of here—come spring, though why, I don't know, with all the money she takes in. I guess we will, if she wants to."

"Then Jessie has found work," I said.

Moses cleared his throat. "Yeah. She's kind of what you might call a doctor. For women, that is. You know how good she was when Johnnie was born. And with Mrs. Amidon, too. Jessie said she thought Mrs. Amidon would have killed herself if she hadn't helped out."

I thought over Moses's words, not quite understanding. Then, of a sudden, I asked, "Does she work on Holladay Street? Upper Holladay Street?"

Moses looked up quickly. "How do you know about Holladay?"

I have learnt that when one is uncertain of a thing, the best way to elicit information is to keep quiet, which advice I sometimes follow.

"You know about it then, do you?" he said when I did not reply. "Well, there are plenty of the most desperate sort of women working the line who need her, and some others, too, who live in society. Those arrive after dark when they think nobody sees them. Jessie says it's funny how they draw up their skirts when she passes on the street, but they're not too proud to go looking for her at night. She makes them pay for it. I guess she's made as much money as any woman in Denver."

Moses reached into the pocket of his vest and extracted a square of pasteboard, handing it to me. To my surprise, because I did not know such women presented calling cards, it read:

MRS. J. CONNOR-EARLEY
Denver City
(Holladay at H Street)

•

Ladies Suffering from Chronic Diseases
Will Find my Commonsense Treatment
Greatly to Their Advantage
Will Attend Calls to Neighboring Towns

While I find such an occupation unsavory, I cannot condemn it. I well remember Charlotte Hoover, who was cruelly deceived at Fort Madison and left alone to deal with the consequences of her folly. When her body was pulled from the river, I told Carrie I wished there was a way to destroy the unwanted child without sacrificing the mother. At home, an abortionist, for that is what Jessie is, would be subject to tar pots and feathers, but here she is a valuable member of the community. I do not know, is that so wrong?

"Where is Holladay Street?" I asked.

"O, I wouldn't go there if I was you. Not that it's all bawdy houses, you understand. Just part of it. Still, it's no place for a lady."

"But I would like to pay my respects to Jessie."

"I'll convey them." Moses cleared his throat. "Ah, she'd be grateful if you didn't tell it about in Mingo, the line of work she's in. Just say I'm taking care of her. Jessie's never worked the line, but folks in Mingo have in mind that she's no good. I wouldn't want to stir up talk." Moses does not care so much about what "folks" think as he does about Tom's opinion, and I believe he does not want his brother to know the truth.

"I keep my own counsel, particularly when it comes to friends, such as you and Mrs. Earley."

Of course, I did not know if Jessie *was* Mrs. Earley, but I hoped to elicit information to pass along in Mingo if it was favorable. Moses gave me an uneasy smile, but he did not remark on his marital state. Instead, he said, "That's a real pretty bonnet."

We spoke a few minutes more about old times, until Moses said he must be at work, and I took my leave, promising to tell Tom I had found his brother well and happy, giving as few details as possible.

———

March 8, 1867. Denver City.

"Why, there is a lady of refinement," said Mrs. Chubb, who likes to watch people pass by the window of the West Lindell. "You can tell she's not from Denver."

I turned and studied the woman. "Indeed, she is not. She is my friend from Mingo!"

Jessie Connor certainly was a lady of style in her elegant black silk suit, trimmed in jet. She wore black kid gloves, the like of which I had not seen since leaving the Mississippi, and a hat that was every bit as smart as my new lilac bonnet. No one would recognize her now as the strumpet Missus once called Red Legs, if, in fact, she ever had been.

Jessie drew many admiring looks as she walked into the hotel, but her glance was for me alone, and the instant she saw me, Jessie rushed over and kissed my cheek. From the corner of my eye, I saw that Mrs. Chubb was impressed with my acquaintance with such a magnificent creature.

After Jessie and I had embraced, I spied a beaming Moses behind her, also dressed in spotless black, with boots polished to a shine. A narrow scarf was tied rakishly about his neck, in the manner of the gamblers at the Mozart. He saluted me warmly, and I presented the two of them to Mrs. Chubb, saying, "You must make the acquaintance of my dear friends, Mr. and Mrs. Earley."

Jessie gave not the slightest indication that the introduction might be in error, and she held out her hand graciously.

"We've come to collect you for dinner," Moses told me, turning to Mrs. Chubb. "It won't be as good as the Christmas dinner Mrs. Spenser spread for me and my brother. She has a way with the Christmas cake all right."

I blushed at his praise, but Moses did not notice, as he had spotted Johnnie. He threw him up into the air, causing Boykins to laugh happily. "If this one hadn't been in such a hurry, me and Jessie would have done the honors with him." Johnnie put his little arms around Moses's neck, to the pleasure of both. "How would you like to take your dinner in a fancy restaurant?" he asked.

"O, we cannot," I said. "I showed Johnnie the sights. Now he suffers from a cold, and I fear he may come down with the croup, as well. Besides, he is ready for a nap."

Mrs. Chubb spoke up. "*I'll* see to the nap. You run along with your friends."

I protested that I could not impose on her twice, but she insisted, saying that when Johnnie awakened, she would bring him downstairs, where she would enjoy the attention of all. I knew she was sincere, so I accepted her kind offer, hurrying to my room with Jessie to change into my navy silk.

As I removed my traveling costume, Jessie observed, "You're not pregnant."

"I lost the baby at Christmas."

"A purpose?"

Of course, such a question was in the worst taste, but I think Jessie intended it as a professional query, so I did not take offense. "Things were never right. I had been sick from the onset. It was God's will."

Jessie snorted. "God's will. La! Myself, I don't trust the man. That's why I'm in the line of work I am. Moses says he acquainted you with it. I don't mind you knowing. Others would judge me for it, but not you. You was nicer to me than anybody in Mingo."

"There were many in Mingo who liked you. Emmie Lou is one. I believe you saved her life," I said. "But you are right to say that I do not judge. I shall always hold you in the highest regard for your attention to me." Then I added impulsively, "Jessie, I like you better than anyone I've met in Colorado."

Jessie bit her lip, then wiped a bit of dust from her eye. "Best we hurry. Moses don't like to be kept waiting."

"Moses is a good man," I said, tying the ribbons of my new bonnet to form a bow just under my ear.

"The best I ever had," she replied.

My friends carried me off to the People's Restaurant on Blake Street, which, despite the rawness of the town, was as dazzling as anything to be found in Fort Madison—or down the Mississippi in Hannibal, for that matter. It was tastefully appointed with walnut tables and chairs and crystal lights hanging from the ceiling. All were transported across the prairie from St. Joseph by oxcart. The most remarkable thing about the establishment, however, is that it is owned by an industrious Negro. Nobody cares in the least that he is a Son of Africa as long as he does his job, and he does it with great success, for the place was crowded and the prices high. Of course, he is very light-skinned.

We were presented with many dining choices, Jessie and I both selecting trout, which I had not tasted before. It is the fish that swims in the mountain rivers, and it was daintily prepared. Moses chose badger, whose dark red meat is solid and sweet. When we had finished, I was invited to select a dessert from among many splendid offerings, which included wine jelly and queen's pudding, both great favorites of mine. But there was just one choice for me, and that was chocolate cake, which I have not tasted since last autumn (and that, having been made by Persia, was not very tasty).

As the waiter set the plate in front of me, Jessie looked up and frowned as someone came into view across the room. I did not turn, for she quickly brought her attention back to me, but I wondered if she had seen one of her "patients." I put the glance out of my mind, however, for I was enjoying the opportunity to relive old times with friends, as well as to taste the excellent cake.

We had a most agreeable time, and I did not want it to end, but at last, the bill was presented, and Moses paid it. When we rose to leave, Jessie stepped beside me, talking earnestly and taking my arm, blocking my view of the restaurant. But she did not block Moses's view, and he said, "Why, look, there's Luke." Moses raised his arm in gesture, whilst Jessie shook her head violently, saying, "La! Do be still." But it was too late. I turned, to see my husband seated at a small table, his hand on the linen cloth, holding the hand of his companion. That companion was Persia.

To my humiliation, Persia looked up and recognized me. She said something to Luke, who glanced our way, his face as unexpressive as if he were studying the prairie grass, but he quickly let go of Persia's hand.

I did not wait for him to come to us to offer explanation, but said, "It is very close in here. Let us go out at once." With a friend on each side of me, I was led into the street, where I took the fresh air in great gulps. Neither companion mentioned the scene inside, but stood quietly with me, waiting for Luke to emerge from the restaurant and give an accounting.

After many minutes, I realized he was not coming. So did Moses, who, without a word, presented his arm to me, and we three walked on, not stopping or talking until we came to an ugly building that I took to be a stable.

"That is the Elephant Corral," said Moses.

"It is famous. Mr. Horace Greeley wrote about it in the *New York Tribune*," added Jessie.

I was grateful for their efforts to turn my mind from Luke's strange behavior, and I replied in a light manner. "When I write home, I shall say I have not 'seen the elephant,' as Mr. Bondurant puts it, but I have been to his home." We all laughed a little too loudly, for the sally was not that humorous. But it allowed us to pursue a new subject, and for that, we were all relieved.

When we returned to the West Lindell, Mrs. Chubb and Johnnie were not to be found in the reception room. I said my goodbye to Moses, but Jessie insisted on accompanying me to the room, as she had not yet held Johnnie. At the door, she stopped me. "You tell Mrs. Amidon, I can send her something if she needs it. And you. You remember if you want a friend, you have one in Jessie. Write me if you need me." She extended another of her cards. "I brung something else for you, too. It's laudanum, for the nerves. I hope you never feel the need of it, but you might." Jessie thrust a bottle of the opium into my hand. Then without going into the room to hold Boykins, she took her leave.

Johnnie was asleep, and Mrs. Chubb explained sheepishly that she had awakened him when we left, so that she might take him to the lobby, where all could enjoy his antics. "He'll sleep awhile longer, as he was tired," she said, then looked closely at me. "You look tuckered out yourself, Mrs. Spenser. Your friends have exhausted you."

I nodded, for I was very tired indeed, though not because of Jessie and Moses.

"What you need is a bath. The hotel will

bring one up for a dime. I'll go right down and order it."

For the past two years, I had bathed in nothing larger than a washtub, and suddenly a proper bath was what I wanted most in the world. I did not care if the cost had been four bits. I thanked Mrs. Chubb, and within a few minutes, a man arrived at my door with a hip tub, buckets of hot water, and a piece of soap that was as soft as flower petals.

At his leaving, I stripped off my dress, the sight of which brought to mind Persia in her robin's egg blue costume, decorated with old gold lace that made her hair shimmer like a heap of bright coins. I compared her habiliments with my own plain costume and remembered that Persia had called it the ugliest wedding dress she had ever seen. I threw it upon the floor and sat down in the tub, scrubbing every inch of myself, as if I could rub out the sight of Luke and Persia. When my anger was washed away, I let the tears come and splash into the water. I leaned my head against the back of the tub and sobbed in self-pity. Then I cried for Mother, who could no longer comfort me, for the little boy I had lost at Christmas, and for Sallie. At last, the hot water and exhaustion brought blissful sleep. When I awoke, the water was cold, and Baby was cooing to me.

It is now very late, past nine o'clock, I should judge, and still no sign of Luke. I cannot explain his faithlessness. Is he still with Persia? Does he regret Baby and me? Does he not care that his perfidy has brought me such pain? I sit in a chair by the window, looking out at the mountain range, which is now just a black shape against the dark sky. The sunset was very angry, with bold clashes of orange and violet that tore into the sky as well as my heart, where it joined the anguish already present there. The noise from the street is harsh and hurts my head. I do not like Denver City anymore. I am sorry I came here.

March 10, 1867. Prairie Home.

We were away but a week, but O, what a great deal of work awaited us upon our return. Luke spends many hours in the field, not only making up for lost time but putting into practice the ideas he learnt in Denver. An agriculturist at one of the meetings proposed that farmers on the dry plains plow their fields in half circles instead of straight rows, claiming such a method keeps the wind from blowing away seed and soil and will attract moisture. The proposal drew much ridicule, but Luke was taken with it, as was Tom when he heard about it. So now the two farmers are plowing the field between our homesteads in undulating furrows. I think a crow flying overhead must think the land worked by a blind plowman with a mule full of rum.

There were many tasks awaiting me, too, for the wind had cracked our precious pane of glass and dust covered every inch of the house. A family of mice had chewed their way into my flour barrel and made themselves at home. Had I been prudent, I would have sifted out their "calling cards," but I threw out the contents, and now I am hard-pressed to fill up my hungry husband until he can go to Mingo and replace the spoilt flour.

This morning, I bathed Baby, using the precious soft soap from my bath at the West Lindell. I had carefully wrapped it in paper and packed it in my trunk, and now it gives Baby relief from the harsh lye soap that we use here. When Johnnie was in bed for his nap, I poured his bathwater upon the earthen floor to settle the dust, then settled Self in a corner whilst it dried. Waiting there were pen and journal. It is time to put down the particulars of our last night in Denver, which I have been unable to do until this time. My mind has been greatly confused.

Luke did not return for many hours that evening, and many times did I pace the floor between Johnnie's cradle and the window. I went to bed but could not sleep, feeling as if a thousand pins were pricking my body. So I was awake when there was the scrape of key in lock, and I saw the familiar shape enter the room.

Luke began undressing in the dark so as not to awaken me, but I said, "I am not asleep. You may light the lamp."

"I see well enough without it," he replied, but I struck the match, for I did not want to discuss the fateful day in the dark.

I gave Luke time to speak, but he was not inclined to do so, and after waiting in vain, I said, "Have you an explanation?"

Luke turned to me, his eyebrows raised, as if he did not understand the question, but I knew he did, and I said nothing, which made him uncomfortable. At last, he asked, "Do you mean Persia?"

I dipped my chin just a little to show that I did, then waited again, but Luke said nothing. "I think I am owed your explanation as to why you were dining with Persia, ignoring your own wife," I said when I could stand the silence no longer.

"And why were you dining with Moses and Jessie without my permission?" There was anger in his voice, although I do not know if it was caused by my demanding an accounting of him or my failure to seek his approval before going out.

"Jessie and Moses are not only old friends; they took charge of Johnnie and me when you abandoned us to visit Persia in Fort Madison," I said hotly.

It was the first time I had blamed Luke for being away during my confinement, and his chest rose as he took a deep breath and replied, "That is not true."

"That you abandoned us, or that your true reason for going to Fort Madison was to see Persia?" I did not like to play the shrew, but I felt I must have an accounting.

"You yourself agreed I should go alone."

"Only at your insistence. But what of the rest? Persia told me last fall that you loved her above me, that you proposed to me only after she refused you."

Luke looked away and did not respond, his silence being answer enough.

"If that is true, what am I to think when I find you with her?"

Luke finished removing his clothes, blew out the lamp, and walked to the window to look out upon the street. He was stark, but my eyes were on him nonetheless, forsaking modesty, because I was very angry.

He stood there for a moment, then replied without turning back to me. "I did not know Persia was in Denver. I was as surprised as you when I saw her on the street, and as she said she was leaving in the afternoon for Central City to meet Mr. Talmadge, I invited her to dine. There was not time to ask you to join us, and I did not think you would want to see Persia, anyway, for she said you were unkind to her last fall."

"She slanders me. It was she who was unkind to me."

Luke turned from the window, then came to me and sat down on the bed. "Persia is unhappily married. If you had seen her up close, you could not have missed the bruise on her face where her husband hit her." Luke made a fist with his right hand and slammed it into his left palm, as though it were Mr. Talmadge he struck. "I can't abide a man who hits a woman. If I'd seen him, he'd be plenty sorry for it." Luke stretched his arms over his head. "That's all I have to say," he added, as if to put an end to the subject.

I would not let the matter lie, however.

"Persia says you still love her." My voice was so small that I had to clear my throat before asking, "Do you?"

Luke stared at me, and I was glad he had blown out the light, because my eyes, already red and swollen from crying, had filled again with tears in anticipation of his answer. Without putting on his nightshirt, Luke drew aside the blanket and slipped in beside me. "Do I?" he asked. "Do you think I would do this if I loved another?"

As he reached for me, I turned away, wanting a clearer answer. But Luke was not to be refused. He fitted himself to my back, as if we were bowls stacked in the cupboard, then put his arms around me, my breasts in his hands, kneading them just as I knead bread. He had not done that before, and it caused such a strange longing in me that, despite my reluctance to permit the marital act, I turned at last to my Darling Boy.

When he was finished, Luke quickly went to sleep. But I did not sleep for a long time, as I pondered his question, which was the answer to my own. I am not satisfied, but I will not bring it up again, for Persia is a closed subject between us.

Chapter 6

June 15, 1867. Prairie Home.

Poor health and the management of our little household have kept me from writing in this book for many weeks. I accompanied Luke to Mingo in April, and the glare of sun on snow weakened my eyes. Luke suggested I put charcoal smudges under them before leaving home, as he does, but vain girl that I am, I refused. I bathe my eyes frequently in a decoction made from herbs that Mr. Bondurant brought me, and I have written away for colored glasses. I shall look very strange indeed in sunbonnet and blue spectacles.

There is another cause for my sorry health. We shall welcome a little stranger at Christmas. Luke has not voiced his desire for boy or girl, but I have my heart set on one of my own sex. I am glad for this third pregnancy, as is Luke, I believe. In my case, it is because it puts the unpleasantness with Persia behind us. I have concluded that I was indeed second choice to Persia, but it no longer matters, for I am now the first and forever choice. Persia is a reminder to Luke of carefree days when he was a Fort Madison swell, unencumbered with care of Prairie Home and family.

I, too, remember aplenty those happy days when Carrie and I sat beneath the arbor in our yard with our sewing, giggling over girlish concerns. Were there ever more joyous times? But I am a woman now, and I find pleasure in family and duty. Life was not meant to be without pain, and easy times do not build character. (O, do I not sound pompous? I am too young for such heavy thoughts.)

I take much comfort from Johnnie. The little fellow celebrated his first birthday in May with a chocolate cake (the chocolate purchased in Denver, even though it was very dear) and a farmer doll bearing the likeness of his father, made by his proud mama. Papa gave him a set of blocks, which the birthday boy lined up in a row before tasting them, thereby proving he has characteristics of both parents—Papa's logical mind and Mama's sweet tooth.

Many here talk of statehood for Colorado in the near future, although we have been turned down twice by our government in Washington, D.C. The designation would help attract homesteaders to this sparsely settled place. We hold our own, although the new residents barely make up for those who leave.

A Russian family moved into the Garfield place. The man told his name, which none could pronounce, excepting Mr. Bondurant, who declared it is "Frog Legs Frank," and by that name, he is now known amongst us. His family is made up of a wife and brown-faced girls, who go about without their sunbonnets. We have not asked if the family is aware of the Garfield homestead's terrible history, for none can speak their strange tongue. That barrier does not deter these good people from adding their voices to ours in praising God at Sabbath services, turning that meeting into a Tower of Babel. Some believe the Russians are Hebrew, but it matters not to me, for one is glad for any neighbors here. I should like to take a cake to welcome them, for they are very poor, and Tom, who has visited, says they live principally on a kind of pancake called hardtack or on prairie chickens they hunt, using dried peas as shot. But I cannot yet bring myself to visit that place of so much sadness.

Fayette Garfield feels as I do, for he has scarce set foot on his old homestead since that terrible day. He is seen in Mingo and at other places where unruly men gather to drink. Mr. Garfield has a way with horses and is in demand as a cowboy, but it is said his mind, which was already affected by the horrors of the war, was broken by Sallie's death. Mr. Garfield must be restrained whenever he sees a savage, but I believe Indians are not solely at fault for his mental state. One must blame Mr. Garfield's origin in the South, where climate often produces a dissolute temperament. Luke encountered him on his last trip to town, but he merely nodded, as he did not care to join Mr. Garfield and the drunken company he keeps.

Another couple has taken up a homestead north of the Osterwald place. "Woodbury Wheeler and wife," said he, introducing both at Sabbath service. She quickly spoke up and offered her name as Nannie. Though Southern, they are not highborn, being Texians, and he has but one arm, having lost the other in battle at Shiloh. When he was told that Luke was in the same battle but on the Yankee side, Mr. Wheeler thought it a huge joke, and neither man bears the other any ill will for the wounds each sustained there. Colorado has made that war seem further away to all.

Because of the number of Confederate men killed in the war, many women of the southland are destined to be old maids. Even so, a good wife must be hard to find, because Mr. Wheeler placed an advertisement in a newspaper for one. Mrs. Wheeler responded, sending a picture of herself and sister, and he, thinking her the prettier one, discovered on his wedding day that his bride was "ugly as sin," as he put it to Mr. Bondurant and me, treating the whole affair as if it were a joke.

Mrs. Wheeler, overhearing her husband, was not the least put off, but said, "Perhaps you are right, Mr. Wheeler, but I am the agreeable one." Indeed, they seem as happy as any couple I ever saw. I should think that here a man would choose a cheerful woman and a hard worker for his life's companion over a tearing belle. But from observation, I conclude that men do not always know what is best for them.

We have a second lady homesteader, a Miss Eliza Hested, who filed on the claim adjacent to Miss Figg. The two women will build a house that straddles the line between their claims, allowing each to sleep on her own land and, thereby, meeting the requirements of the law. Both are brave to come to this place without a member of the male sex to protect them. I told Tom he is quite the lucky man, for he lives in the only part of Colorado Territory where the available women outnumber the single men.

Yesterday, Husband invited Johnnie and Self to go for a ride in the wagon. We drove many miles across unfamiliar prairie to the southwest, and I thought perhaps Luke had found a new tree and we were going for a visit. Then we crested a hill and saw before us a village of tiny dugouts, each inhabited by a burrowing animal as fat as a woodchuck, called a "prairie dog." The pups wiggled their stubby tails and barked when they saw us, not in warning, but in welcome, for they are friendly creatures. But when we came close, they turned tail and scurried into their holes.

Johnnie was enchanted with the little village, clapping his hands and saying, "Doggie, doggie," for he is such a clever fellow and already speaks words. Luke carried him near to the burrows, keeping a sharp watch for rattlesnakes, as they like to sun themselves in the village before supping on prairie dog. In only a minute, the curious animals reappeared, and knowing we intended them no harm, they went about their business.

It was a fine outing. Luke is the best of fathers, taking more than a little interest in our boy. He said the other day he wished he had thought to name him Shiloh John Spenser so that he might be called Shiloh, which is Hebrew for "place of peace." I am glad he did not.

Tom brought us the slip of a yellow rosebush that he acquired from an emigrant who stopped at his homestead. She had several of them, wrapped in burlap and watered daily. So Tom traded her a crock of butter for it. As the butter was from our cow, the rose properly belonged to us, Tom said. Someday, I shall have a hedge of yellow roses along the house. I carefully water the slip, and this morning I was rewarded with a sliver of green.

My birthday has passed, and I received from Husband a fine wooden dough bowl, which he himself had made, and from Carrie an autograph album, which is much appreciated. I shall ask all my friends and neighbors to sign it—those who can write, that is.

July 8, 1867. Prairie Home.

Moses, who is yet in Denver, sends Tom copies of the *Rocky Mountain News,* and when finished, Tom delivers them to us. Little matter that the events contained therein occurred many weeks prior. As we are not up on the news, it is as fresh as today's milk. Tom's visits are doubly welcome now, for himself and for the intelligence he brings of the world outside.

This morning, whilst Luke was in the fields, Tom arrived in a hurry, and after much clearing of the throat, he asked if I knew what was about.

"O no!" cried I with alarm at his troubled countenance, thinking he had read something in the paper. "Not the President? Has President Johnson been shot, just like Mr. Lincoln?

Tom quickly shook his head.

"What is it, then?"

"Mrs. Amidon. She has not mentioned it to you?"

Having been ill, I had not seen Emmie Lou since my return from Denver, and the Amidons have been absent from Sabbath services. "Is she all right?"

Tom looked uncomfortable and muttered, "I shouldn't have brought it up, as it is private. I thought because you are the only one in whom she confides, she might have discussed it with you. I only asked because, well, Amidon is acting strangely, and I need advice on how to deal with him."

"Luke says he is quick to anger but does not know why. You must tell me the particulars, Tom." After a moment's contemplation, I asked, "Is Emmie Lou in danger? O, I hope her husband is not a brute like Mr. Osterwald."

"No, not that."

Tom did not continue. So I prepared tea, taking out the dear-bought English stuff, another Denver purchase. Even on the hottest day, good tea creates a cozy atmosphere in which to share confidences. I built up the fire in the stove and set the kettle upon it, then turned back to Tom. "I won't breathe a word of it, even to Luke, if you think I shouldn't," I said, hoping to encourage him. "Perhaps there is something I can do for Emmie Lou."

"No," Tom replied. "The only one who can help is Amidon, but continence is not his way."

Though I had begged for the details, I was shocked that Tom would be so frank. "Sir!"

He knew at once he had misspoken and asked me to forgive him.

I told him the fault was mine for pressing him. "I know that Emmie Lou is greatly burdened in that way. You may as well tell me the whole of it."

"It was something I overheard and none of my business," he said after I turned my back to him to pour the tea.

"Quite."

"I went to the Amidons' to ask for the loan of a sod plow. When I got there, the house was dark, and I believed everyone was asleep. So instead of knocking, I listened, intending to leave if I heard no sound."

I handed Tom his tea, but he set it aside and gnawed on his fist for a moment.

"Then I heard a loud banging from above, the bedroom door, I suppose it was. Amidon demanded to be let in. He said he was her husband and had his rights, and he ordered her to turn the key in the latch. Emmie Lou cried that if she did, she would be dead in a year, and she begged him to stay away from her. I think he would have broken down the door if he wasn't so proud of the millwork in the house. He seems to hold its welfare in higher esteem than his wife's. Perhaps Emmie

Lou let him in, because the pounding stopped, and I slipped away as quietly as I'd come."

I sipped my tea. "Poor Emmie Lou. A woman has few rights in marriage."

"A man ought to learn to control himself."

At that moment, Johnnie, who had been playing so quietly on the floor that I had all but forgotten him, lifted his baby arms to Tom to be picked up, and so our conversation was over.

I suppose I should be shocked at the changes in me. Such a conversation with a man not my husband would not have been permitted two short years ago, but in Colorado Territory, we put conventions aside.

I resolve to call on Emmie Lou soon. It is unlikely she will confide in me, but she may find the presence of another woman to be some consolation. This place and Mr. Amidon have worn her out.

⁓

July 24, 1867. Prairie Home.

My eyes are better, but my condition makes me a poor companion this summer. Though I try to keep a cheerful countenance, Luke knows I suffer with this babe. My understanding of the situation is that each pregnancy gets easier, but my experience is quite the opposite. With Johnnie, I would not have known I was enceinte had it not been for my misshape. I pray I can carry the child to term, for I want it very much. This little stranger, now more than three months along, is not only a creation of Husband and Wife, a precious bond between the two, but a playmate for Johnnie and a completion of our little family.

Knowing I need rest, Luke hitched up the team and went to Mingo today with a dear little passenger—Johnnie. Save for the few hours in Denver, Baby has never been out of my sight since his birth. I miss his happy presence but know he is with a companion who will care for him as lovingly as I do.

Being alone was such a strange sensation that I did not know what to do with myself. So I pretended I was a bride, and as in my first days in this place when Luke was away, I prepared a bath in the tub outside, singing gaily, not thinking until I was finished that Tom might have chosen this time to call and was scared away by my sounds of "Nelly Was a Lady." That being the case, I am glad he was frightened off, because had he come closer and found me à la Eve, he would have concluded that Mattie was *not* a lady.

We see little of Mr. Bondurant lately. Luke says he is not cut out to work in the fields, but only to make whiskey, which he sells less or more to the Indians.

August 1, 1867. Prairie Home.

The last mail at Mingo brings the wonderful news that Carrie, too, awaits the arrival of a baby at Christmastide. I feel closer to her than ever. Was there ever a time we did not do things in tandem?

Johnnie returned from his trip to town

with Papa in fine spirits. He is such a manly little fellow, and Luke pronounced him the best traveler he has ever seen, to the dismay of Johnnie's mother, who had assumed the honor was hers. But she will not be jealous of her Boykins and so humbly accepts the assignment of the second place.

August 13, 1867. Prairie Home.
So pleased was Luke with Johnnie's companionship that he has once again taken him to Mingo. I had thought to make it a threesome, but the little stranger who is to be in just four months had other ideas, and so we two stayed at home. The minute Luke was out of sight, I crept back into bed and stayed there the better part of the day, not rising until half after nine, when I felt my domestic duties could no longer be put off.

Johnnie is the best boy that ever was. He is steady on his feet and loves to chatter. I try to develop his mind by pointing to objects and naming them so that he will learn such words as house and chair and horse. Luke caught me at it and naughtily indicated the cow, saying, "Elephant." Husband does not often joke, and I burst into laughter. A gold-seeker can now "see the elephant" at our Prairie Home and not trouble himself with the mountains. I point to Carrie's picture and say very clearly, "Pretty lady," and Johnnie attempts to repeat it. What a smart boy I have!

Yesterday, after Luke inquired whether I was raising a girl, I cut Boykins's hair for the first time, an event that occasioned tears on Mother's part. But Johnnie enjoyed the attention, and he laughed as he threw the severed curls into the wind, all but one, which his mother saves in this little book.

Our crops do somewhat better this summer. Luke believes our success depends on development of a drought-resistant grain. He talks of returning to Fort Madison after harvest to consult with agrarians, though how a farmer on the Mississippi can advise on dryland crops, I do not know. On one point, I am clear: If he goes, Johnnie and I shall accompany him.

My favorite hour is sunset, which begins with prairie and sky both blue. The setting sun turns the grasses golden. The sky is swirled and streaked with pink and scarlet and lilac; then slowly it turns to claret, and both land and sky fade into blackness. I am finding much to like about this place.

August 15, 1867. Prairie Home.

Tom came in his wagon to fetch the three of us for a call on Mr. Bondurant, but Luke had gone to the lady homesteaders, who had asked his advice on harvesting. I protested that I could not go with Tom, saying it was not proper for a married woman to accompany a man on a social call without her husband's permission. Of course, such manners are not much observed here, but after our conversation about the Amidons, I felt the need to distance myself a little from Tom.

Nothing would do but that I go, however. Tom gave me no reason, but from his insistent manner, I knew it was a matter of some importance. Besides, at the idea of riding in a wagon, Johnnie clapped his hand and chatted away, and I could not deny him the pleasure.

"He's so smart, you'd almost believe he's saying real words," Tom observed.

"He is."

"You are the finest mother I ever observed."

I blushed furiously, because even Luke has not paid me such a compliment, although I hope he believes it to be so. Sometimes, Tom is too familiar.

"Is Mr. Bondurant ill?" I inquired.

"I think he has never been so healthy." Tom blushed himself, for what reason I did not know.

When we arrived at Mr. Bondurant's place, everything seemed in perfect order, including its owner, who rushed to meet us.

"Get you down," he called, muttering something over his shoulder, which I could not make out. He picked up Johnnie, throwing him into the air, which made Boykins squeal. Then he helped me from the wagon, all but hugging me, so glad was he for our visit.

"You have told her, then?" Mr. Bondurant asked, hopping from one foot to the other in his excitement.

Tom shook his head. "I thought I'd let you do the honors."

The smile left Mr. Bejoy's face. "So you're ignorant of it?"

As I looked at him in confusion, someone came from the soddy and stood quietly in the doorway. I stared in such astonishment that Mr. Bondurant turned and beckoned to the figure, who was dressed in the tanned skins of animals.

"This be Mrs. Bondurant. We get along fine. You bet. Her people named her Bird Woman, but I call her Kitty." There was as much pride in his voice as if she had been a white woman.

Kitty was pretty in the way of the Indian maiden, very young and shy, her eyes on the ground like any blushing bride. Still, that ground was knocked up from under me, and I blurted out, "An Indian?"

"Arapaho," Mr. Bondurant said.

"Arapaho women are known for their chaste ways," Tom added.

I did not know what to reply, and I am ashamed to record here that upon meeting Kitty, I could not even extend my hand to her, for fear of that hand being stained with Christian blood. Mr. Bondurant himself had told me on our trip to Colorado that the only good Indian was a dead one, and I could not understand how he could choose a savage for his bride.

His disappointment in me was clear, as was Tom's, and we stood awkwardly, excepting for Johnnie, who sat down in the dirt and played with sticks he found there. Mr. Bondurant muttered something to Kitty, who went into the soddy, returning with tin cups of cool water. Before I could stop her, she handed Johnnie a scrap of buckskin.

"It's a doll. My Arapaho ain't so good, and she thinks Johnnie's a girl. She made it herself. Handiest woman I ever saw," Mr. Bondurant said. "There's nothing like an Indian squaw for work. Come inside and see for yourself. Kitty can't do nothing but that she does it decent."

Mr. Bondurant entered the house, but Tom held me back to whisper, "I know you're angry with me, but I couldn't tell you, for fear you wouldn't come. Ben's counting on you. O, he doesn't expect you to throw a housewarming, but he hopes if you treat Kitty nice, the others will, too. If Kitty's not welcome, then the two of them might go off and live with the Arapaho."

"I thought he didn't like savages. He's told me as much."

"Love does strange things to a fellow. Besides, he's learned to know them better and says Indians are people, just like white folks. He thought you'd agree."

"He has no right to presume." I entered the dark room, which was lighted only by the doorway, letting my eyes get used to the dimness. My nose needed no time to adjust, and I was aware that the Bondurant place no longer smelled like the home of an old batch, for now it was filled with the sweet odor of prairie grasses. When I could make out the room, I observed it was as tidy as any home I ever saw, with blankets neatly folded and household items in place. The walls were hung with beading, which Mr. Bondurant informed me was the work of Kitty's hands. "She sews 'most as good as I read," he said with a wink.

I could not help but laugh at his jest, which eased the tension a little.

"Sit," Mr. Bondurant ordered, and we did so. "How come us to marry?" He asked the question I had not, then answered it himself. "I'm not attached to batching." He nodded at Kitty, who went without, returning with plates heaped with stew. "I already teached her to use plates, but she won't touch the cookstove. She'll like it come winter."

I was not hungry, and I did not care to eat something prepared by an Indian, for I did not know what it contained, but Tom and Mr. Bondurant "dug in," as the saying is here, and at last, I sampled the fare, finding it was as good as any stew I ever prepared, and certainly better than any *I* had cooked over a campfire.

"Very tasty," I told Kitty, who watched us eat but did not join in. She frowned at my words, not understanding them. So I repeated slowly and loudly. "Very tasty."

"She ain't deaf," Mr. Bondurant said, then turned to Kitty and said something in her language.

She lowered her eyes and replied to Mr. Bondurant.

"She says, 'It's no botherment.' "

"Won't she join us?" I asked.

"Indian women don't eat with their men, just stand around taking care of them and eat what's left over, if there be leavings," Mr. Bondurant explained.

"Well, I think that is a very poor policy indeed," I said hotly. "Women need sustenance as much as their men. It is my observation that the Indian woman needs more, because she does most of the work." I looked at Mr. Bondurant to defy me, but I found he and Tom were laughing instead.

"You're not so glad she's here, but you take her part," Mr. Bondurant said, and as he was right, I joined the laughter.

After we had eaten, Kitty sat down with us, and in a few minutes, she was playing with Johnnie with such warmth that this mother's heart softened toward her.

I do not approve of the amalgamation of the races, but Mr. Bondurant's consort shall not be scorned by me. I will not condemn the union of one who has proven himself so faithful a friend. To convey that conclusion, I extended a hand to Kitty as I left—to her confusion, for she is not familiar with our custom of shaking hands.

When Luke returned that evening, I told him of Mr. Bondurant's companion, and he said he had heard as much that day. The Smiths are outraged, and others are not fond of having a savage in our midst, but as for Luke, he thinks it is not his affair. "Out here, we make allowances," said he. His response surprised me a great deal, for he has very high standards, but upon reflection, I believe him to be right. I, too, make allowances for the ways of the country.

⁓

August 22, 1867. Prairie Home.
The gossips are at work, and our neighbors are much vexed with the new Mrs. Bondurant, declaring Mr. Bondurant guilty of mongrelization. At our last meeting, the Sabbath group spoke more about Kitty than the Savior. Some of the displeasure comes because none knows how this union came about. Mr. Bondurant has enlightened no one on the particulars of his matrimonial partner. There is some thought that he bought her with a barrel of whiskey. Mr. Bondurant was heard to say that "if nobody don't like my way of going about this interesting business, I don't care. It's none of their funeral."

Mr. Garfield heard about Kitty at Mingo, and it is said he was in a rage, calling her, "Our nig."

⁓

September 1, 1867. Prairie Home.
Mr. Bondurant brought Kitty to call on *me*. She presented Johnnie with the gift of an Indian top, patiently showing him how to spin it, but Boykins had his own idea and uses it for teething. As I had baked a dessert for our supper, I served refreshments. Kitty was pleased with the coffee, but she showed confusion when presented with a fork for her rhubarb pie. She watched Mr. Bondurant, then

copied him, doing about as well as I would eating the pastry with a Chinaman's chopsticks. In many ways, Kitty is the ideal helpmeet, smiling much and talking not at all.

Mr. Bondurant told me Kitty's people have been poorly treated by many of our race, and he knows of more than one occasion when white men have shot Indians for sport. "The Indians was willing to share the land, but white peoples just want it all. And they'd rather murder the Indians than live peaceably with them," said he. Upon reflection, I believe there may be some truth in what he says. Perhaps I should revise my views of the Red Men. If all were like Kitty, I would have no objection to any of them.

When the two callers left, Kitty jumped upon her horse, which was unsaddled, and rode off, the best horsewoman I ever saw, but perhaps that was because she rode astride like a man. I should think that painful.

As she rode off, an interesting thought presented itself: Perhaps Kitty can attend me in my confinement. She is clean and gentle, and Jessie once said the Indian woman knows a great deal about herbs and medicines to ease in parturition.

Mr. Bondurant and wife were scarcely over the horizon and I had barely returned to my tasks when the Amidon family halloed the house. Poor Luke, for the Amidons made quick work of what remained of the pie, and now he shall have nothing for his dessert.

"I've come to say good-bye," Emmie Lou said as Mr. Amidon watered the horses.

"Elbert doesn't want me to speak of it, but you have been a true friend, and a note would not do. We're going east."

"O, I shall miss you."

"We leave next week."

"Who will care for the farm?"

"Elbert won't accompany us. Only the girls and I are going."

"I shall count the days until you return."

"You don't understand. I won't return." Her eyes followed Mr. Amidon as he rubbed down the horses. "O, Elbert will say it about that I've gone only for a visit, but I shan't be back." She sniffed away tears, for her little ones were playing nearby and she did not want to alarm them.

I put my hand on hers. "I shall miss you, Emmie Lou, but I understand. This is a hard place in which to find happiness."

"I've found Hell and Colorado are the same, although I am at fault, too, for I was ill-prepared for the hardships."

"As were we all. You saw how it was with me, with my Delft plate and silver spoons. Why, I had calling cards printed just before I left home."

Emmie Lou laughed, then was quiet for a moment. "I think you know the way it is with Elbert. Mrs. Connor gave me a potion of rhubarb and pepper. I took it in the spring, when I thought I was pregnant again. I should not care quite so much about this infernal child-bearing if I was among my own kind, but you are the only one of my class in this wretched place, and we don't see each other but once a month at most. Elbert doesn't understand a woman's need for friends and family."

"Men don't," I agreed. Then I inquired as to where she would go.

"Philadelphia. That's where my people live. They've encouraged me to return, as they don't care much for Elbert, and they fear I shall succumb to hysteria if I stay. I should have listened to them and never come here in the first place."

"Perhaps Mr. Amidon will go east later on."

"Never! He has said it! We had quite a spat, and he told me, 'Go yourself, then, and let us be done with it.' "

"Will you divorce?" I asked boldly.

Emmie Lou examined her hands, which could have belonged to a woman twice her age, so rough and worn were they. "It's not my intention, but Elbert may want to marry again one day. I care for him. I do not want to disgrace him." She sniffed back tears. "I wonder that you can stay in this place. Colorado is fine for men and mules, but not for women.

"I think it is not so fine for mules, either."

With Emmie Lou gone, this journal, more than ever, is my valued confidante.

~

September 8, 1867. Prairie Home.

Now, it was Kitty's turn to be forgotten at Sabbath services, as everyone talked of Emmie Lou's departure. It is the general opinion that Emmie Lou is at fault in the marriage, being too refined for this place, that being considered a great imperfection. I could not violate her confidence, so I said only that I believed she had gone for a visit.

"Mark my words. She won't be back, that one. She's too conceited, and not cut out for work," said Missus, who has often been the recipient of the Amidons' hospitality. "Ain't this the place, Old Smith? A piano in one sod house and an Indian squaw in another."

"A piano?" asked Miss Eliza Hested, who had never visited the Amidon house. "A piano out here on the prairie?"

"A nice home for pack rats is what it is," Missus told her.

"I shall ask Mr. Amidon to sell it to me if he doesn't want it. We'll have the next Sunday services at our place. Do you agree, Anna? I told you I could play the piano, and now you shall hear for yourself."

Tom offered to move the instrument, but they refused, declaring the two of them were strong enough for the job. That was foolish of them, for Tom is an elgible bachelor and would make a fine husband for either.

Emmie Lou was wrong to say Colorado is not a good place for women, because both the lady homesteaders thrive here. They say they like the fresh air and freedom from convention. Miss Figg wears the bloomer costume when about her work, and Miss Hested, it has been observed, dresses in men's trousers! So I believe Colorado is a fine place for a certain kind of woman, but I am not sure what kind that is, or whether I am one.

I must record that Johnnie walks and says many important words, among them *Mama* and *Papa*. The other day, he looked at Carrie's dear picture and announced, "Pret' lade." Now, is he not the dearest boy? His sister or brother does not have his sweet disposition, and gives me much discomfort. My back aches so at the end of the day, even though Luke helps me with the heavy work. Colorado Territory may do for a particular woman, but I think I can safely relate that it is good for *no* pregnant woman. Well, I believe I can stand it for another three months or so, when Baby should arrive.

Now, here are some remarks about Husband. His hard work and knowledge of agriculture have won the respect of all neighbors. He is often consulted on things agrarian, though none has copied his unusual method of plowing in circles. He is the best papa, taking Boykins to Mingo whenever he goes in the wagon.

Luke does not often solicit my opinion, but when he does, he listens with care, giving my remarks the same weight as if they came from a man. He does not want to know my opinion unless it is asked for, however, so I have learnt not to offer it. Luke seldom points out ways for me to improve, as he did when first married. At times, I believe he finds me to be a thrifty and efficient manager of the household, but at others, he has too much on his mind to take notice.

Luke is partial to my rhubarb pie, calling

it better, even, than his mama's. Is this not the basis for a happy marriage?

⁓

September 18, 1867. Prairie Home.
Here is the story as Tom tells it.

He accompanied Mr. Bondurant into Mingo on Tuesday last. Immediately they reached the town, Mr. Bondurant was accosted by Fayette Garfield.

"They say you've living man and wife with a filthy savage," Mr. Garfield bellowed so all could hear.

The taunt made Mr. Bondurant very angry, but, respecting Mr. Garfield's piteous circumstances, he ignored it.

"Hey, you, Bondurant. Can't you hear me? You're no better than a dog. You're laying with an Indian squaw."

"Go to hell, Garfield. I have went here for a purpose, and it ain't to argue with a fool." Mr. Bondurant turned away, although his jaw was taut and his fists clenched. "I despise such as that," he told Tom.

"Your damned black-headed bitch is a red nigger, and you're a yellow nigger for fearing to fight me."

Mr. Bondurant could not ignore further insult and struck Mr. Garfield a hearty blow, knocking him to the ground.

Mr. Garfield turned aside and vomited, for he was very drunk, whilst Mr. Bondurant stood over him, ready to strike again. One of Mr. Garfield's confederates held Mr. Bondurant's arm, however. "Leave be. "It ain't a fair fight, him liquored up the way he is. Go along. We'll take care of him."

"Come, Ben. Garfield's crazy," Tom said, leading Mr. Bondurant down the street.

Mr. Garfield shouted threats and curses at their backs, but instead of following them, he withdrew with his friends to the stable.

Hoping to defuse the situation further by removing Mr. Bondurant from the scene, Tom took him into the saloon and bought him one or two glasses of whiskey. Mr. Garfield then rid himself of his restraining friends and quit the town, riding off at a tear. All were relieved, although Tom did not trust Mr. Garfield, fearing he would waylay Mr. Bondurant along the road. So Tom insisted on accompanying his friend home. They saw no signs of Mr. Garfield, however, and by the time they reached the Bondurant place, Tom concluded things between the two men would go no further.

"You best stay for dinner. Kitty's a good cook—if it ain't dog meat. I never cared shucks for dog," Mr. Bondurant said.

Being assured by the remark that the bride would not serve canine stew, Tom did not need a second invitation, for, as I well know, he does not care much for batching.

"Now, where's she got to? It's usual for her to come and take my horse. There's nothing like an Indian woman to care for a man." As a cooking fire burned outside, they knew Kitty was not far away, although she did not answer Mr. Bondurant's call.

He was not greatly alarmed at Kitty's

absence, for she often went into the fields to snare jackrabbits or gather grasses and herbs. Instead, it was Tom who felt something was amiss, and he insisted they search for her.

They found Kitty several rods beyond the barn, shot at close range. A hole as big as a fist had laid open her flesh, and her body was covered with other wounds. The killer, not satisfied with taking Kitty's life, had removed the knife from her belt and thrust it again and again into her chest, until the ground was soaked in her blood. The knife lay beside Kitty, covered with gore and dirt. When the fiend had finished the foul mutilation, he had scrawled his explanation in the earth beside Kitty.

O, that I ever taught Mr. Bondurant to read! He was the one who spied the letters and took their meaning! He knelt on the earth beside Kitty and pointed to each word as he spoke it aloud. "An eye for an eye."

"Now what for did he do that?" Mr. Bondurant said, his voice breaking. He was silent for a minute, collecting himself. Then he vowed, "I'll follow him to hell if I got to."

But first, the two men wrapped the young bride's body in sweet-smelling grasses, then in a shroud made from a white buckskin that had been Mr. Bondurant's wedding gift to Kitty. Tenderly, they placed her in a grave that they dug in the prairie at a place where Kitty often stood and looked out over the plains. Mr. Bondurant scattered what he called "Kitty's pretties" over her, and the two men replaced the sod. Tom said a word of benediction, but instead of adding his own prayer,

Mr. Bondurant once again pledged revenge.

"Kitty was a peaceful woman," Tom told him. "This is no way to honor her memory. It's not what she would want you to do."

"You don't understand Indians. It don't matter what she wants. It's what she *expects*. To the Indian way of thinking, vengeance ain't up to the Lord. Kitty won't never rest easy if I let Garfield get away. I aim not to forget it." His voice broke as he added, "She was my pleasure piece. She warmed me."

"I'll go with you."

"I'm obliged to you, Tom, but it's 'tween me and him. Best you go about your business."

As they argued, there came the sound of a horse in the distance, and, thinking Mr. Garfield was returning, the two sprang to their weapons.

Mr. Bondurant raised his rifle, but Tom urged caution. "You can't see who it is. If it's Garfield, you'll have your chance."

The men watched until they recognized the figure of the new Russian neighbor, Frog Legs Frank. Greatly agitated, he drew rein but did not dismount. Instead, he yelled something in his gibberish.

In the same manner in which he had treated me after Sallie's abduction, Mr. Bondurant calmed the man. Then he patiently questioned him, forcing him to speak the little English he knew.

"Man... hurt... come" were the words he uttered.

"The Russians live on the Garfield place," Tom said. "Maybe Garfield's gone there.

God knows what he's done. This man has a wife, too." They mounted up, then followed the Russian.

Frog Legs Frank did not lead them to the house, however, but turned along the river near Sallie's rock garden. They rode a quarter of a mile beyond, following the streambed as it dropped into a gully. The bank rose at a sharp angle, until it became a cliff, and where it was steepest, Frog Legs Frank stopped and pointed. In the water just beyond lay the bodies of a horse and rider, and I hardly need record that the man was Mr. Garfield. The Russian had seen man and animal cartwheel over the edge of the precipice, but when questioned, he said he was too far away to tell if Garfield took his own life by spurring his horse or if, in his drunken fury, he forgot the cliff was there.

Mr. Garfield broke his neck in the accident. Still, he had not died instantly, but landed facedown in the water, where he drowned. Whether he was conscious as the waters closed over his face, only God knows. Mr. Bondurant chose to believe he was, and he said that Mr. Garfield had died in anguish.

Mr. Garfield's death was for the best, all agree. We are of divided opinion, however, as to whether Mr. Bondurant would have had the right to kill Mr. Garfield if he had caught him. I am among those who say Mr. Bondurant has the same rights as any man, no matter what his wife's race. Others believe that Mr. Bondurant himself was at fault for bringing an Indian into our midst. Among them is

Mr. Osterwald, who insisted, "A white man for an Indian squaw ain't a fair trade."

As I have learnt, there are no crepe veils in Colorado Territory, as we have neither time nor desire here to observe the traditions of mourning. Most expressed sympathy at Kitty's death. One or two took cakes to Mr. Bondurant. Now, as was the way with Sallie, we say no more about Kitty. Mr. Bondurant prefers it that way and is intent on removing all traces of his wife. He burned her belongings, saving only the finest example of Kitty's beadwork, which he presented to me. Were it not for that piece, and the little top that Kitty herself gave to Johnnie, we would have no sign that she had ever been amongst us.

⌒

September 24, 1867. Prairie Home.
Now a word about our little farm. One would think I was not a farmer's wife and a farmer's daughter, so little do I tell of our progress in the fields. As for the harvest, it is not what we would have taken in on the Mississippi. In fact, except for potatoes, it is very poor, although we have done better than our neighbors. The credit is to the Fort Madison seed and to Husband, who knows more about farming than any man twice his age. The field that was plowed in circles did no worse than the others. Still, it did no better, and I believe Luke will not repeat the experiment, for he took much teasing on that score. (It did not come from me. I have learnt to keep my mouth shut about some things.)

In August, Luke talked of returning to Fort Madison following the harvest, but when I announced he would take two traveling companions (and perhaps return with three), he reconsidered. Being more fertile than our fields, I am glad, for this third pregnancy weighs heavily on me, and I was not anxious to walk to Iowa and back.

I did present the idea of spending the winter in Iowa, however. We would leave as soon as our harvest was over, allowing ample time to reach home before the early-winter arrival of Baby. When first the possibility occurred to me, I was quite overcome with excitement at the thought Carrie and I would be together for the births of both of our babes! But Luke would not hear of it. I renewed the idea twice more, but it angers Luke now, so I shall not bring it up again.

He says it is out of the question that we stay with my family in Fort Madison, for it would hurt his mama's feelings. But he does not want to impose on Mother Spenser for the winter, either. Well, neither do I, so perhaps it is best we stay here.

I think Mr. Bondurant would be quite put out if I had the baby in Iowa, for he has hopes of officiating again. He keeps his feelings about Kitty inside, never mentioning her name and acting as much like his old self as is possible. Perhaps it is the Indian way of mourning. Once, when Luke referred to Kitty, Mr. Bondurant put up his hand to show the subject was unwelcome.

October 4, 1867. Prairie Home.

I awoke yesterday with pains gripping my belly, and, after thrashing about, I woke Luke, telling him my time had come and that he must go for Mr. Bondurant. Poor Luke has had no experience with such things (he was not here when Johnnie was born, of course, and I was not aware until after the fact that the second baby had slipped away). So he was in a great state, not knowing whether to do as I asked or to attempt to calm me. When I said that without Mr. Bondurant, he would have to do the honors himself, Husband left at once.

As fear of the unknown is greater than dread of a known event, no matter how painful, I was not greatly worried. If Johnnie's birth was any indication, there was sufficient time for Luke to ride to the Bondurant place and return before the baby put in an appearance. So, between the pains, I built up the fire in the stove and filled the teakettle. I arranged the birth table just so, and even set out Johnnie's breakfast, knowing Boykins would be hungry before the big event was over.

Of a sudden, however, the contractions worsened. I felt a great wrenching and cried out, waking the poor little fellow, who looked at me in alarm. When 'twas over, I rushed to his side to comfort him, taking down his top and favorite book. The pains had been coming about four minutes apart, but now their frequency increased to such an extent that one scarcely stopped before the next began. I was doubled over with the hurt, scaring both Self and Johnnie.

"Mama's all right," I whispered, hoping to ease Boykins's fears, if not my own. I did not remember such searing pain as this before, but I told myself that was because two friends had been there to share it with me.

Then came a pushing so great, I knew the baby would be born before Luke's return and that it must be delivered by me alone. Since I could not attend to myself while lying on the table, I snatched up the sheet and spread it across the floor, then lay upon it, groaning and straining. I heard a great sob and looked up, to see Johnnie, his eyes wide in terror as he watched his mother, but there was nothing I could do to calm him. I tried hard not to cry out, but I could not avoid it, for my body was torn apart. At length, came a great cramping and pushing, and in a moment, a tiny bundle of tissue emerged.

Satisfying myself that the babe was a girl and alive, I quickly wrapped her in a flannel cloth and set her beside me, for I was hemorrhaging and had to attend to myself. I believed that to be the prudent course, for if I continued to bleed, I should become senseless, useless to either of my babies. But, O, that I had neglected myself to hold that tiny body.

"Look, Johnnie, a sister," I said after I had staunched the bleeding. Unwrapping the little bundle, I held up the baby for Johnnie's inspection. But as I did so, she made a pitiful cry, gasped for breath, and was still.

Frantic to restore her, I put my finger into her mouth to remove a blockage. Finding none, I held her upside down, slapping her to open the tiny lungs. Then I put her wee mouth to my own as if my breath would sustain her. "Breathe, breathe for Mama, Sallie," I cried, believing God would not take from me one who already had a Christian name.

Luke and Mr. Bondurant found us there a few minutes later, Johnnie crouching in his bed in terror, Self leaning over Sallie, beseeching God to save her. Mr. Bondurant took the little body and examined her, then shook his head. "She's too small. She ain't got lungs," he explained, placing Sallie on the bed, but I snatched her up and refused to relinquish her, even to Luke, for she should not grow cold without her mother's arms around her.

"I named her Sallie," I said, and Luke, who was overcome with emotion of his own, nodded his approval.

Too weak to stand, I sat in the rocking chair and sang a lullaby to Sallie, stroking the yellow down on her head. I called Johnnie to me. He crawled into my lap and placed his hand next to mine on Sallie's head, laughing at the touch. The tears scalded my face, knowing this little playmate had been cruelly snatched away from him.

Luke put his arms around the two of us and held us close, without speaking. Then he and Mr. Bondurant went to the barn to make a coffin. When they had finished, Luke returned to the house and asked for his daughter. With tears in his eyes, he held Sallie to his face and kissed her, then laid her gently on a pillow.

"Where shall we bury her?" he asked.

"Under a tree."

Luke nodded and helped me to my feet, but I could not stand and so I crumbled onto the floor. He picked me up and set me on the bed, then held me close a moment. "Stay here, Mattie. I'll see to it."

"Wait," I said. "My wedding dress."

Not understanding, Luke removed the dress from the trunk, nonetheless, and brought it to me. Summoning all my strength, I ripped the silk skirt from the bodice and tore off a length of it. "Wrap her in this. It is the best I have."

Luke tenderly folded the precious lump of flesh in the blue silk, then said, "Come, Son. We must bury Sister." He put coat and shoes on Johnnie. Then hand in hand, those two mourners, accompanied by Mr. Bondurant, went on their sorrowful mission.

⌒

October 21, 1867. Prairie Home.

Yesterday, Luke took me for my first visit to Sallie's grave. He has fashioned a cross and scratched upon it her full name, Sallie Susannah (for my mother) Spenser. Someday, I shall plant a yellow rose next to the marker. The little plot was decorated with an arrangement of dried weeds and bright leaves. We do not know who left them, but we think they are the work of Tom. Despite my vow to keep tears to myself when around Luke, I could not stop the flow. Luke, I know, grieves over his daughter's death in his own way. For him, it was a double blow, as he never held Sallie whilst she lived.

I am recovering better than can be expected after such a loss of blood, but I am very tired. I feel greatly the need of a woman's comfort, not having seen one of my own sex since before Sallie was born, but who would I want for a visitor? Certainly not Missus or Mrs. Osterwald. There is no one here in whom I can confide except for Tom and Mr. Bondurant, and I find them wanting, for they are men.

Luke took Johnnie to Mingo today. Poor little fellow. This is a sad place.

November 2, 1867. Prairie Home.
Tom, who tries to take our minds off our sorrows by bringing interesting news, called yesterday to tell us about the beeves that are now being herded from Texas to the new town of Abilene in Kansas, thence shipped to eastern markets. It is all the talk among the cowboys that our section of Colorado Territory will be cattle country one day. I asked how many cows could be grazed on a 160-acre homestead with sparse grass and little water, but men do not always care for logic, particularly when it comes from a woman, and neither Tom nor Luke replied.

I continue to improve. Luke helps me when he can, but with little enthusiasm. He has drawn inward, denying both of us the comfort of our mutual sorrow. O, that Carrie were here to put her arms around me!

December 27, 1867. Prairie Home.

We endeavored to make this a memorable Christmas for Johnnie's sake, and I believe that we succeeded. The three of us entertained Tom and Mr. Bondurant at Christmas Eve supper, even though those two stalwarts were forced to ride through snow as high as their horses' bellies to get here. Tom said it was not necessary for Secretary of State William Seward to spend $7 million on the purchase of frozen Alaska, as the country already has more than enough snow in Colorado.

I served a fat sage hen, our traditional Christmas bird, and the spiced oysters that I had purchased for the occasion in Denver. Tom contributed a can of peaches and brought me a cookie cutter in the shape of a heart, which he fashioned from tin. Mr. Bondurant presented me with a small spice cupboard with a cunning drawer. He had requested a dried apple pie for dessert and declared my offering "the best these grinders ever chewed, by ginger"—even after I told him that my supply of dried fruit was gone and the "apples" were nothing more than broken crackers soaked in water, which all thought was a clever trick. That inspired Tom to teach us a song he had learned in the army, a spoof sung to the tune of "Hard Times Come Again No More." It is called "Hard *Crackers* Come Again No More." We have declared it part of our repertoire of Christmas music.

We were swept up in our traditions, this being

our third Christmas in Colorado, and gathered around the "Christmas bush," about which were placed many favors of the season, including the lovely Berlin work calling card case from Carrie.

Boykins was much pleased with the wagon made by his papa, the harmonica from our guests, and the tin soldier purchased in Denver by his mama. He held it high, shouting, "Pret' lade," whilst Luke passed round the cigars I had bought for special occasions. Husband pronounced himself as pleased as punch with the tintype of Wife and Son (though I hope the mother has not changed as much as the babe since it was taken last spring), as well as the pocketknife from Tom, who had ordered it from Moses in Denver.

I am the proud possessor of a new butter paddle, which Luke made. It is as fine a paddle as I ever used. Luke joked that he would have presented me with a lilac bonnet, but the one he saw in Denver was snatched away before he could purchase it. I replied, in the same manner, that a bonnet would have been more practical but that I should try to find a use for his gift. Then, securing a piece of string, I tied the paddle to the top of my head. It was our first joke in a long time, and I hope it means we both are healing.

⁓

December 30, 1867. Prairie Home.
I cannot close the old year without recording my joy over Carrie's news, which Luke brought home from Mingo today. I hope she

will recover quickly from the birth of her precious daughter. My dear friend does me great honor in naming her little one Mattie Rose. Can there be anything but happiness in the year ahead for all of us?

Chapter 7

January 28, 1868. Prairie Home.

Luke is much withdrawn of late, one minute finding fault, the next becoming oversolicitous. His emotions are due to Sallie's death, I believe, and I try to help him deal with the loss as much as I can. Last week, thinking to show my love for him, I initiated the marriage act, the first time I have done so. I placed my hand on Luke, causing him to stiffen, then drew myself to him. I trembled at my boldness, but my desire to give Luke pleasure was greater than my fear that he would find me wanton. He has not mentioned my action, of course, and I do not know if it gave him surcease.

It is clear that Johnnie lifts his spirits. Luke took Baby to Mingo today. I do not like it, fearing they will be caught in a blizzard, but said nothing, for both enjoy it, and I know Luke will take every measure to protect his son. I no longer find pleasure in solitude, as I once did, for my time alone causes me to brood over my little girl. When the weather warmed at noon today, I walked to Sallie's grave, the first visit since Christmas. The little mound is covered with snow, but Luke's cross stands firm. The dear marker fits this place better than any lamb or cherub carved from marble.

~

February 16, 1868. Prairie Home.

At dark three days ago, Mr. Bondurant knocked and asked Luke to step outside, which was cause for curiosity, as there is little he says that is not suitable for my ears, too. When the two returned to the house, Luke took down the pistol and told me not to expect his return until morning.

"Indians?" I asked.

Luke shook his head, and Mr. Bondurant reassured me. "Winter time, them's too busy keeping warm for making mischief."

"Then what is the matter?"

The two men regarded each other, and Luke replied for both, "There's nothing for you to fear. Bolt the door. Don't open it to anyone but me or Ben or Tom. No other man, no matter who he is. This is important, Mattie. Do you understand?"

Knowing further inquiry was useless, I nodded and quickly turned our supper into sandwiches, wrapping them in a napkin for the men. As the two went to the barn for Luke's horse, Mr. Bondurant called over his shoulder, "Don't worry none, Mrs. Spenser. We got business. That's all."

Of course, I did worry, for having no hint of the matter, I feared a great many things— prairie fire, tornado, epidemic, Rebel marauders, crazed animals, even the outlaw brothers James from Missouri, whose criminal activity excites many in Colorado Territory. Still, as I could do nothing, I went to bed.

The men did not return until sunup. Both were tired, but so agitated that they did not want to sleep. So I mixed biscuits and fried side meat, keeping my curiosity to myself and waiting until such time as an explanation would be voluntered.

Both watched me without comment until at last, Mr. Bondurant said, "She'll hear about it. 'Twould be best to tell her the truth and have done with it." As I turned to them, Mr. Bondurant glanced at Luke, for he would not confide in me without permission from Husband. "She's got the right. Mrs. Osterwald was her friend."

This intelligence changed the situation considerably, and, believing the events of the night were now my business, I asked if Lucinda were all right.

Before replying, Luke went to the door and opened it a crack to look off into the distance, turning something over in his mind. He returned to the table, blowing on his hands, for it was bitterly cold without. His nose was still red from hours in the snow, and I feared he would take ill. I added more wood to the cookstove to build up the heat in the room so he would not suffer.

"You know about Lucinda Osterwald, the state in which she lives," Luke began. "Lived, that is."

My knees weakened. I dropped the cooking fork and slid into a chair, for fear I would fall. "Is she dead?"

"Yes," said Luke, reaching for the fork and placing it upon the table.

"Perhaps it is best. Hers was a bitter life. Was it another 'fall'?"

The two men looked at each other before Mr. Bondurant muttered, "Murder. Plain and simple. You bet."

"Lordy, it was at that," I said hotly. "Mr. Osterwald is as cruel a man as ever was. There should be a law that prevents a man from striking his wife, but I suppose he'll not be punished for it."

"She tried to run away," Luke said. "She made it as far as Wheelers'. Not knowing how things stood with her, Wheeler only thought she was queer and had wandered off. So he rode to the Osterwalds' to alert them of her whereabouts. Osterwald and Brownie followed him home and dragged the woman out of bed."

"Wheeler said the men were so mad, they stunk, but the woman belonged to them, and it weren't the Wheelers' place to stop 'em. Wheeler, the durn fool, said he would have if Mrs. Osterwald had put up a fuss, but she prob'ly knowed it only meant a worse beating if she done it. She didn't say a word, and he'd be hanged if he'd interfere in his neighbors' business. Maybe she reckoned her time had come," Mr. Bondurant added.

I had forgotten the meat, which began to burn, and I jumped up from my chair to pull it off the fire. Then I removed the biscuits from the oven and placed all upon the table with just two plates, for the news had quite taken away my appetite. I waited for the coffee to boil and settle, then poured it into three cups before returning to my chair.

"That was five days ago. The situation didn't set well with the Wheelers, 'though they didn't tell a soul till Tom stopped by yesterday. Tom was alarmed, of course, and went for Ben, and the two of them rode to the Osterwalds'." Luke stopped talking to bite into a biscuit, but he didn't chew it. He nodded to Mr. Bondurant to continue.

"We thought we'd just make a sociable call and in the bargain check to see was she all right. We wouldn't have saw her if we hadn't come in cross the field instead of by the road. Tom's idea that was, to sneak up on 'em, without they saw us. She was out back by that draw. They'd tied her up."

"The animals!" I exclaimed. "As if she'd have the courage to run away again!"

"They tied her up," Mr. Bondurant repeated softly. "Outside. To a fence post. Naked. She was froze solid."

"O! How beastly!" I cried, clenching my fists until the nails broke through the skin and drew blood. The coffee in my stomach sent up a sour taste.

"They'd strapped her. We saw where the blood was froze on her. A blacksnake whip was throwed in the snow beside her, like they was going to go back and beat her again. Tom said he'd whip both of 'em with it, but just then old Osterwald poked a rifle out the door, and I knowed he'd shoot us both if we got closer. So I told Tom we'd ride on by and settle with 'em later."

"That's when Ben came for me, and we rode for Amidon and Wheeler. Tom collected the others," Luke said.

"We rendezvoused at Tom's to figure what to do."

"Vigilantes," I observed.

Luke, thinking I was critical of the action, explained, "When there isn't any law between here and Denver, we have to abide by the law of God as we understand it."

I nodded, for rather than disapproving, I quite agreed. The two men ate silently for a few minutes, neither willing to go on.

"Was it Brownie or Mr. Osterwald or both of them who tied her up?" I asked, swallowing hard to keep the coffee from boiling up into my throat.

"Each blamed the other," Luke said. "We'll never know for sure. They were as evil as any men I ever came across." He was still a minute, as if deciding whether to tell me something, and when he spoke, he was too distraught to look me in the face. "Brownie was the father of Lucinda Osterwald's last child. When the thing was born, Osterwald smothered it. That must have been why they came west, for fear someone would discover what they'd done. Mrs. Smith found out when she took care of Mrs. Osterwald last winter. The poor woman blurted it out during her delirium. When Mrs. Smith asked for the truth of it later, Mrs. Osterwald begged her to keep the secret. Mrs. Smith agreed, for what reason, I don't know, because she is a terrible gossip and likes nothing better than shocking others. Perhaps she hoped to extract something from Mrs. Osterwald later on. She told no one but her husband, threatening him if he didn't keep silent. He did as ordered until last night, and that decided us upon our course of action."

I put my hands over my face to block out the horror and discovered tears there, which I was not aware of having shed. I wiped them with my fingers, mingling the tears with the blood on my nails.

"When we got there, Brownie and Mr. Osterwald denied everything. They claimed she'd run off again. Of course, knowing Tom and Ben were likely to return, they'd cut the poor woman from the post, but we saw strips of flesh frozen to the wood. The body was laid out like cordwood, hidden under a stack of kindling. I never saw..." Luke swallowed a few times, then got up and went outside.

"Brownie's always been off his feed," Mr. Bondurant said. "I guess Osterwald went stark mad when his wife took off like she done. After we found the body, Osterwald said the wife deserved what she got for shaming him, said what was between man and wife weren't none of our affair."

I did not reply until Luke returned and sat down, his head in his hands. "Thank God you apprehended them. I believe they will hang. A jury would never set them free," I said.

Luke glanced up at Mr. Bondurant, then turned to me, and, pronouncing each word slowly and distinctly so's I would not misunderstand, he said, "We are farmers, not peace officers, and there are occasions when we must deal out justice with our own hands. We have neither the time nor the means to take those two to Denver for trial. I think no man will take issue with what we did. We gave Mrs. Osterwald a Christian burial. I myself said the words over her. The Osterwald men... well, they're gone. No one need ever fear them again."

"Then—"

"It's done. You mustn't repeat any of this. The Osterwalds are gone, and their place is burnt to a cinder. We shall mention the name only when necessary," Luke said. After he finished speaking, Husband looked very tired, so weary, in fact, that I thought he might fall asleep at the table.

"You must lie down," I said, taking his hand and leading him to the bed. I invited Mr. Bondurant to rest, too, but he refused, saying he would go home. I think he was not in need of sleep so much as whiskey.

As Mr. Bondurant put on his coat, Johnnie awoke, and, seeing father and friend, he demanded to be held. I told him he must be quiet, but both men rallied and insisted on playing with Boykins, teasing him and tossing him into the air. I think that innocent child did a little to erase the monstrous events at the Osterwalds' for both men, but not for me. I am heartsick over the death of one more innocent woman in this place and cannot help but wonder who will be the next.

February 23, 1868. Prairie Home.

All in the neighborhood attended Sabbath service and were much subdued, although not one word was spoken about the Osterwalds. Someone must have told the lady homesteaders, because they were quite as melancholy as the rest. When Miss Hested noted that there were none of her favorite pasties on the table, following the service, Miss Figg whispered a quick word, and Miss Hested was quiet. Pasties were always Mrs. Osterwald's contribution.

February 25, 1868. Prairie Home.

Luke to Mingo again yesterday. He goes 'most every week now. I am glad to have him away, for his moods are blacker than ever. At times, he stares at me with such intensity that I am quite unnerved, but when I inquire the reason, he only scowls. I believe he broods over the Osterwald situation. Nor has he forgotten our little Sallie. The past few months have been hard on him.

Tom stopped by, the first time except for Sabbath service that I have seen him since the Osterwald farm burned down—which is the way we put it. He did not enlighten me on the events of that night. In response to my vague inquiries, he replied something about moral laws, adding that the Osterwalds are better forgotten.

He was more anxious to talk of Jessie and Moses, who are spending the winter in Denver again but will go to the Swan River, high in the mountains, as soon as spring arrives. The area is one of the older diggings, but Moses has intelligence that it may be "hot" again. In the meantime, Moses writes, they do very well in Denver, by which I conclude that Jessie does well, for she is the one with the income. Tom does not appear to know what business she is in, and I, of course, have not informed him.

Then we fell to talking about poor President Andrew Johnson, whose certain impeachment will mean lack of confidence in the greenback, and, in turn, a harder time attracting capital to our corner of the country. I am of the opinion that the President is self-willed, obstinate, and unfit for office. But such faults are not cause for casting him aside, said I, for if they were, who amongst us could be President? Tom, however, believes the President will be gotten rid of, for Mr. Johnson is an obstructionist and proved himself a true copperhead by denying statehood for Colorado. I replied I was not sure the Southerners thought so well of him, remembering Sallie Garfield calling Mr. Johnson a "renegade, a demagogue, and a drunkard."

"All three in one man? Even General Grant did not rate such a compliment from the Rebels," said Tom, and we had a good laugh. We are in agreement that General Grant, who is Tom's own hero, not only for his brilliant military battles but because he lives near Tom's old home in Jo Daviess County, will be our next President.

Our discussion was so lively that we forgot the time, until we heard the return of the wagon. Tom stayed to supper so he could elicit Luke's opinion on our President, but, to his disappointment, Husband was deep in his own thoughts and not much for politics.

⁓

March 7, 1868. Prairie Home.

I am put out with Luke for taking Johnnie to Mingo today. There appears to be no danger of snow, but the weather is bitter cold, and I thought it wrong to expose so small a child. Luke disagreed, saying that if he is to be a Colorado boy, growing up with the country, Johnnie must be tough. Indeed, Husband accused me of coddling our son, saying I had tied him too tightly to Mama's apron strings. Luke has found fault with me in every way in recent days, so I said no more.

I believe he took heed of my concern, however, for Luke asked me to me dress Johnnie in so many layers of clothing that he looked like a boy twice his size. Luke took a change of garments for both himself and Johnnie in case the weather turns wet, packing the clothing in a little trunk (not the one in which I keep this journal, for I should never let him have access to it). Wrapped in a buffalo robe, they went off in high spirits, so I waved gaily, despite my misgivings. Johnnie waved back, though he could scarcely lift his little arm, so encumbered was it with sweaters and coat.

Their departure has put me out of sorts, although my monthly sickness, with the attendant backache, shares the blame. O, that it were summer and I could indulge myself with a leisurely bath in the "garden." It is too cold to bathe even indoors, though I build up the fire. The wind is so fierce, even our thick sod walls fail to keep out the drafts. Luke means well with Johnnie, but I shall worry until they are safely home.

It is nightfall, and Luke and Johnnie are yet away. As there is no storm, I do not know what delays them. I thought perhaps the cold made Luke keep Baby in town for the night, but upon further reflection, I do not believe that to be the case, for Luke should have finished his errands and been on his way by midafternoon, when the sun was yet out. Besides, there is no lodging in Mingo excepting for the saloon, and that is hardly suitable for Boykins. I fear the two have met with an accident, and I have knelt the past half hour in prayer, begging God to keep them safe. Next time, I shall make use of foot instead of knee, by putting it down when Luke insists on taking Johnnie to Mingo in such cold.

⁓

March 8, 1868. Prairie Home.
The thermometer stood at seventeen below zero, and midnight had come and gone when Luke returned home. I gave him a tongue-lashing such as he has never before received from

me. He bore it in silence, as if deserving the rebuke. Though wrapped in a buffalo robe, sleigh robe, and the warm homespun blanket Luke carried in the war, my baby was chilled to the bone. I held him close and rocked him to warm the little fellow, then put him to bed, surrounded by stones heated on the stove and wrapped in cloth. Nonetheless, the chills turned to fever before dawn arrived, and I spent many hours answering Johnnie's pitiful cries for water. I fear he has contacted catarrh or la grippe.

Luke is upset over Baby's condition, but to my inquiries as to their whereabouts yesterday, Luke gives not the slightest satisfaction, saying only that the road was bad and the time got away from him. When I remarked I did not understand how six or eight hours passed without his knowledge, Luke murmured it was not a wife's place to question her husband.

"It is a mother's place to know the whereabouts of her son," I retorted. Of course, I should not have spoken to Luke in such manner, but I had been frantic with worry, and his lack of concern for Johnnie made me bold.

Luke is contrite—a virtue he has never shown before—and spent today in the barn, coming into the house only for meals. He is in the barn now, though the cold there is fierce. I am greatly fatigued but cannot sleep, for fear of missing Baby's call. Johnnie is fitful, even when I rock him, having developed a cough that racks his hot body. I apply an affusion of vinegar and cool water to break the

fever, but I dare not make him too wet, for fear
the chill will return. I also doctor him with
febrifuge tea, made of snake and valerian
roots.

March 10, 1868. Prairie Home.
    Mr. Bondurant called today, and discovering
Johnnie's illness, he went home and returned
with an infusion made from wild-cherry bark.
He claims it is better than febrifuge and
cures all ailments, including his rheuma-
tism. I am grateful for the infusion, as Boykins's
symptoms are worse. When Tom arrived later,
having been told of Johnnie's condition by Mr.
Bondurant, I asked that he write a letter to
Jessie requesting her advice. Tom agreed to
do so at once, riding to Mingo to post it this
very day. With any luck, we shall receive a reply
within the week, though I pray Johnnie will
be well by then. O, that there were time to write
home for help! Never have I felt the need of
a woman friend so keenly as now that my
precious baby is ill. I do not tell Luke the depth
of my despair, confiding it only in my journal.

March 11, 1868. Prairie Home.
    Exhaustion caused me to fall asleep this after-
noon. When I awoke, Luke was holding a
cup of water to Johnnie's parched lips. I
jumped up, but Luke ordered me to rest,
saying it was his turn to attend to our little
patient. When Boykins closed his eyes, Luke

took my hand and said he was certain Johnnie would recover. I believe there were tears in his eyes. As Luke finds it difficult to admit to an error, this was as close to an apology as I should expect, and I forgave him with all my heart. How can I remain angry with a father who loves our son so?

Tonight, Johnnie's throat is badly swollen, causing him great difficulty in swallowing, and he cries out in pain when he moves his little neck. I wash his face and comb his hair to soothe him, but it does not help.

March 12, 1868. Prairie Home.

Delirium has set in. Johnnie frets, calling, "Papa" and "Mama" in his sleep, and once he cried out, "Pret' lade," which made me laugh, the first time I have done so in many days.

Luke is much underfoot now, going from house to barn and back again to see if Johnnie's condition has improved. I think up chores for him to do to occupy his time. Each morning, Luke spreads hay upon the floor of our Prairie Home for a carpet, then sweeps it up and replaces it the following day. The hay keeps the sickroom fresh. My rag rug, which I save for good, is set upon the hay, for I think it warms the room and cheers it, too.

Though it is too early for a reply from Jessie, Tom rode to Mingo, and he says he will do so each day, until it is received.

March 13, 1868. Prairie Home.

The delirium continues, with Johnnie calling out the same three names. I no longer laugh when I hear the cry of "Pret' lade." The fever and fitfulness are worse, and I am sick with fatigue and worry. God knows, I would give my life for my son. Yet I am powerless to cure him. Why is there not some woman nearby to offer me aid and comfort?

March 14, 1868. Prairie Home.

Johnnie awoke this morning with an angry red throat, sprinkled with white spots, confirming my worst fears. My poor boy has scarlet fever. I read and reread the instructions in *Dr. Chase's Recipes* in hopes of discovering something previously overlooked that will help him, but there is nothing more to be done. Johnnie's eyes are dull and do not focus on Mama's face.

Tom rode to Mingo in threatening weather today, but there is still no word from Jessie. Pray God that she has not left for the Swan River.

March 15, 1868. Prairie Home.

All at Mingo know of Johnnie's condition and leave the room when Tom walks in, for fear he will bring the infection. Tom told us about it in hopes of amusing us, as he finds it queer that men who are frequently exposed to Indians, outlaws, and drunken fights are afraid of a child's disease. Mr. Connor tells Tom to stay away until Johnnie is well, but Tom insists he will return each day, until he receives the letter from the Denver "doctor," as if that will cause Mr. Connor to hurry the mail.

Mrs. Wheeler sends word that the Southern treatment for scarlet fever is pulverized charcoal and spirits of turpentine mixed with a little milk, which I have concocted, but Johnnie refuses it. Tom bought precious apples for apple tea, of which Baby sipped a little.

Johnnie's skin is deep red with a rash, and I rubbed him with bacon grease before wrapping him in flannel. While Luke sat with Johnnie, Tom and Mr. Bondurant took me outside for a walk, saying if I did not get exercise and fresh air, there would be two of us to be doctored. Having cared for me once before, said Tom, they did not relish tending such an obstreperous patient again.

⌒

March 16, 1868. Prairie Home.

Johnnie is in a coma, no longer repining. This state is worse than any before. No word from Jessie. Baby is in God's hands.

⌒

March 17, 1868. Prairie Home.

I left my boy's side for only a moment to put the hotcake batter into the pan for Luke's breakfast, when Johnnie took a long, deep breath and shuttered, his little body trembling gently for a few seconds. Then he was still, and I knew in that instant, his life had gone from him. I dropped the griddle onto the floor and rushed to the bedside with a prayer that it was not so, but Johnnie lay quietly, his sightless eyes turned to the ceiling. O, poor boy, that his last moments were spent without his mother's arms around him! I picked up the dear form, which was very light, for he had lost much weight during his illness, and sat in the rocking chair, just as I had with Sallie, praying, "Not my will, but Thy will be done." But, O, I did not mean it!

Then, as if pretending my boy was only asleep, I sang to him his favorite songs, "Old Dan Tucker" and "When Johnny Comes Marching Home," until Luke, who was doing chores in the barn, returned to the house.

He saw the griddle on the floor and rushed to the rocker. I shook my head, for my grief was too deep for me to speak.

"Is he gone?" Luke whispered, refusing to believe what his eyes told him was so.

I nodded.

"O, my soul!" Luke knelt upon the dirt floor beside me and took the little hand into his own. Then he broke into ragged sobs. I put my hand on his shoulder, but he only cried the harder.

"It was God's will," I struggled to tell him.

"No," Luke cried. "It was mine. O, blame me. The fault was mine. Forgive me, Mattie."

"Hush."

Luke cried for many minutes, his face

against my skirt, and when the sobs ended, he asked to hold his son, lifting up his arms to receive Johnnie.

I do not know how long Luke and I sat there grieving, when, without knocking, Tom burst through the door, a letter in his hand. "It's come. Jessie saves the day...." Tom stopped when he saw the scene before him, and, shaking his head once or twice as if to make it go away, he gasped, "No! No! Not Johnnie, too!" He slumped onto the bed, his face in his hands.

Mr. Bondurant arrived a few minutes later, for Tom had called out to him as he galloped past, telling of the letter's arrival. Johnnie's death was as hard on that faithful friend as Kitty's had been. He did not cry, but he set his stony face and said again and again, "Hellfire! Hellfire!"

And so our little band gathered quietly around the body of the one we loved so well. I draw strength from their love, and from Luke's, and without it, I do not know how I could go on.

⌒

March 18, 1868. Prairie Home.

I wanted to bury Johnnie yesterday with but little ceremony, surrounded by the four who loved him most, but the others said Johnnie was beloved of many who would want to say their final good-byes, and they have persuaded me to hold the service tomorrow. Luke used the carved drawers of Grandmother's little commode, which I brought from home, to make the coffin. The lining is what remains of my China silk wedding dress. I washed my precious boy with great care, cut a lock of his hair, which I shall save in this book, then dressed him for eternal rest in the night-shirt Carrie made for his Christmas present. I know God shall recognize him, even without the name so lovingly embroidered upon it.

Mr. Bondurant dug our baby's grave under the tree, next to Sallie's. Tom takes our sad news to the neighbors.

When Sallie died, Luke kept his grief to himself, but he turns to me in this great sorrow. Last night, we held each other as we never have before. Although I did not care to do it, I allowed marital relations, even encouraging Luke to show him I did not place the blame for our mutual tragedy on him. I thought the act would give him release and allow him sleep. I myself found no release.

⁓

March 19, 1868. Prairie Home.

I do not believe I have ever seen so many people gathered together in Colorado Territory as came to pay their respects to Johnnie. Among the mourners were the lady home-steaders, Mr. Amidon, the Smiths, the Russians, the Wheelers, and several residents of Mingo who are friends of Luke's and who admired Johnnie from his trips to town. To my surprise, Mr. Connor was among them. They feel keen-ly the loss of one who was a great favorite amongst them, and several told me stories of

Johnnie's clever remarks and winning ways. Though they are not my kind, these people are good, and I took comfort in their heartfelt presence.

The service was brief and to the point, for I wanted our friends to remember the joy of Johnnie's short life, not the sorrow of his passing. We recited together holy verses, then sang Christian hymns. As Luke could not speak, the service ended with a prayer from Tom, asking God to accept this little boy who could brighten even the heavens.

As the men replaced the earth and sod over the tiny coffin, the women set out a dinner, sharing their meager supplies, as everything has been scarce this winter, excepting snow. They left behind such a generous store of cakes, stews, and other edibles that I shall not have to cook for several days. I put out my best china and silver, for the day was in honor of Johnnie, and as I gathered up the things, I saw my prized Delft plate had been broken in half. What does it matter, when I have suffered so great a loss?

The folks stayed only a little while following the ceremony, for it was a blizzardy day. The Smiths were the last to leave but Tom and Mr. Bondurant, and as Mr. Smith picked up the reins, Missus settled herself in the wagon and turned to me with what I believed would be a final word of comfort. Instead, she said, "He'd be amongst us now if not for the Lord's vengeance. He punishes the son for the sins of the father."

She saw my confusion and added, "Keeping

a little tyke in the cold like that just to wait for the woman. I seen it myself, and I knowed Mr. Spenser to be a sinner, even if he didn't leave in the conveyance with her, as most thought he would."

I was thunderstruck at her words. But I was determined to keep a quiet face, depriving Missus of the satisfaction of knowing her gossip had hit the mark. For the instant the words were spoken, I knew how Luke and Johnnie had spent those long hours. Luke had taken Johnnie to see Persia, who must have come to Mingo on the stage. Luke had kept my poor boy in the cold wagon as they waited for her to arrive. Then slowly I felt a sense of horror slip over me as I remembered the quantity of clothing Luke had taken for both of them. No, Luke had not gone merely to see Persia. He had intended to run off with her, and to take Johnnie with him! I knew it as surely as I knew my son was dead. At that moment, as I stood by the grave of my little boy, I knew that Luke did not love me, that he had never loved me. It was Persia he had always cared for and wanted, and he had made up his mind to have her. And he had planned to steal Johnnie from me and give him to her, to leave me alone in this house on the prairie while he and Persia stole off like thieves with my boy. O, Luke was right to blame himself for Johnnie's death. His perfidy killed our son.

The revelation made me feel faint, and I would have crumpled had not a strong hand reached out to support me—Tom's hand. I turned, to see Tom standing next to me, Luke behind him. Both had heard Missus's words.

I looked to Luke to deny them, praying he would say something to make my belief groundless, but he would not meet my eyes. Instead, Luke muttered some excuse about accompanying Mr. Bondurant on an errand that would not wait. Not giving me a chance to protest, he went to the barn for Traveler and was off.

"Is she right?" I asked Tom when the two of us were alone.

"She is a gossip. You know she is up to no good. Goddamn her. It is not right at such a time!"

"If Missus knows, everyone does. You've been to Mingo a dozen times since then. You knew."

"Mattie, it's between you and Luke, and none of my business. Whatever Luke did, Mrs. Smith is right. He's been punished beyond measure. He's lost his son."

"*My* son. I did nothing, but I lost my son, too, and my husband, as well."

"No," Tom said. "You didn't lose him. He came back to you, didn't he?"

"Came back! Came back!" I screamed. "My son is dead. I have no use for the one who is responsible for that. I don't want Luke back. How could I? He should have gone with Persia. If he had, Johnnie would be alive."

"You don't know that. You will never know that. Luke needs you more than ever."

"But I no longer need him."

The words that flew out of my mouth stunned me, and I believe they did Tom, too, for instead of arguing, he led me into the house, ordering me to sit whilst he fixed tea.

"Do all in town know?" I asked.

Tom searched the shelf for the good tea. "There is not one in Mingo who thinks Luke other than a fool, for everyone admires you, not Mrs. Talmadge, myself most of all," he said in way of reply.

When he had finished with the tea, Tom set a cup before me and sat down with his own. "A terrible thing has happened to you, Mattie, and I worry for fear it will destroy you, just the way this place destroys every woman of breeding who comes here. You must stand by Luke. He is all you have."

But I do not have Luke. I have nothing. By betraying me and taking my most precious possession, my husband has destroyed all feeling I have for him.

Tom offered to stay until Luke returned, but, pleading my weary state, for I have not slept a night through since Johnnie took ill, I begged him to return to his homestead. Tom understood, and as I promised I would go directly to bed, he withdrew.

I cannot go to bed, however, because so many questions about Luke and Johnnie and Persia crowd into my mind. How could he marry me and take me to this place when it was Persia he loved? Why did Luke try to take my dear boy from his mother? Does he wish I had died with Sallie so that he and Persia and Johnnie could be together? I must have the answers. I tell all to my book to keep from falling asleep, for I intend to have it out with Luke before the day is ended.

It has been many hours since Luke left, and he is yet away. Perhaps he only pretended to accompany Mr. Bondurant home and in truth has left to join Persia. A moment ago, as I rose to wash the teacups, I put my hand upon the hot stove and did not feel the the heat until I smelled the flesh burn. Am I devoid of all feelings? Did all my love die with Johnnie?

March 20, 1868. Prairie Home.

I have slept for more than eighteen hours, a sleep harder than any I ever had. The clap of doom could not have opened my eyes. Yet, when I awakened, the events of the previous day were as clear in my mind as if they had happened only minutes before. Perhaps it would be better if I did not remember them so well. But I do not want to forget, so I confide all here.

Luke returned not long after I had set aside my journal, finding me seated at table, reading my Bible, which I had turned to in search of calm. He said as he entered the room that he was surprised to see me awake. I deserved rest after the many hours I had spent at Johnnie's side, Husband declared with a solicitousness he has rarely shown toward me before.

"Do you truly believe I would sleep just yet?" I asked, not getting up, but closing the pages of the Holy Book.

Luke removed his coat and took his time hanging it on its peg. "I suppose not."

"There is food on the stove if you are hungry. Our neighbors were very kind." I did not offer to bring the food to him, however.

"No, I'm not hungry." Luke shifted his weight from one foot to the other, as if waiting for an invitation to join me. He appeared not to know how to proceed, wanting me to take the lead. "Shall I get a plate for you?" he asked at length, but I did not reply.

I had thought of nothing but Luke and Johnnie and Persia in the hours I had been alone. Still, I did not know how to proceed. So I was silent for some minutes before asking, "What do you have to say for yourself?"

"There is nothing to talk about."

"There is a great deal to talk about, and I must know it all," I replied hotly. "I have the right to question you, and you must answer truthfully."

I thought Luke would disagree, for he will not be told what to do, but instead, he took his seat at table across from me and responded at once. I am sure that in the previous hours, he had given much thought to this interview and wanted it finished as quickly as possible. "I said there is nothing to talk about because it is done. I waited for Persia in Mingo. She wrote from Denver, where they had gone in February, that she intended to leave Mr. Talmadge. It was a poor match. She was returning to Fort Madison."

"Was it your intention to go with her?"

"Affairs between Persia and me are done with, Mattie." Luke's face was drawn, and he looked much older.

"That is not the answer to my question."

"I do not want to hurt you."

"You are late in deciding that, for you have already done so." I was surprised that I could speak with such force to one who had so recently been the center of my universe. "I want the truth, plain spoken, though it is painful to both of us."

As he thought over my words, Luke got up from his chair and went to the stove, cutting himself a piece of johnnycake. With his back to me, he said in a rush of words, "Yes, I suppose I did plan to go with her. You don't understand how close Persia and I were. It was thoughts of her that got me through my injuries at Shiloh. Ever since I was a boy, I'd planned to marry her. I never thought otherwise until I'd filed on the homestead and returned to Fort Madison. While I was away, Persia had turned into a belle and a flirt. She said mine was not the only offer of marriage she had received. There were a dozen others. She had not made up her mind which one to accept but knew one thing: The man she married must provide her with fine clothes and a brick house, not calico and a dirt shack on the prairie."

Luke turned back to me, and I could tell by his face how much Persia's words had hurt him, but his pain was as nothing to my own. "I did not understand then that Persia was teasing, that her answer was only part of the bargaining that takes place between man and woman. I believed it was final. I knew I needed a wife here, because I did not care to live alone. So when Abner confided his intention to propose to you, I considered you myself and found you to be suitable. Persia was always jealous of you—your wit, your cleverness. I suppose a part of it was to cause her pain." Luke sat down again. "There, I've said it as plain as I can. I did not believe asking you to marry me was wrong, because I thought I would be a good husband." Instead of eating the corn bread, he set it on the table and picked at the crumbs that fell from it.

"You married me for spite of Persia, then? You never cared for me?"

"That's not altogether right."

"What part of it is wrong?"

"I wouldn't have married you if I hadn't had some feelings for you. I did not misuse you." Luke looked up from the crumbs. "It is not easy for me to say these things to you."

I knew that to be true, for Luke dislikes speaking of his feelings, but I did not care. "Cry shame! Do you think it is easy for me to hear them?" In fact, I did not want to continue the conversation, but I knew I must have it all. "When did you determine to leave me for her?"

Luke shifted in his chair and looked about the room, his eyes stopping on Johnnie's little bed before they returned to me. "We spoke of it when I was in Fort Madison, but I would not abandon you in your condition. I'm not altogether devoid of conscience, Mattie. I hope you will believe that. We talked of it in Denver, too, but Persia would have nothing of it then, for she was enjoying Mr. Talmadge's money."

"Did you commit adultery there?"

Luke did not reply to the question, but his face flushed and he looked away, and I had my answer. "You said to me once you wanted a house with a veranda here, where we could sit on a swing when we were old. I told Persia—"

"You told Persia!" I interrupted with a cry of anguish. With that fresh revelation, I slumped down in the chair, pulling my elbows tight against me, drawing inward. Luke had told Persia the things I had said to him in love. Had he told her my hopes and dreams, too? What else had he revealed to her—my headaches, my fear of storms, my weakness for bonnets? Had he confided how I had initiated the marriage act and that I liked it when he fitted himself to my back and put his hands on my breasts? I burned with the shame of it. Luke had betrayed not just my body but my soul, and the latter, I think, was worse.

I was silent while I collected myself, then forced myself to continue with the interrogation. "You have been corresponding with each other since the beginning, since our arrival here. It was the reason for your frequent trips to Mingo. You went for her letters." These were not questions, but statements.

Luke nodded. "Persia wrote a few weeks ago, saying she had reconsidered, that she would desert Mr. Talmadge. He appears to be a kind man, but he is a cruel husband. It was my intention to leave with her, not for Fort Madison, but for Oregon or California. The homestead would be yours. I'd planned to put it in a letter to you." Luke broke off a piece of the bread and chewed it, but his mouth was dry, and it took him a long time to swallow. He got up and poured himself a cup of the cold coffee that was left from morning and gulped it down.

"Why didn't you go with her?"

"Persia refused to take Johnnie with us. She didn't want him."

"Not want Johnnie!" I could not believe my ears. How could Persia not want my precious little boy? I understood my husband far better than she, for I knew Luke loved Johnnie above all others, even Persia, and would never give him up.

"When she said it, I was glad." Luke set down the cup and looked at me, his eyes glittering.

I stared at him without comprehension.

"Don't you see? The scales fell from my eyes, and for the first time, I saw Persia as she is, foolish and vain, not fit to make a home here or to raise Johnnie or to overcome hardships without complaint, as you have. She is as shallow as the Platte. Why, it was as plain to me as anything, and plainer still that I didn't love Persia. She was part of all that I chose to leave behind in Iowa. I don't know why I hadn't seen it before. I had come to love you and did not even know it. When I realized that, I wanted to set out for home immediately and would have, but I couldn't leave

Persia alone in Mingo. The stage had been damaged on the road, so I was forced to wait until it was repaired and on its way."

Luke set down the cup and came to me, standing by my side and looking down at me. "I was determined that things between us would be different. I have not been a good or affectionate husband, but I mean for that to change. You'll see, Mattie. Do you understand what I'm saying to you? I love you, dear."

For three years, I had waited for Luke to say those words, but they meant nothing to me. My heart was stony against him. Luke reached for my hand, but I drew it away. "It is too late," I told him.

Now that all had been said, I felt a weariness so great that I did not know if I could take the few steps to the bed. As I rose, Luke put his arm about my waist and led me across the room. He helped me remove my dress and put on my nightgown. I do not know if he slept beside me last night, because I was asleep the instant I lay down, and when I awoke, he was gone, whether to the barn for chores or for good, I do not know. It does not matter.

March 29, 1868. Prairie Home.

Tom or Mr. Bondurant calls every day. I appreciate their attempts to cheer me, but I do not respond well. Tom says they fear I shall fall into melancholia over Johnnie's death, and perhaps he is right. Luke has begun the spring plowing. I envy him his work. There is little for me to do except for cooking and washing, which are performed in a dreamlike state.

Sometimes I see Johnnie as plain as life and reach out for him, only to break into weeping with the realization he is gone forever. O, my poor boy!

I spend much time contemplating my future. If Luke had gone away with Persia, I should have returned to Fort Madison. All there would know I was a scorned woman. Still, I would have begun a new life among those who care for me. Society does not think much of a woman who has been deserted, but it is far less kind to a one who is herself the deserter. So I could not leave Luke, no matter the reason, for I should be an even greater embarrassment to family and friends. O, that Luke had come to his senses just a few weeks earlier! Johnnie would be alive, and we would be the happiest of families. I brood on how to repay the bitterness he has brought me.

∾

April 7, 1868. Prairie Home.

Luke inquired whether I would attend Sabbath service on Sunday last, and upon reflection, I concluded it was a good idea, for I have not left our homestead in weeks, and I felt the companionship of others, along with the worship of God, would lift the spirits of both Husband and Self.

That was not to be, however, for the instant I arrived, I perceived all were watching us with curiosity, as Persia's arrival and departure were common knowledge. A few, such as the lady homesteaders, of whom I am quite fond, showed heartfelt sympathy for my loss of Johnnie and were anxious to know if they could do something for me. Others, however, looked at me with less or more pity, which I cannot abide.

Only Tom acted in a natural way, teasing Luke that he had seen no fields plowed in circles on our place this year. Then he inquired of me if I would knit him a pair of mittens in exchange for one day's *straight* plowing with Luke. I replied pertly that if I were to knit the mittens for him, I should expect a day's help in the kitchen for them. The lady homesteaders laughed, but others seemed disappointed that I was able to hold up my head.

The drive home was melancholy, for I remembered the same ride with Johnnie in happier times, his sweet voice repeating the Sabbath songs just sung. By the time we reached home, I had a headache, and I went to bed at once, a scarf tied tightly about my forehead. Luke prepared dinner without complaint, though I did not eat a morsel. He reached for me in the night, and I was shocked that he would think of his own gratification at such a time. How could he ever again be my Darling Boy?

April 10, 1868. Prairie Home.
I shall make a greater effort to become the old Mattie, for I do not care for cheerlessness and self-pity, particularly in Self. I have con-

cluded that even if I no longer care to be a wife to Luke, there is no other choice open to me. I will not burden those at home by returning to Fort Madison, and I could not earn my keep, even as a teacher, in Denver or any other place. So I must go on and make the best of it.

Having reached that decision, I concluded to resume my domestic duties with enthusiasm. This morning, I looked about the little house and found it in a disgraceful state of untidiness, so I set out at once to give it a good airing. I hung bedding and clothing in the sunshine, then cleaned cupboard and blackened stove. When Luke came in for his dinner, I told him I had taken the grass from the tick and made twists for the stove with it, and unless he wanted to sleep in the oven, he must bring new grass before bedtime. He seemed much pleased with my sally, and he brought it at once.

I did not rest in the afternoon, but swept the dirt floor with my sagebrush broom, then washed it, though I could wash the floor all the way to China before I got it clean. I intend to make a jelly cake for dinner, but I cannot go back into the house until the floor is dried hard. So I sit on the bench in the spring sunshine to record these words, having conveniently placed journal in pocket before completing my housekeeping tasks. Tomorrow, I shall undertake the washing.

⁓

April 11, 1868. Prairie Home.
Luke was much pleased with the jelly cake,

but I could not eat it, for my state of sadness had returned. I was not fit company. One moment, I am industrious and cheerful, the next, overcome with lassitude. It is an alternative to anger, which I keep under control, sometimes only with great effort. I have just completed the wash and am fatigued from the heavy work of lifting and scrubbing. I dropped one of Luke's shirts on the ground and cried when faced with having to begin on it again. I shall be sorely tried on my resolve to take up housewifely responsibilities cheerfully.

My mood improved when Tom called with the first dandelion of the season, which he presented to me with as much flourish as if it had been a dozen roses. He stayed to supper, making it seem like old times. Moses urges Tom to give up the land and take his chance in the gold camps. I advised him he is more farmer than miner and said we should miss him keenly if he left. Tom says he gives a change more thought than he had expected.

Luke has asked whether I want him to remove Johnnie's bed, which takes up much space in our cramped house, but I cannot yet bear to see the room without it and the little Postage Stamp quilt Baby loved so much. I waited until Luke had gone out before sitting down on the little fellow's tick and giving way to tears.

April 15, 1868. Prairie Home.
Luke proposes to add a wooden floor to our soddy, saying we have lived long enough as

"cavemen." When the harvest is over, he will cut sod to add a second room. He asked what I would think of writing home for a slip of honeysuckle to plant beside it.

Here is an odd thing: We have never again talked of Persia, except for Luke saying he had burned her letters and all other reminders of her. Luke has put her out of his mind. I wish I could do the same. I think I can forgive him the adultry, but will I ever overcome the greater betrayal of the private part of me?

The yellow rose beside the house made it through the winter and is sending out green leaves.

April 20, 1868. Prairie Home.

On impulse, Luke announced he would drive to Mingo and invited me to accompany him. As he has not been to town since his trip with Johnnie, he has much to accomplish there, including the purchase of lumber for our floor. I have not seen Mingo in many months and thought the air would do me good. But upon reflection, I declined, for I am not yet up to an examination by townspeople who know of Persia. Luke left very late, after dinner, just as large flakes of snow began to fall. I have heard of these heavy spring storms, called "willow-benders" in Colorado—though not here on the plains, as there are no big willow trees. So I begged Luke to postpone the trip. He replied his mind was made up, but that if the storm turned bad, he would respect it by seeking a bed in town.

He inquired whether I would be safe if left to myself overnight. He does not remember that he was not concerned about leaving his wife alone for many nights two years ago, when he returned to Fort Madison.

I believe a night alone will be good for both of us, for we have been too much in each other's company. Still, I do not like being by myself in this blizzard, which puts me quite as much on edge as the thunderstorms of summer.

~

April 21, 1868. Prairie Home.

Hearing a noise without and thinking Luke had braved the heavy storm after all, I threw open the door, to discover Tom, covered with snow and nearly frozen. I helped him into the house, ordering him to remove his wet clothing while I put his horse into the barn.

Upon return, I found Tom wrapped in a blanket, his clothes spread over the stove to dry. As he was chilled and I feared he would take a fever, I got out the little supply of medicinal whiskey Mr. Bondurant had given us and poured a dram into a teacup. On impulse, I poured some for Self, and using the old chipped cups, we toasted each other with as much style as if we were drinking from the finest crystal.

Tom and Mr. Bondurant had been on the road home from Mingo, when they encountered Luke on his way there. The storm being very bad, Husband had already concluded to spend the night in town and requested that one of them inform me of his plans. I told Tom he should not have taken the trouble but that I was pleased he had done so, for I was glad of his company. The storm had affected my nerves, and I was in need of companionship. "I am greatly afraid of thunder," I told him, then laughed at myself, for there is not much thunder in a blizzard.

"I suppose we're all afraid of something, even when our brains tell us it makes no sense," he said, to my surprise, for it is my experience that men do not show much sympathy for feminine weakness.

Tom's clothing needed time to dry, and I knew he was hungry after his long, cold ride for my sake. So I got out the waffle iron to make a treat, remembering from Tom's visits during the days Luke was in Fort Madison that waffles were his favorite. Preparing the familiar supper brought to mind those happier days of two years ago. I had not been in such high spirits since before Sallie's death, as we chattered of all manner of things, settling several questions of social and political importance. As we dined, Tom became serious, saying he had almost concluded to join Moses in Middle Swan, a gold camp on the Swan River, high in the Rocky Mountains.

"O, Tom, I could not bear it if you left. I have no close friend here but you," I told him. "Why would you go?"

I thought Tom would respond with a sally, as he often does in order to avoid serious discussions, but instead, he was silent for a moment, as if thinking over his reply. Then he said, "How could I not go? It's not easy to batch. I can't stand the loneliness. Sometimes, it is so still at my place that I think the world around me has died, and I talk to myself out loud just to hear the sound of a human voice. I'm surprised I made it through this winter, and I know I can't spend another alone."

"Why, you're not alone, Tom. You have us, and I need you more than ever now."

"That's why I've stayed so long. Ever since Mrs. Talmadge's first visit, when I saw how things stood with Luke, I knew you needed me. But there is nothing I can do for you now, and I cannot bear to see you so unhappy. Don't you know the truth of my feelings?"

Until that instant, I had thought of Tom as only a dear friend. But as I looked at him over the teacup, I saw a different man, one who had come to my support again and again when I had been neglected by Husband. I could not think how to reply.

"I can see you didn't know. Well, that's no surprise to me. You are too fine to think me capable of any but the most respectable feelings for you. Now that you see how it is, you know I cannot stay." Tom rose and came to my side, and before I could stop him, he had knelt beside me, his arms around me, his face against me. I stroked his hair, which is not coarse and honey-colored like Luke's, but fine and almost black, with threads of gray running through it. "Say you care a little for me, Mattie."

"Of course I do. You have been so good to me."

"Say I mean more than that." Tom stood and pulled me to my feet, his arms around me. "I think of this when I cannot sleep," he said, and kissed me with far greater tenderness than Luke ever had. He kissed my neck and my eyes and the top of my head, and as he did, I felt the sorrow and pain of the last few weeks slip from my body. I held tight to him as he pushed me gently to the bed.

I was loved better last night than in three years of marriage, finding satisfaction in union that I did not know was available to me. For a few hours, there was neither sadness nor guilt, but only love, and when it was done, I felt as if my body and soul were whole once more.

Tom rode off before dawn into a starry night clear of snow. As he left, he asked me to go with him to the Swan River. He says his mind is made up, for after the night, he has no choice but to leave. If I remain with Luke, Tom does not want to be about, and if we are to be together, as he hopes, it cannot be here. So there is another course open to me, after all, one I never dreamed of.

I no longer love Luke, and I care for Tom very much, but do I love him enough to live my life under the condemnation of others? Could Tom and I find happiness when we have acted contrary to all moral dictates? Was my union with him one of love, or was it a way of seeking to even the score with Luke? There is no one whose advice I can ask, so I write all down in my precious book, hoping, as I do so, that I can see my way to a decision.

The sun had not long broken the horizon when Mr. Bondurant shouted from without, inquiring how we had weathered the storm. I quickly put away my journal and opened the door, replying I had been warm and snug.

"The trip home must have pret' near used up your husband," he said.

"No, he spent the night in Mingo. Tom came by to tell me before going back into the storm. I hope he is safely home," I replied brazenly. Tom and I had agreed to say he had stopped for only a few minutes.

Mr. Bondurant eyed me strangely, then turned toward the barn, where a single set of tracks made by Tom's horse led from its door to our house and thence to the horizon. "I'll check on the livestock." Mr. Bondurant urged his horse forward, riding over the tracks as if to obliterate them.

When he had finished and returned to the house, he said not a single word about the tracks, but sat down to a breakfast of "slap-jacks," as he calls them, and talked about the storm. By the time he left, the sun was hard at work melting the snow, and the telltale prints were gone.

I am confident Mr. Bondurant will never reveal what he saw, but he forced me into deception, and so that is what things have come to. Now I wonder how I shall face Luke.

⌒

May 12, 1868. Prairie Home.

As the weather has been poor, Luke is much underfoot, giving me no time to be alone with journal or thoughts. I maintain a calm surface, but I am in turmoil within. I tell myself what I did was recompense for Luke's perfidy, but a woman's lapse from virtue always seems the greater sin. Luke knows nothing of my wrongdoing, does not even suspect it.

Tom has visited twice, and he was so agitated and pale that Luke remarked on it. Husband stayed by Tom's side during both visits, giving us two only a few precious minutes together.

"Luke isn't worthy of you," Tom whispered, but I put my finger to his lips, for I would not let him speak ill of Luke, even under the circumstances. So Tom inquired if I was all right and whether Luke knew what had happened between us.

"Yes to the first, no to the second," I replied.

"I will never forgive myself for the wrong I did you."

Luke returned just then, so I could not reply.

⁓

May 16, 1868. Prairie Home.

When I heard the horse riding hard, I thought Tom had come again, but it was Mr. Bondurant, who tied his animal to our hitching rail and burst through the door. Skipping the formalities, he blurted out, "Tom's gone. He's riding to Denver to join up with Moses. Then them two and Jessie heads for the gold fields. The durn fool. I told him he ought not to go until he sold out, but no, by ginger, he were in a hurry and said he'd made up his mind."

"Without telling us? Without saying farewell?" I asked, for I could not believe what I had heard.

"He's some pumpkins, Tom is. He told me to say it for him."

"Tom's been strange lately, but it's not like him to act impulsively. He's always been a cautious man," Luke said.

I did not hear Mr. Bondurant's reply, for I went outside to sit on the bench, as I was greatly confused, wondering whether Tom thought my lack of a reply to his proposal meant I had turned him down. Perhaps he had not meant his declaration of love after all and had spoken only in the heat of passion.

I sat impatiently, hoping Tom had given Mr. Bondurant a message to be delivered to me, and when at last he came without, I whispered, "Is there a word for me?"

Mr. Bondurant turned his face so that I could see only the blind eye and said softly, "Tom don't think he'd be able to say good-bye to you. He says to tell you he'll write."

That was not a satisfying answer, because I had hoped to receive instructions for going to Tom. Yes, I have made up my mind to join my future with Tom's. It is not my decision; I believe it has been made for me.

⌐⌐

May 19, 1868. Prairie Home.

In hopes of finding a letter from Tom, I persuaded Luke to carry me to Mingo, saying I needed several purchases that could not wait. Now that Luke no longer expects letters from Persia, he is not so anxious to go to town, and he was surprised at my insistence. Still, he seemed pleased to make the trip for my sake.

There was no letter, and I am frantic to hear from Tom, for a reason that I do not care to put down on paper.

～

May 22, 1868. Prairie Home.

When Mr. Bondurant called, I inquired whether he had heard from "our absent friend." He replied that he had not but would come immediately if he received a letter, for Tom's handwriting is poor, and Mr. Bondurant will need someone to read it to him. I have never seen Tom's handwriting.

Yesterday, I heard Luke whistle "When Johnny Comes Marching Home," and I was taken with a great fit of weaping for my own Johnnie, and for myself, too. I am surer than ever that I am enceinte, and that is the reason I must go to Tom. He does not know, of course, else he would write for me immediately.

Luke brought me a bird's nest he found on the prairie. Skill-fully woven within was a tiny little curl. I believe it to be one of those that Johnnie had thrown to the wind when I cut his hair last year.

～

May 25, 1868. Prairie Home.

Luke has gone to Mingo, and I pray there

is word from Tom, even a letter written to both
of us with a message between the lines saying where I may join him.

Luke has become the tenderest of husbands. I would not believe such a change
possible in a person if I had not experienced
it myself. But it is too late.

⌒

May 26, 1868. Prairie Home.
No letter. Did God take Johnnie from me
because my wickedness was foreordained?

⌒

June 2, 1868. Prairie Home.
Still no word. Today, I remembered Mother
saying a good name is above all price. I no
longer have one.

⌒

June 5, 1868. Prairie Home.
A family named Richards has moved onto
Tom's homestead. I do not know the particulars of how they acquired it. Luke is anxious
for me to meet them, for they are an educated
couple from Ohio, near to our age, with a little girl of two years. Kathleen Richards (whom
Luke declares is as pretty as Carrie) is gently bred and bewildered by the country, and
Luke says I can be an inspiration to her. I have,
at last, the possibility of a close woman friend,
and a husband who has grown far more atten-
tive than I ever dreamed, but I care about none
of it. If I did not carry another man's child,

I wonder if things might have worked out between Luke and me. I am paralyzed with self-loathing for my deceitfulness, and I pray to join Tom.

⁓

June 12, 1868. Prairie Home.

Luke awoke me on my birthday yesterday with a bouquet of wildflowers and said that he had ordered a sewing machine as memento for me. It should arrive before summer is over.

I said I did not deserve such a fine gift, as indeed, I do not, and Luke replied he hoped it was appropriate for a "mother," for he believed I had a secret I was keeping from him. I told him he was mistaken.

⁓

June 15, 1868. Prairie Home.

Mr. Bondurant came for a visit and stayed so long that Luke at last excused himself, saying he had work in the fields. Waiting until Husband was away, Mr. Bondurant withdrew an envelope addressed to him, with a second envelope inside, upon which was written my name. "This come from Tom in my letter, the first letter I ever got. Tom set down in it that I was to give the envelope to you in private," he said. "It sat in Mingo a week or more, since I ain't been to town."

Knowing I was anxious to read it, Mr. Bondurant withdrew.

Here is his letter:

Middle Swan, Colorado
June 2, 1868

Beloved Mattie

Each time the mail arrives, I am first in line at the counter, which is a board laid across two whiskey barrels in a saloon, in expectation of receiving a favor from you. Now my hope is used up, and there is nothing for it but to believe such response has been rendered. If you intended to reply to my previous letter, even to send me on my way, you would have done so by now. I would make the long ride to Mingo if I thought I could change your mind, but I know it would do no good and only cause you embarrassment. I believe I was right in taking the coward's out by writing for your answer instead of forcing it from you in a personal interview. I chose that way because I could not bear to hear a refusal from your lips.

Perhaps this is best for us both, for what kind of life do I offer you, beginning as it did with the breaking of a Commandment. I was wrong to ask you to violate your sacred marriage vows, as well. You are too steadfast and good to put aside duty.

Being fed up with Middle Swan almost at once, as they found the gold used up, Moses and Jessie are determined to seek better prospects, and now that I have given up all hope of receiving a message from you, I say ditto. Ho for Montana! Moses is checking now for news respecting the Indians, and if all is as it should be, we leave at sunup.

Dearest Mattie, the thing was done. I had one night of purest bliss. Can any man say more? My heart is overcome with tenderness when I think of it. But it is worth my soul to take it back, for I did not intend the act and live in anguish with the knowledge I have caused you pain. You know from my first letter, sent the day after I left, that you have no cause to doubt the sincerity of my feelings for you. That you forgive me and remember me only as one who loves you with tender and exclusive affection is my daily prayer.

Though I shall not contact you again, you have not heard the last of Tom Earley. I have as much right as any man to discover a rich gold mine, and I will succeed or be found trying. So when you hear of such an event in connection with my name, you will know it is only the second-best thing that ever happened to

Your very sincerely devoted
Thompson Earley

⁓

July 24, 1868. Prairie Home.

It appears I shall recover, and so shall the babe I yet carry. For a long time, I am told, it was thought neither of us would survive. I was senseless for many days, and without the tender nursing of Mr. Bondurant and Kathleen Richards (the young wife who now lives in the Earley place), I should have died. O, my sad heart! If only I had done so! By what rights should either this babe or I live?

After reading Tom's missive, I was consumed with self-pity over the lost letter, my mind as black as a beehive. I knew that as my only course was to remain with Luke, I must rid myself of this child conceived in sin. Then with great bitterness, I realized the only one who could help me do so was Jessie, and she was with Tom, both lost to me forever.

In desperation, I drank huge quantities of bitter tansy tea, and when that failed to produce the desired result, I made a decoction of rhubarb and pepper, mixing it with the laudanum Jessie had given me in Denver. Then I took a dose big enough to kill a horse, as the saying is—but it was not sufficient to kill the baby or me.

Luke found me senseless on the floor, and when he could not rouse me, he went for Mr. Bondurant. That kind friend declared I had eaten tainted food or was suffering from a complication of pregnancy. If he knew the true cause of my illness, Mr. Bondurant uttered no word of it. He has confided that Luke did not leave my side until he was assured I would recover, and Luke himself told me he had concluded that if I died, he would leave Colorado Territory.

Now that the danger is past, I am under orders by Husband and friends to rest. So I lie in bed with time enough to write but little to say.

There is no solace in confiding in my journal. Why should I record the events of my life when I take no interest in them? I have neither enthusiasm nor hope for the future.

When I awoke from my long illness, I was not the gay bride who had started these pages, but a tormented woman whose life henceforth will be duty.

This book has become a burden to me, and so I put aside my pen, perhaps forever. In time, I shall destroy this once-beloved companion, upon whose pages I have written so faithfully. But I cannot do so now, for it is yet too much a part of me. I could no more toss it into the flames than I could burn away my own arm. So I return it to its hiding place in the trunk. Perhaps one day I shall take it out and in reading its story rediscover the joyful young girl who just three years ago began its journey. Pray God that she is not lost forever.

January 12, 1869. Prairie Home.

Just before dawn on this day, I was delivered of a healthy baby girl, who is named Carrie Lorena. She favors her mother.

Epilogue

Mattie Spenser never wrote in her journal again. Still, judging from the wear on the diary's leather cover, as well as the rusted safety pin that had replaced the original strip of leather securing the flap, I think she must have taken the volume from its hiding place and reread it often.

As I closed the diary and slipped the flap through the safety pin, I felt a sense of disappointment at the lack of resolution. It was as if I'd read a book all the way to the end, only to discover that there wasn't any end, that the last page was missing. I wanted closure (a word that certainly wasn't used in Mattie's day), and I hoped Hazel could provide it.

Her portable radio was on, turned to some talk show, which meant Hazel was home. So gathering up the diary and the transcript that I'd printed out for her, I pushed open the side gate that separates our two yards and found Hazel sitting on her patio. Her feet, clad in Nikes, were propped on a footstool. A stemmed glass was on the table at her side.

"Oh, hello there," she said when she saw me. "I'm having a martini. Can I fix you one?"

I shook my head.

"Every time I see him, my doctor warns me against liquor, says it isn't good for me, but my stars, what harm will it do at my age? Cut me down before my prime? I can't think of a better way to leave this world than loaded, can you?" Hazel shook her head as she switched off the radio. "I don't know why I listen to that drivel. It just makes me mad. Sit down, dearie."

But I was too excited for small talk and blurted out, "I read your grandmother's diary. I transcribed it onto my computer and made you a copy." I set the journal reverently on the table and dropped the printout on the footstool next to her feet, noticing that Hazel still had great legs. I wondered if Mattie had had good legs, too, and if anybody ever knew it.

Hazel glanced at the computer copy. "Why, isn't that nice of you. Honestly, with the way those old people wrote, I never could have gotten through that diary. Was it any good?"

"Oh, Hazel, it was wonderful. You ought to donate it to the Western History Department of the library or the Colorado Historical Society. But read it first, and the sooner the better, because I've got some questions about your grandparents."

"And you want the answers before I kick off. Well, don't worry about that. Mother lived to be older than God, and I suppose I will, too." She drained the martini glass. "I'll get to it this week. It's nice to have an excuse to stop packing. That surely does tire a body."

Hazel picked the olive out of her empty glass and threw it into the bushes next to the house. At my look of surprise, she said, "Yes, I know what you're thinking. Why bother to put an olive into the martini when I'm not going to eat it? Well, that's the way Walter made martinis, and I never thought to do otherwise." She chuckled. "I had a martini every night of my life after I got married, but Mother pretended I didn't drink. She had a wonderful sense of humor, just like her own mother, she said, but she was awfully straitlaced. She got that from her father."

"Was your mother's first name Carrie?"

Hazel looked stumped. "I don't rightly remember. Isn't that awful? She always used Lorena. But now that you mention it, I believe Carrie may have been her first name."

"Did she have brothers and sisters?"

Hazel shook her head. "Not any who lived, anyhoo. Birth control being what it was back then, it wouldn't surprise me if there were other children, who died, or miscarriages, but you didn't talk about such things." She looked down at her hands. "Children don't much run in the family." Hazel sighed, then looked up. "Mother absolutely adored my grandmother."

"What was she like, your grandmother?"

Hazel thought a minute, twiddling the stem of the empty glass between her fingers. "I hardly remember her. She was tall, I know. We were all of us tall. In my mind, I see her wearing a big apron that went all the way around her and standing in the barnyard with her feet apart, leaning forward. I'd forgotten how farm women stood like that. She seemed awfully old to me then. But I was a little bit of a thing, maybe four or five when she died.

I don't suppose she was out of her sixties. Who knows, she might have lived to be as old as I am if she hadn't been killed in the accident."

I moved the printout and sat down on the footstool next to Hazel's feet.

"My grandparents died together. Their car turned over. The accident made the newspapers in Denver because it was the first fatal automobile crash out there in Bondurant County. And then they were quite prominent, too. My grandfather was a rancher. He came out here as a homesteader, but the land wasn't much good for farming. So he turned to cattle and built up quite a spread. I suppose he bought out everybody around him. My grandmother was an educator of some kind. I don't know exactly what she did, but there was a school named for her in Mingo. They left quite a bit of money to Mother, and she used it to build this house. She saved some for my education. I went to Oberlin."

Hazel reached up and pulled a yellow rose from the bush that shaded the patio and held it to her nose. "I remember my grandparents' funeral. All those people dressed in black." She was lost in thought for a moment, and I waited for her to continue. "Walter and I went out to the Mingo farm. I think it must have been in the early fifties. Whoever bought the place from Mother abandoned it during the Depression. The house had fallen in, and one side was completely overgrown with these same yellow roses. Walter took a clipping for me, and I planted it here."

"Was there a big veranda with a swing?" I asked.

Hazel shook her head. "There was a porch all right, but if there was a swing, it was long gone. I remember Walter pointing out where there was sod under the siding. The ranch house had been built around the original soddy." Hazel looked off into the distance for a moment. "What I remember most is the floor—wide pine boards that had fallen through. Wildflowers had grown up through the rotted places."

When I went out for the paper early the next morning, Hazel, dressed in the same Nikes and denim skirt and blouse she'd worn the day before, was sitting on the swing on the front porch. "I read the diary. I stayed up all night to do it, and I've been waiting here since four this morning for you to get up." She waved aside my look of astonishment. "Do you have any coffee, dearie? No cream or sugar, you know."

I went back inside, poured coffee into two mugs, and set them on a tray with some doughnuts left over from yesterday. "You can see why I was so anxious to find out about your grandparents, can't you?" I asked, letting the screen door bang behind me. I handed coffee to Hazel and sat down on the porch steps in the morning sun with my own cup.

"The passion of it is what startled me so," Hazel said, watching the steam rise from the cup, which she held between the palms of both hands. "She was just an old lady to me. How can someone so old be so vulnerable, so... so sexual?" Hazel looked up at me. "Good Lord, when she died, she was twenty or thirty years younger than I am now. You don't suppose somebody will say that about Walter and me, do you?" Hazel blushed, then ducked her head and quickly sipped her coffee. "To think that after churning the butter and chopping the kindling, my grandmother turned into Mary Astor."

To my quizzical look, Hazel explained, "Oh, you know, that actress in the 1930s. She recorded all the juicy details of her affair in her diary, and her husband made it public when he divorced her. Back then, it was all quite the scandal. I thought it was rather tacky of him."

I asked Hazel if she wanted a doughnut.

"The plain one. Chocolate gives me migraines. I must have inherited them from my grandmother." Hazel shook her head. "She didn't know about chocolate, poor woman."

"Did your grandmother ever mention Tom Earley?"

"Not to me. Mother never spoke of him, either. You don't suppose he discovered a famous gold mine, do you?"

I told her he had not, at least not that I could find out. I had gone through my mining books, but I couldn't find even a mention of Thomas and Moses Earley. I'd even called the Western History Department, but it had no record of either name.

Hazel finished the doughnut and brushed the crumbs off her skirt onto the porch floor. Then she picked up a box lying beside her on the swing. "I brought you some things. This picture came from Mother's photo album. It's Mattie." Hazel handed me a square card with an oval tintype in the center, showing a young woman, her head held high. The pink hand-tinting emphasized her high cheekbones, but her eyes were blurred because she'd blinked when the picture was shot. Her long hair was parted in the center and drawn back.

"I want you to have the eardrops she's wearing there. And the breast pin she wrote about in the diary, too. Mother left them to me, but I don't wear them anymore." Hazel took them out of the box and handed them to me. I protested that they were too valuable, but Hazel waved away my objections. "They'll just be stolen where I'm going. Go ahead. Take them." She put them into the palm of my hand.

I slipped the old-fashioned wires of the earrings through the holes in my ears. Then I examined the brooch. One stone was missing, and the gold showed signs of wear, but whether that was due to Mattie or Lorena or Hazel, I didn't know. "I'll treasure them," I said, looking up at Hazel, who smiled at me.

"Oh, and here is something else. It was on one of the bookshelves. I thought Mother saved it because she liked birds." Hazel handed me a bird's nest and pointed to a tiny curl that was woven into it.

"Johnnie's hair?" I asked

"I expect so."

"What do you think happened after the diary closed?" I asked, touching the little curl with my fingertip. "Do you think Luke ever found out the baby—your mother— wasn't his daughter?"

An automatic sprinkler system went on across the street, and Hazel looked up, startled. She watched the water spray out, the little droplets shining in the early-morning sun. Then she turned back to me. "That's the odd thing of it. Mattie was wrong."

I looked up at her in astonishment, shifting a little because the sun had moved and was shining into my eyes. "Luke, not Tom, was my grandfather." Hazel nodded for emphasis. "Mother always said she looked just like her mother but that I was the spitting image of her father. I should have brought his picture so you could see. Just look at these ears." Hazel brushed back her hair and cocked her head so I could get a better look. "And this." She untied her Nike and slipped out her foot. "Six toes. I've got those same spots Luke and Johnnie had on their bodies, too. I guess they've been in the Spenser family since time out of mind. Mother hated them. She said it was like being born with liver spots. You'll have to take my word for the spots, because I'm not going to unbutton my blouse to show them to you. So there isn't the least doubt about who my mother's father was."

Hazel sipped her coffee thoughtfully. "I bet Mattie intended to get rid of that diary but never had the chance because she was killed so suddenly. Otherwise, I don't know why she'd keep it around. Good thing Mother never found it, because she'd have burned it along with the family papers she destroyed just before she died. I bet you Carrie's letters were among them."

"What a shame." I closed my hand over the brooch and felt the pin prick my skin. "Were your grandparents happy when you knew them?"

"I was too young to notice if they weren't."

I sighed. "I guess we'll never know what happened after the diary ended. Do you suppose Luke found out about Tom? Maybe Mattie and Luke ended up hating each other for the rest of their—"

"Like the characters in *Ethan Frome*?" Hazel interrupted.

"That's a possibility. After all, as Mattie wrote, she didn't have any options. She had to stay with Luke, and they must have lived on together for what, thirty or forty more years?" I picked up Hazel's cup to get her more coffee, but she put her hand on my arm and gave me an impish grin.

"Don't be so quick, dearie. There is an ending of sorts. I brought you something else. This morning, when I finished reading Grandmother's diary, I went back to the carriage house and turned that trunk upside down. Then I stretched my arm through the hole in the lid and felt around and discovered this. It was caught in the lining. That's why we didn't spot it when we found the diary."

Hazel waited for me to set down the cup before she reached into the box and brought out an envelope. "You read it while I get the coffee. Now, go on." She got up from the swing and went inside.

I studied the envelope, which was tattered and dirty, as if it had been handled often. Mattie's name and address, written in pencil, were so faded that I could scarcely make them out. I removed the single piece of paper, which was folded once, and smoothed it out. The letter was written in pencil, too, but it was easier to read, since it hadn't rubbed against the inside of the trunk all these years.

Fort Madison,
Iowa
June 11, 1902

Dear Old Girl

I see by the calendar that you are a year older today. I wish I was at home to wake you up with a kiss and a hug and a yellow rose from the bush by the porch, but instead, I send you this bit of lilac. I cut it off a branch next to the parlor window out on the McCauley farm. I went to the old place yesterday, and you'd be mighty pleased. Jemima and Husband keep it as fine as they did three years ago when you and I were last there.

Well, I thought I'd surprise you and get that fellow in Mingo to lay pipes to the kitchen so you'll have hot and cold running water instead of the pump. But Carrie said, "Thunderation, Luke! What woman wants

318

a kitchen sink for her birthday? You get it for her just for putting up with you all these years. Then I'll help you pick out a hat for Mattie." Well, I guess I know what my wife likes better than Carrie Fritch does. Carrie wears her hats as big as a turkey platter, says it's the fashion here, but I know that's not for you. I'll look for a little purple one, like that bonnet you bought on our first trip to Denver.

Carrie's loaded me down with so many homemade geegaws that I hardly have room for a hat, even if I do find one. She says next time I'm not welcome here without my wife. I could hardly tell her Fort Madison in the summer makes you think you'd fallen in a barrel of treacle, or that you feel closed in when you can't see a horizon. So I said you wanted to be with Lorena now that she's due. Carrie and Rose are as excited as hens about seeing Lorena's baby, but Carrie says the visit will have to wait until after harvest. That way, Will can go along, too.

O, here's a thing you'll be interested in: Will tells me there's talk about "contour plowing," as he calls it. Seems that the rest of the world is getting wise to what me and that fellow over on the next farm did near forty years ago, plowing circles on our place. Remember, there were two brothers named Earley, but I'll be hanged if I can recall their first names. We gave it our best all right, but rain never did follow the plow the way we thought it would. The land wasn't meant for farming. Good thing we turned to cattle. Will's showed me a new hay baler he thinks I ought to get. I wish you could *see it, for I value your opinion. What would you think if I bought you a hay bailer instead of a hat? I suppose you'd speak your mind about it. You can do that all right.*

Being out at the old place put me in a sentimental mind, for I got to thinking of that day so long ago when I came a-courtin'. I thought I was a right smart catch back then, but I learned pretty fast that I was the lucky one. If you hadn't stuck by me when we lost the boy, I think I'd have gone as crazy as that fellow whose wife was killed by Indians. Then the Almighty gave us Lorena, and things just got better after that. Since you know me good, you know I'm not much for putting my feelings down in words, and I guess I've said more here than I ever have.

Well, Mattie, if I was there, I'd come up behind you and give you a hug and take your breasts in my hands, the way I like to. Now, don't blush when you read this or say we're too old, because there's life in the old man yet.

Come Tuesday, I'll board the cars that will take me toward the sunset and our Prairie Home. I'd like it mighty good if you'd welcome me with a rhubarb pie from that old clump we set out our first year in Colorado. Give my love to Lorena and save a good measure for yourself from

Your Darling Boy
Luke Spenser

If you have enjoyed reading this large print book and you would like more information on how to order a Wheeler Large Print Book, please write to:

 Wheeler Publishing, Inc.
P.O. Box 531
Accord, MA 02018-0531